Not for Love or Money

By

Linda Sealy Knowles

Forget Me Not Romances, a division of Winged Publications

Forget Me Not Publisher
~ Where stories take flight~

ISBN: 978-1-959788-62-1

<u>Dedication</u>

to

Toni Money

When it comes to true friendship I couldn’t have asked for a better friend. She makes me want to be better than I am.

Prologue

"Please, Papa, don't ask me to honor your wish. I don't love him, and I can't bear to be near him. Please, I 'll do anything you want, but not that." Horrible memories flashed in her mind, but she closed off her thoughts of the past. Jocelyn buried her face into the mattress of her dying father's bed.

"My daughter, I'm sorry. I've been unfair to you, but if you do as I ask, I can go to my maker, a happy man. That way, I will know that you're taken care of. You'll live the lifestyle I've always given you," Mr. James Norwood struggled to breathe.

"What have you done? The last time we spoke about our future, you never said anything about not having money for me." Jocelyn wiped tears from her face and held her papa's hand close.

"I gambled with a full house, but Luke won with four aces. I kept betting money I didn't have, so I signed an IOU when that wasn't enough. Now, the man wants his money. All I have is this house and land."

"Why do I have to marry the banker's son? What does that have to do with your gambling?"

"Mr. Sullivan, the banker, bought my note. He said he'd tear up the IOU if you marry his son. I told him you'd agree."

"Oh, Papa, how could you use me like this? I want to

please you, but I can't this time." Jocelyn surveyed her lovely surroundings. Once, the governor had even asked to purchase this mansion.

Her father's words came in gasps. "Come closer, child. I don't have long on this earth, and I must know you'll be taken care of. Tell me that you'll obey me."

"I can't Papa, I can't. Please don't make me do this . . . Papa?" His head slumped to the side. Jocelyn pushed away from the bed. "Get the doctor quick." A moan escaped. "Oh, Papa, I promise. I'll do as you wish."

"I love you, Jocelyn.

****

Jocelyn's pleas had fallen on deaf ears, and months later, she was still in mourning. Although it was customary to wait a year to marry. Since the banker was a well-known businessman in town, she hoped Mr. Sullivan would allow her time to mourn her papa's death.

Unfortunately, the banker wouldn't listen. Mr. Sullivan had no patience and demanded that she marry his son in two weeks or he would toss her out in the street, penniless.

While Maria, her elderly personal maid, dressed her in her lovely wedding dress, Jocelyn couldn't stop crying.

"Please Miss Jocelyn. Don't cry. You'll ruin your beautiful face."

"I can't help it, Maria. I'd rather live in a shack and scrub floors than let that creep put his hands on me. I think I'm going to throw up." She raced to the bathroom and slammed the door.

As she retched over the sink, someone was knocking on the bedroom door, and she heard Maria open it.

****

Maria looked toward the bathroom, then opened the bedroom door. Mr. Sullivan's voice boomed, "Is the bride ready?"

"No sir. Just give her one more minute."

Marie knocked on the bathroom door. "Miss Jocelyn? Are you ready?" When there was no answer, the old woman eased open the door and gasped. The beautiful wedding dress covered the floor, and the bathroom window stood wide open. Jocelyn had fled. Marie covered the smile on her face, collected herself, and then headed slowly to the bedroom door to give the groom's father the unpleasant news.

Chapter 1

In Midland, about fifty miles north of Perryville, Texas, Jocelyn stood staring at a bulletin board on the wall of the post office. She pulled her bonnet closer to her face as she viewed a large poster that read;

Attention single ladies and widows. *Brides needed in Amarillo, Texas. The men who want to marry will pay a three hundred fee for a bride. Brides-to-be must pay a $50.00 fee to travel to Texas on the Brides' wagon train. Sign up on the 2nd floor of the Freedom Hotel on Main Street. For more information contact George Campbell."*

Jocelyn eased away from the notice and strolled down the old wooden boardwalk. She counted in her head how much money she had sewn in the hem of her shift. During the two weeks of waiting to marry the banker's son, Maria, had helped her sell many items that had belonged to her mother. They had sold over two hundred dollars' worth of jewelry, paintings, and small figurines. This fund helped her to escape Perryville without being seen. While plotting her escape, she had hidden a carpet bag with small items she might need. Careful not to remove anything from the house that someone would notice, she packed a few of Maria's dresses and a few pieces of her mother's jewelry to have as keepsakes. Then dressed in Maria's clothes, she'd purchased a ticket on the Pacific Railroad to Midland,

Texas. She only dared to use some of her money, so Midland was a reasonable distance away.

Her eyes took in the whole street before she headed to the corner café for some dinner. Black and white posters about her disappearance hung in windows and on lampposts on Main Street. She felt like a criminal, and she would be treated like one if caught. Add to that a reward was offered for any information as to her whereabouts.

Sitting at a table in the middle of the café were three young women discussing the wagon train that would carry brides to Amarillo, Texas. They were three beauties who didn't need to marry sight unseen, but listening to their conversations, it was obvious they needed to escape, just like her.

"We'll sleep in a covered wagon or on the ground and have to cook our meals," one of the girls said.

"I can't cook. My ma did all the cooking, and I had to do everything else. But my Pa hit me for the last time," another girl swore.

"I can't wait to get going," the third girl finally spoke. "I'm sure my brothers are looking for me now. So, I'd better head back to the room before they find me.

All three of the young ladies left the café. Jocelyn looked around the place and found she was the last customer. A robust woman walked over to her table. "What'll you have, honey?"

"A bowl of soup and a ham sandwich, please."

When she returned with Jocelyn's order, she asked, "Have you signed up to be a bride on the wagon train leaving in the morning?"

"No, but I must admit I was thinking about it." Jocelyn gave the woman a shy smile.

"Me, too," said the waitress as she slid into a chair at the table. "I want to get out of that hot kitchen and find a nice man to take care of me."

Jocelyn didn't think this woman needed a man to care

for her. She stood nearly six feet tall and was as round as a barrel. Her hair was her best feature. She wore it braided on top of her head like a crown.

Jocelyn shrugged. "Nice to meet you. I'd like to go, but I don't intend to be a bride. There's not a chance I'll marry a stranger and be tied to him for the rest of my life. I can cook and clean, so I could take care of a home or be a cook for a rancher and his hands."

The big woman leaned forward. "What will you do when the man finds out that he paid your passage, and you don't honor the contract?"

"I'll just hope he understands."

The large woman shuffled in her seat to lean toward Jocelyn. "How would you like for me to travel with you to Amarillo? We can look out for each other. It will be a hard, rugged trip, but I can drive a team of mules, and I've cooked over a fire many times. I don't believe a pretty gal like you has ever done any hard labor, am I right?"

"Well, I'm not as fragile as I look. My mama taught me to care for our home, and I worked beside our hired help. She insisted that our cook teach me. Mostly, she wanted me to stand on my own feet and never depend on a man to survive. As a result, I'm educated, a good cook, and I can care for livestock, sew, and make my own clothes. So you see, I'm not helpless just because some say I have a pretty face."

"Mercy, I admit I was wrong about you, but I know it's not safe to travel alone. As for me, I'll feel better having you as a traveling companion. My pa never allowed me to attend school, so I can't read. You'll be able to help me understand what I'm getting into," Cassie laughed. "Now that I think on it, I feel like you. I don't want to marry any yahoo just because he paid for a bride."

Jocelyn wiped her mouth and placed the napkin down on the table. "Well, I believe if we get to sign on with the other brides, we'll make a good team. So, if you're sure you want to go with me, we'd better find the hotel and hope that George fellow will let us travel with the others."

"Atta girl! I need to tell Henry I have to run an errand. By the way, my full name is Cassie Rowe."

"My name is . . . Call me 'J', she smiled at Cassie, and both of them laughed.

****

The clerk told them where they would find Mr. George Campbell. As they entered his office, Mr. Campbell, sitting behind a large wooden desk, looked the two girls over from their heads to their toes before offering them a seat.

"What can I do for you, ladies? Do you want to travel on my bridal train and marry up with a handsome, wealthy cowboy in Amarillo?" He shifted his cigar from one side of his mouth to the other. 'Well, speak up. I ain't got all day."

Cassie lifted her chin. "My name is Cassie Rowe and I do want to sign up to go with you. I'm a cook at the City Café and ready for a change."

"Yes. . . . I've seen you there. Your food is good, but you look too old to snag a husband."

Jocelyn stepped in front of Cassie. "Mr. Campbell, I don't appreciate you speaking to my friend in that way. Cassie is not ready for the grave. She's just tired of working twelve hours every day. Older men will appreciate a woman who can cook and care for them and herself."

"I'm sorry, Miss Rowe. I didn't mean to be rude. Please forgive me." Mr. Campbell turned his focus on Jocelyn and his eyebrows lifted. He looked at her as if she were a prize horse. "What about you, young lady? Are you ready to travel on my bridal train? I have many men willing to pay your passage, that is, if you can survive the long, hard trip."

"I assure you, Mr. Campbell, I'm stronger than I look. But, there is one thing that you have to understand before I sign your contract."

"What can that be? It's a straightforward contract

stating you agree to marry the man I choose for you. The gentleman will pay me your passage before you marry."

"That's just it. I don't intend to be a bride. I want to travel with you, but not as a bride-to-be."

"Look, lady, I ain't giving no free ride to Amarillo. I'm only taking willing women who intend to marry." He replaced his pen in its holder. "I furnish each wagon with plenty of beans, potatoes, flour, lard and sugar. Barrels of water are tied to the sides of the wagons. They cost a pretty penny, so I can't afford freeloaders." He stood and gave them a stern look. "Besides, many men have waited months for a wife. If you don't want to marry, then catch a train or a stagecoach to take you wherever."

Jocelyn sighed and turned to Cassie. "Don't let my decision keep you from traveling with Mr. Campbell. I'm sure some man will be looking for a nice lady who can cook and is a hard worker. I was hoping to get a good job as a cook on maybe a farm or ranch, but it looks like I'll have to secure a job as a hotel maid, for now."

"I don't want to go without you," Cassie said. "Please, Mr. Campbell, you can see for yourself that my friend is a beauty. She's an educated decent lady. Any man would love to have her working for them—whether she'll marry or not."

Mr. Campbell stood and walked to his window. He looked down at the street and watched the people rushing from one side to the other. He remembered a certain Matt Colburn who said he didn't need a wife: he just needed a woman to cook on his ranch." He turned to face her. "All right you can go."

Mr. Campbell returned to his desk and peer at Jocelyn over his wire-rim glasses. "I don't think Mr. Colburn wants to get married. But Amarillo has very few women, so he hired a man to cook, and the ranch hands nearly lynched him for burning the food all the time. This man I'm thinking about is a tough young man. He has a fierce temper, and I find him hard to deal with."

Jocelyn posted her hands on her hips. "Look, Mr. Campbell, if this rancher doesn't like me, I can work on his ranch until I pay off my passage. Then, he'd would have a new cook for a few months and get his money back."

"Once Matt gets a good look at you, he'll most likely want to marry. He'd be crazy not to," he chuckled. "Matt's a strange fellow so who knows what he might do?" He sized Jocelyn up again and finally leaned back in his chair. "Fair warning, you'll have to pull your weight on the wagon train. There will only be a few men traveling to protect the train from bandits, rustlers, and drunken, rowdy men who want to rob, steal, and have fun with the women. My men will hunt for fresh meat and share it with the women, but they don't drive the wagons or care for the livestock. The women do everything. What do you think about these rules?"

"I agree with your rules as long as it's in my contract that I will not be a bride." Jocelyn turned to Cassie, "What do you think?"

"I feel the same about marrying." Cassie gave Mr. Campbell a hard stare.

"Fine. I'll have your contracts ready to sign in the morning, but you must keep your traps shut about the conditions I'm granting you both."

Jocelyn and Cassie gave Mr. Campbell their fifty dollars and hurried out of the office on to the boardwalk. "You got any money left?"

"My name's Jocelyn and yes, I have some. Why?"

"We need to go and purchase a few personal supplies for the trip. We need some men's britches to wear under our skirts. They'll make moving around on the trail so much easier. Also, we need to purchase some medical supplies in case we get scratched, cut or bit by a critter."

"Goodness, Cassie, how do you know so much?"

"My folks traveled a lot before my pa decided to settle

down. My ma wore my older brother's pants and shirts, and always had bandages to care for wounds. So, let's learn from her and take care of ourselves."

"Let's go, and I need to purchase a few undies because I left home so fast, I didn't take time to pack," Jocelyn remarked as they headed to the dry goods store."

"So, like some of the other girls, you're a runaway from home?" Cassie asked.

"Let's just say I had to leave. I'll tell you about my life while on the trail. The law doesn't want me, so don't fret about my personal life—for now."

Chapter 2

The following morning, Mr. Campbell's clerk assigned wagons to all the ladies. The trail guide told them to go to the corral and pick out four mules and hitch them to their wagons. Cassie reached for Jocelyn's arm. "Come on, gal. Let's show these men we can take care of ourselves. First, we'll pick out the biggest strongest mules and lead them over to our wagon. I'll let you hold their heads while I hitch up. Although, I haven't had to do this in a long time, I haven't forgotten how to do it."

Once the girls hitched the mules, Cassie and Jocelyn carried each mule a bucket of water and gave each a juicy red apple. "Now, I know why you purchased a bushel of apples," Jocelyn laughed. "I thought you were going to bake apple pies for the whole train."

"If you treat your animals well, they'll gladly follow your instructions," Cassie said. "That's something I learned from my pa." Cassie revealed as she watched a man herd about ten milk cows by their wagon.

"Maybe, we can get a reduced price for a pint of milk each day if I help milk. What do you think?"

When she didn't receive a response, Cassie noticed the strange look on Jocelyn's face. She turned as pale as a ghost. "What's wrong, gal? Are you sick?"

"No, I need to hide," she whispered. "Those men are looking for me." Jocelyn visibly began trembling.

Cassie looked over Jocelyn's shoulder and saw three men coming their way. One was the sheriff of Midland whom Cassie knew well, one was Mr. Campbell, and the other two were strangers. "Come quick and get in the wagon."

"No, they are searching the wagons."

"Hurry, climb inside. Those men will never find you," Cassie said, as she pulled the front and back curtains closed. Then Cassie lifted boards from the floor. There was a hidden crawl space between the bottom and top of the floorboard. "Get in and lie on your stomach. You'll be able to breathe. I'm going to set boxes on top of you."

Jocelyn lay down in the shallow crawl space and breathed from the cracks on the bottom of the floor. She could hear the men telling the sheriff to look in their wagon.

The sound of footsteps and male voices got closer to the wagon. Summoning her courage, Cassie pretended to be folding her clothes. What are you fellows looking for?" Cassie asked as the sheriff pulled back the curtain at the back of the wagon.

"We're searching for a young lady that ran away from home."

"Where'd she run from?" Cassie asked, pretending to be interested.

"Perryville, Texas. Ever heard of it?"

"Sure, I lived in that small town when I was younger. So, who is the girl you're looking for? Just maybe, I might know her family."

"Her folks are dead. She's a runaway bride, you might say," chuckled the young stranger searching for Jocelyn.

"Mark, keep your remarks about our client to yourself. It's no one's business but the sheriff's."

"Sorry," he said as he moved closer to Cassie. "I just found it funny that the gal ran away from a rich fiancé," he whispered.

"All right Sheriff, we're burning daylight," Mr. Campbell yelled. "I don't remember signing on a lady with the description you gave me, and you haven't found her on my train. So, if you don't mind, we'll be pulling out in ten minutes."

"Thanks for allowing me to search. These men will feel better knowing the lady they're looking for isn't on your train. Good day." The sheriff nodded to Cassie and the other ladies standing nearby.

Cassie climbed on the wagon bench and touched the lead mule to move out. The team immediately began following the wagon in front of them. "Miss Rowe, take care of my valuable cargo," Mr. Campbell said, and gave her a wink.

As Cassie watched the three men ride away from the wagon train, she gave the lead mule its head, quickly removed the boards, and helped Jocelyn from the crawl space. "You all right, honey?"

"Yes, thanks for your help." She brushed the dust off her clothes. "Do you have spices stored in here? I could smell garlic or something like that."

"Yep, when I told Henry I was leaving, he fixed me a box of things I would need on the trail. He gave me a twenty-pound bag of dried beans, a small basket of eggs, a container of sugar, jars of jam, and white lard for baking. And look, he even gave me this big skillet. You'll need these things, he said."

"It looks like we have all we need for a while. So, let's go and begin our new life."

****

The first day was long and hard for two women who hadn't worked outside in years. Jocelyn only worked outside when she chose to work in her mother's lovely flower garden. She had worn a large bonnet, so the hot sun never touched her complexion.

Cassie had worked in Henry Jerkins' café for the last

five years. She walked to work before sunrise and returned home in the moonlight. The most challenging work she did was to help wash dishes and mop the kitchen floor.

Both ladies took turns driving the wagon. Once they stopped for the midday meal, Cassie watered the mules while Jocelyn built a fire and put the coffee on. Cassie unfolded a small table that she had tossed in with her supplies and whipped up some griddle cakes to eat with strawberry jam.

The three ladies in the café two days ago walked over to Cassie and watched her cook. "Those flap jacks sure smell good. Do you think you could share a couple with us?"

She looked up. "Hi, my name is Cassie. First of all, these are called griddle cakes. There's only flour, sugar, eggs and milk in them. You gals can cook them without any trouble."

The youngest of the three girls' smiled. "I'm Janet, by the way. Wish that were true, but I can only cook soup. You know where you toss everything in a big pot and let it stew over the fire for hours."

A slight woman who looked older than her years shielded her eyes from the sun. "I'm Martha. That's more than I ever cooked. My ma made me work outside with my pa. Oh, I cleaned and mopped the house, but she never let me work in the kitchen." Her sad face held a faraway look.

The pretty blonde spoke up. "My name's Tonya. To tell you the truth, Miss Cassie, out of the three of us, Janet is the only one that knows anything about cooking," she walked over and sat on a stump.

"What did you plan on telling your new man about cooking for him?" Cassie asked.

"Surprise!" All three girls said in unity and laughed.

Cassie looked at the girls and shook her head. "All right, if Jocelyn doesn't mind, I'll cook for all of us, and you can take turns helping me. That way I can teach you to cook before we reach Amarillo." Cassie took a plate and passed it to one of the girls. Before she turned it loose, she said, "We're going to need your supplies to help with the food."

"Of course. Just let us know when you need something, and I'll bring it over." The girls looked at each other and one asked, "Deal?"

"After we eat, we clean our dishes, put things back in the wagon, and secure the fire. We will work as a team." Cassie waited for all the girls to agree.

The girls ate their fill and asked Cassie who she wanted to help clean that day.

"Jocelyn will help me today. I'm going to soak some dried beans while we travel the rest of the day, and tonight it won't take them long to cook. I ain't a gourmet cook, but you won't go hungry."

"Did you water your mules?" Cassie asked as Jocelyn peeked out from the back of the wagon.

"Yes, Janet did that as soon as we stopped," Tonya replied.

"Jocelyn, these three girls want to share our cooking and fire while we're traveling. They don't know how to cook, so I'll give them a few lessons, so their new men won't starve." Cassie laughed. "Do you care if they join us?"

"No, I don't mind." Jocelyn looked at the girls. "While in the café, I believe I overheard one of you say you were running away from home. Will we need to hide you?" She peered at each girl. "If we get another search party like we had this morning?"

"Me," Martha said. "My brothers are probably looking for me, but I'm not going to go back. I'm tired of being tossed in our cellar for days just because I smiled at a man in town. My pa is mean, and my brothers follow his orders."

"You don't have to be afraid with us," Cassie said,

putting her arms around the sad girl. “We’ll all protect you.”

Chapter 3

After Jocelyn and Cassie had finalized a deal with the three girls, the days were easier for all of them. Each lady had an assigned duty to perform each day. Janet helped Cassie with the milking each morning while the other girls set up the table and prepared the fire. Martha had discovered a large grate in the back of their wagon to help cook over the open fire. Jocelyn made the coffee and she and Tonya would go to the open field and bring in their mules. Jocelyn had learned from Cassie how to hitch the team to the wagon.

After the milking, Cassie cooked a big breakfast. It wasn't long before the men smelled the aroma of good food. Cassie laughed and invited them to have a biscuit with jam and a cup of coffee. The men were thrilled to have food prepared by a woman cook.

After two of the girls cleaned the camp and secured the fireplace, Cassie put a pot of dried beans on to soak while traveling. Everyone would have a big appetite after a long day of traveling.

While walking beside the wagon, Tonya began to sing. Later, she admitted to being raised in the church and knew many hymns by heart. She had a beautiful, clear voice, and everyone close by enjoyed her singing.

After dinner one night, a lovely young lady stopped by

the girls' wagon. She had a guitar and asked if she could join them. "My name is Betty Wilson. My traveling companion has gone to bed already, and I'm lonely. I heard someone singing and I hoped to add my music to the voice."

"Oh, I'm the singer," Tonya said. "Please play something for us."

"I will if you'll join in," Betty smiled, and she strummed her fingers over her instrument. Betty played the tune of *Amazing Grace.*

"That's my favorite," Tonya said. The two joined together and the music soothed everyone's spirit. As the stanza was near the end, Jocelyn began to sing the second verse. Everyone stood still as her voice floated all through the camp. "Whoever is singing has the voice of an angel," one lady said. It wasn't long before many other ladies on the train gathered. When the song ended, everyone applauded, and a few asked for more.

"Goodness, Jocelyn, we had no idea you had such a lovely voice," Tonya said.

"Why don't we plan a few songs to sing and play together?" Betty suggested. "We could entertain everyone on the wagon train after a long, tiring day."

Jocelyn agreed. "Let's start tomorrow night."

"Yes, I'd like that." Tonya stood and said, "I better go to bed, but I enjoyed singing with you two."

****

On the third night on the trail to Amarillo, a thunderstorm with heavy sheets of rain and hail fell upon the covered wagons. The men had their hands full, corralling the mules and horses together. They tied the animals to a long picket line. In heavy rain gear, several men stayed close to the animals to ensure they didn't get spooked and break away.

Jocelyn admitted to Cassie that she was afraid. They could feel the strong wind and hear the hail pounding the wagon canvas. Fortunately, they had only minor leaks in the canvas. Cassie suggested that they lie in their beds and keep still. Finally, after hours of thunder and lightning, the heavy rain stopped. Cassie put on her boots and checked the top of the outside canvas.

Jocelyn climbed out onto the ground. Their wheels were sunk in mud, and she was sure all the wagons were in the same condition. They'd need to use the mules to pull them out of the thick, axle-deep mud.

Once the sun came up, everyone could see the damage done to the campsite. Most wagons weathered the storm, but potholes covered the ground. Jocelyn jumped over several small ditches of muddy water, and the tail of her skirt got coated with the awful black mud. She stepped out of the muddy skirt and tossed it on the tailgate. It felt good to be in her men's britches and plaid shirt.

Many of the ladies were excited to see her wearing britches. "Where did you get them?" one lady asked. "I want a pair."

"Cassie and I bought them to wear under our skirts, but I'm not going to wear those heavy skirts again while out on this nasty, wet trail."

"The first town we come to I'll buy myself a pair. I don't think the men will fuss about our new dress code," laughed Maureen Sanderson.

"I don't care what they think or say. We have to take care of ourselves, and these britches help us move around easier," Jocelyn commented. "Cassie, let's move this wagon onto higher ground before we start breakfast. I'll hitch our mules while you help the girls gather theirs."

After the girls were covered from head to toe in mud, the mules cooperated and pulled the wagons about fifty yards away to drier ground. The girls laughed and tossed mud playfully at each other.

Once the mules were watered and the brake was set on the wagon, Cassie and the girls pitched in and cooked a big breakfast. As a habit, the men showed up to have coffee and eat. They made a few comments about Jocelyn and Cassie's attire, but the girls didn't pay them any attention. Jocelyn didn't care that the men gave her sly glances.

****

While on the trail, the train scout rode back to the wagons. He spoke to several men and they all seemed to agree. "There's a nice creek running beside the trail. We want everyone to form a circle with the wagons and we'll stop. Everyone can bathe and wash their clothes. The water looks clear enough to refill our water barrels."

Loud voices carried down the train as the women jumped from their wagons and rushed to the water's edge.

"You men get lost for a while. We're going to post guards to make sure you don't get your eyes full of naked women," Cassie said as she glared at the men sitting on their horses.

The women gathered their dirty linens and bars of scented soap. After scrubbing their garments clean, they hung them on the outside of their own wagons. Many women stripped down to their shifts and washed their bodies. This was the first water the train had come upon that was suitable for swimming and frolicking.

****

"It feels so good to be clean all over," Tonya said to herself, using a rough white towel to dry herself. After her body was as dry as it could be, she wrapped her long, brown hair with the towel and sat in the late afternoon sun enjoying watching people swimming in the lake. Just then she heard a movement behind her. "What are you doing over here, Ray?" Tonya asked, surprised to see the young man. She grabbed the towel from her hair to cover her chest. He stood there with a smirk on his face. "I just wanted to see your lovely body."

"You'd better git before I scream," she said, bolting to her feet to run back to the camp.

Ray was too fast for her and grabbed her around the waist as she rushed past him. Tonya wasn't haven't any of his attention, so she shoved him backward. Suddenly, a long snake slithered beside Ray and bit him on the hand. He grabbed his pistol out of his holster and killed it with one shot.

The explosion of the gun drew screams from everyone in the water. Ray kicked the snake away and looked down at the bite mark on his hand. He knew he would be in trouble because he wasn't supposed to be near the women.

"What going on here?' Jackson Mills, the lead man on the train, yelled.

Tonya hollered from where she hid behind a tree. "A snake bit the man, and he shot it."

Cassie hurried over to Ray and demanded to see the bite marks. "What kind of snake was it?" she asked as she examined the top of his hand.

Another man picked up the snake, allowing it to dangle. "It was a brown rattler. You'd better get that poison out of your hand as soon as possible, or you'll be dead tomorrow."

"Come to my wagon," Cassie said. "Jocelyn, build a fire and heat my sharpest knife. Do you or one of your men want to care for his wound?"

"No, you go right ahead and do your best. But, be quick about it," Jackson Mills said.

****

While Martha mopped his brow, Cassie cut the bite mark open and squeezed it, but nothing was forthcoming. There was only one thing she could do. Without hesitation, Cassie sucked on the wound and spit out the venom many times, praying she got all the poison out of his hand.

During the night, Ray suffered from a high fever and was delirious. He cried out and moaned for hours. Cassie and Martha kept cool, wet rags on his forehead and over most of his body. The hand swelled to twice its size.

Despite their efforts, late into the night, the young man passed away.

Cassie climbed down from the wagon. Jocelyn, Tonya, and Janet raced to her. She only shook her head, trudged over to a stump, and sat down. “We did all we could,” Cassie said. “One of you girls, go and tell Mr. Mills.”

****

The following day, while the breakfast was cooking, Jackson Mills ordered the men to dig a deep hole to bury Ray. Another man chiseled his name on a rugged cross. Once they were finished, the whole group gathered together.

Mr. Mills said a few words over Ray, and everyone sang, “Shall We Gather at the River.” Tonya began singing, but soon broke down into tears. The music continued while the other ladies completed the song.

“Everyone, get ready to pull out as soon as we’re finished here,” Mr. Mills said as he picked up a shovel and began tossing dirt into the grave.

When the train stopped for the midday meal, Mr. Mills asked everyone to gather. “I want to thank Cassie and the other girls for helping Ray. It’s a shame that this accident happened, but from what Tonya told me, this wouldn’t have happened. When I give an order, it is for everyone, men and women. I mean for it to be followed. Please remember that I am here to lead you to Amarillo, and I want everyone to get there. I can’t be worried that some of you will not obey my rules. If you have a problem, please come and talk to me. That’s all I have to say.”

“Mr. Mills, I’m so sorry about what happened to that young man. I hope you aren’t mad at me. I tried to make him leave.” Tonya said, wiping tears from her face.

“No, I am not mad at anyone. I am sad that Ray died so young, but as I said, if he had obeyed my rules, he would be here today.”

Chapter 4

The following week was long, and the trail was challenging, but everyone managed to handle their mules or walk alongside the wagons. Cassie and the girls cooked, milked the cows and fed themselves along with most of the men.

"You know, Miss Cassie," one of the younger men called to her. "If you aren't assigned to a man already, I may have to toss my name in the ring for you. I ain't never eaten such good food in all my life. Can't imagine how good your food would be in a nice kitchen with a good stove and oven."

Everyone laughed, especially the men. "Since when have you been the marrying kind, Jimmy?" Carl Moore asked as he stuffed a biscuit in his mouth.

"Since I've been eating a hot, delicious meal three times a day," he replied.

"I hate to break up the party, folks, but we'd better get on the trail after you clean this campsite. I would like for us to travel a good distance today. We'll be near the river tomorrow and need plenty of daylight to cross." The wagon master continued along the train giving orders to the other wagons.

Later, after a grueling five hours, the river came into view. It looked swift and was overflowing the banks. "I don't like the looks of that water," Jocelyn said. "I hope we can find a shallow place to cross."

Early the next morning, Jackson Mills called everyone to a meeting about crossing the river. "Folks, our scout has ridden up and down the river looking for a safe place for us to cross. But, unfortunately, with all the rain, the river is pretty high for miles. I've crossed this river several times, but we and I mean, all hands, have to help build a large makeshift raft to float the wagons across."

"Why can't we drive across the river?" A young lady yelled.

"Crossing this river is a risky endeavor. Once in the river, your wagon wheels could drop into a hole, causing it to overturn, or you may get into quicksand. Your wagon will bog down, making it impossible to get out causing the wagon to capsize." Mr. Mills blew out a breath. "If the water was calm and shallow, it's possible that none of these things would happen. As I said, I've crossed here many times without problems, but the water is different today. I suggest we build a sturdy raft and float one wagon at a time. This will be slow and take a while, but I want to get you to Amarillo safe and with your belongings."

"What do we do first?" Cassie stepped forward and asked. "You've brought us this far, so Jocelyn and I are ready to trust your judgment."

"Thank you, Miss Cassie. How about the rest of you?"

The ladies nodded and prepared to do whatever was needed to build the raft.

"After a good breakfast, I'll need a few of you to help the men chop down some trees for logs. First, the logs must be scraped, and carried down to the water edge. I need some of you ladies to grab a pick and shovel. Next, we must cut down the brush along the riverbanks to move wagons down the incline and into the water. I only want women that can swim to work on the banks. We don't need to have anyone swept into the river and drown."

Cassie raised her hand. "Mr. Mills, I need to stay at the campsite and cook food for everyone. I can cook a large pot of stew and biscuits for the evening meal and make cold sandwiches for the midday meal."

"That's a wonderful idea. I'm sure everyone will be too tired to cook, and we all need nourishment," Mr. Mills said. "Eat your breakfast, and let's all get to work."

****

Jocelyn looked down at her hands. They were no longer the soft, delicate hands she'd had before beginning to chop limbs and leaves from the trees. She was sure her back was broken, but she didn't dare complain. Instead, she found privacy in the bushes and wiped tears away from her eyes. Never had she worked so hard in all her eighteen years, but she knew she had to pull her weight and do her part. Mr. Mills wanted to move everyone across the river safely, and she hoped his plan worked.

It took two days to cut enough logs to make several rafts. Two of the men wrapped a long, strong rope over each log to hold them together, while the women poured river water over the makeshift rafts. Mr. Mills had suggested this so the logs would lie straight. Tomorrow, he would take a small wagon and run it upon one of the rafts to see how it fit.

After everyone had eaten a bowl of hot stew and biscuits, the ladies went down to the river, washed, and changed into dry clothes. Many of the men stretched out on the ground, while others continued to pour buckets of water over the rafts.

Jocelyn was proud of the hard work that they had accomplished. Tomorrow, they would begin crossing the river. First thing, she and the ladies emptied their wagons of personal items and tied them together to be placed on a raft to float across.

****

After Cassie had served everyone coffee, Mr. Mills picked out a small, empty wagon and had the men push it down to the riverbank. The men and women had to tilt the raft and guide the wagon onto the center of the logs. Two men tied the wheels down so the wagon wouldn't roll forward or backward. Once the wagon was on top of the raft, the men, along with many of the women, pushed and shoved the raft down the bank. Four strong men were in the water to hold the raft in place. Mr. Mills called for the women to replace the men, so they could cross holding onto the raft.

One strong mule was hitched to the front of the raft, and it began swimming across the river. Several times the mule swayed sideways and nearly caused the raft to tilt, but the women yelled to each other to hold the raft straight.

After an hour, the mule finally reached the other side of the river. He shook and jerked forward, begging to be turned loose. One of the ladies crawled out of the water and unhitched the animal.

The women jumped and waved to the wagon train still waiting on the other side. Everyone cheered and clapped with joy that all their hard work had been successful.

Carl Moore called to Mr. Mills. "I have a suggestion. A man needs to ride the back of the mule to keep him going straight across."

"Good idea. That's the answer to our problem," Mr. Mills said.

As the sun went down, Mr. Mills called a stop to the wagons crossing the river. They would begin again in the morning with all the personal belongings of the ladies. Over half of the wagon train would camp on the other side of the river. The water seemed to have calmed, and Mr. Mills prayed that it would remain that way tomorrow.

The men built a bonfire on both sides of the river. Everyone was wet, cold and hungry. Cassie had fed some of the people sandwiches at the midday meal but many of the others had already crossed over with no food.

"Listen, folks, I know you're hungry and cold. Some of you can retrieve a blanket or two to help you sleep, but don't unpack all your belongings. In the morning, we'll get an early start and cross the river as fast as we can. I'm happy with our progress today, and I'm proud of those ladies that made it across. Now, get as much rest as you can. Good night," Mr. Mills said as he walked into the bushes.

The next day, all the ladies, wagons, and personal items successfully made it across the river. Mr. Mills motioned for Cassie to come to his wagon. "Cassie, please recruit some of the ladies and see if you can cook something hot for everyone to eat. Breakfast food would be great."

"I'll do that right away. Some of the ladies are already making hot coffee, and pancakes. We'll have something ready in a short while." Cassie rushed back to her fire and signaled for her friends to come and help.

Once everyone had eaten their fill and were ready to go to bed, Mr. Mills said he had some good news. "Ladies, this wagon train is only about twenty-five miles away from Amarillo. If the weather holds, we should be camped on the outside of town in a few days."

The ladies clapped and laughed. Their future was to begin only in a few days.

****

Moore, the wagon train scout, rode into the center of the wagons. "Amarillo is just around the bend," he yelled, slapped his hat down over his chaps and rode his horse around in several circles. Several of the mules rose up on their hind legs and bellowed while the ladies were running to the horseman and screaming with joy.

"Settle down, everyone," the train master yelled. "That's great news, but we have things to do before entering the outskirts of town. So, everyone gather around and take a seat in a big circle." Mr. Mills rushed to his wagon and retrieved his list with instructions needed to prepare the brides to meet their new husbands. As the ladies sat down, they hugged each other.

"Ladies, or should I call all of you 'brides'? We've made a long, hard trip and I'm so proud of all of you. "You made it without harm and without losing your personal belongings. That alone is a miracle," he said, as the ladies laughed at his humor.

"There's a nice lake down the road. We'll park near the bank. All of you can take a nice, refreshing bath and unpack your best duds. We'll notify the men we will be arriving into town in the morning. Mr. George Campbell has arrived, and he'll conduct the meeting. I just want to say thank you for helping my men, and me have a successful trip. If you ladies want to, you can cook up all of your food and have a big party tonight. The men from town won't be allowed near this area. So, spend the day getting ready and have a big celebration tonight. You all deserve it."

The next morning came too soon. The wagon train rolled into Amarillo and their future.

****

Freshly groomed men were seated in the meeting house, nervously waiting for George Campbell to appear.

"They're here!" a young boy about ten-years-old shouted. All the men jumped up from the pews and cranked their necks to the room's back door.

Mr. Campbell waved his hands for the men to be seated. "The ladies will come to the front of the room, and I'll call your name to come and claim your new bride. Please lead her outside, introduce yourself and take a few minutes to get acquainted. He took a seat and watched the parade of ladies enter the meeting room and stand on the foot-high platform. One of the women, a beautiful lady, stepped out of line and took a seat on the back row with some other men. They gave her a stare, tipping their hats and smiling broadly. She seemed to ignore them as she watched a large, older woman, take her place in front of the room.

Mr. Campbell stepped forward and waited to gain their attention. "Welcome ladies and thank you for making the long trip to Amarillo. Each bride-to-be has been given the name of their chosen bridegroom. I worked hard in matching each bride to a husband. Yes, I read your likes and dislikes and your future desires. Indeed, I spent many hours playing matchmaker." All the men laughed, but the ladies eyes were busy scanning the room.

"Get on with it, Campbell. I'm not getting any younger," an older man shouted from the back of the room.

"All right. I will ask each lady to step forward and read the name of her new bridegroom. Once you hear your name, please come forward and claim your bride." He stepped back and wiped his brow.

The first lady to step forward was Tonya. A man whistled and several others comments as to her beauty. "Lucky dog, for sure," one man said loud enough for others to hear.

"Mr. Stacey Brown," Tonya said as she bowed her head and looked down at her feet.

"That's me," a nice-looking farmer shouted. He practically raced forward and seized Tonya's hand. She reached for his firm hand and looked over her shoulder at Janet and Martha. Both girls nodded at her and smiled, causing Tonya to smile back at them.

****

Cassie stepped forward and read the name. "Willy Winters."

"Hell no, I'm forfeiting my money," he said, jumping up from the pew. He scooted past several men and raced out of the room. Cassie stared down at her feet with every bone in her body embarrassed.

Jocelyn's heart was broken for her friend. Cassie didn't need that weasel of a man anyway. Before she thought it through, Jocelyn dashed to the front of the room and wrapped her arm around Cassie's waist. "Come with me," Jocelyn said, as she led her friend out of the room.

****

"Hey, Campbell, who's the lucky fellow to get this young beauty?" Tiger Jordon said as he stepped in the aisle and stopped Jocelyn and Cassie. "If she doesn't have a groom, I'll give you four hundred dollars for her."

"No, I'll give you five hundred," another big farmer announced.

"I'll pay you one thousand," a Golden Slipper gambler declared loud enough for the whole town to hear.

"Quiet. That young lady is Miss Norwood, and she belongs to Matt Colburn. His foreman will take her to his ranch." Mr. Campbell waved his hand to allow her to pass.

"That's not fair. He's supposed to be here. You said that yourself," a man shouted. "Seems like he broke the rules, so she's up for grabs."

"Mr. Colburn is out of town. We didn't know the exact date the wagon train would arrive, so he's not at fault. Please allow Miss Norwood to pass."

Cassie and Jocelyn had made it out to the boardwalk when a young man came running up.

"Miss Norwood, I'm Mr. Colburn's foreman. He asked me to take you to his ranch and get you settled."

"Thank you. May I bring my friend with me?"

"I'm sorry, ma'am. He only said to bring you." The foreman shifted from one foot to the other.

"It's all right, Jocelyn. I'll get settled in the hotel and start looking for a job tomorrow. You go on with this nice young man. Don't your worry, I'll be just fine."

"I'm sorry the little weasel embarrassed you, but you wouldn't have married him anyway," Jocelyn said with a small smile.

"You're right. I wouldn't have acted a fool in front of the whole town, but I was preparing to let him down gently. Our contracts say we don't have to marry," Cassie whispered.

"I'll come back into town as soon as I can. We can't lose touch with each other. You're the sister I never had." She waved goodbye to Cassie as the foreman helped her into a beautiful carriage that had a painted golden brass sign on the door that read *Colburn's Cattle and Horse Ranch.*

Chapter 5

A flash of nerves swept through Matt as he prepared to enter the parlor in his ranch house. He checked the cleanliness of his fingernails, his belt buckle, and the buttons on the front of his denim. He'd arrived home late and rose early to take a bath before meeting the woman that George had chosen for him.

Matt sighed and took a deep breath as he entered the room where his new bride awaited. Her beauty made him stop in the doorway. She stood to her feet, her chin high, and met his eyes. He swallowed at her inspection of him. He waited for her to look away, but her crystal blue eyes locked on his, as if she was scrutinizing his inner soul.

Her lovely, blond hair was pulled back from her oval face, which was tanned, most likely from the drive. He guessed she was as curious about him as he was her.

"Miss Norwood, I'm Matt . . . Colburn." He stumbled over his introduction. A red flush stained his cheeks. *Why am I tongue tied? It's not like I 'm a young fool looking to court a stranger who just happens to be the most beautiful woman I've ever seen.*

Matt had planned his speech, rehearsed it, and committed it to memory. He was going to advise her that they needed to marry. Although he'd never intended to get married, he'd heard so much about this girl and saw that she was a beauty. This time his men weren't exaggerating. So, what the heck? She was everything he dreamed his bride would be.

She was still staring at him and waiting for him to speak.

He started to speak again, but her rosy lips were slightly opened, showing pretty, straight white teeth. Her cheeks were pink, and she had a small button nose. Her beauty made him forget his thoughts. Finally, he found his voice. "I'm sorry I wasn't at the meeting house to greet you, but we need to set a time to meet the preacher tomorrow and get hitched. I mean, married."

****

A blush rose on her smooth cheeks. She stepped forward and said, "Mr. Colburn, did you not get a copy of my contract from Mr. Campbell?"

Matt's hands were sweaty, but he resisted wiping them on his pants. He decided to speak plainly and openly. "No, I didn't read the contract. George told me it was a standard contract stating I would pay three-hundred dollars for your passage to come to Amarillo to be my wife. He chose you for me . . . so, what's the problem? Are you unsatisfied with me? It can't be my home, or this ranch, because it's one of the richest in the state."

Hesitating, Jocelyn smoothed back her hair. She appeared to be trying to hold back her temper. "There is a problem, sir. My contract states that I will be your cook, not your bride."

He paused for a long moment, then summoned the courage to speak his mind. "Let me see your copy of the contract. I need to know what my money bought."

Jocelyn walked over to her carpetbag and pulled out the paper. Matt reached for the contract, saw that it was signed, and gave a short snort of laughter. "You have promised yourself to me."

"No! I told Mr. Campbell I only wanted to come to Amarillo and be a cook, not a bride." Jocelyn slapped her hand down on the kitchen counter. "I should have known that old fool would trick me."

He leaned against the side of the stove and watched the lovely girl wring her hands. The young woman was so mad that her tears nearly overtook him. Matt was a nice man and he hated to see a woman cry, must less be the cause of the tears. She was so beautiful, and he wanted her to be more than a cook. Matt paced the room, waiting for the girl to pull herself together. Maybe if he allowed her to move in and cook for his men, he could change her mind about marriage. He didn't want to be a brute and make her hate him. Like a wild filly, it would take him time to gain her trust. In time, maybe he could make her like him first. Later, he would fight to win her heart and perhaps convince her to marry him.

****

Why didn't the man say anything? Her temper was getting the best of her. She glanced around the room and saw a small tray with a teapot. Infuriated more than when she was told that she only had two weeks to marry the banker's son, she hoisted the teapot to throw it at him, but he grabbed her hand, and none too gently, set the teapot back on the table.

"Stop right now," he ordered. "Get hold of your temper. Everything you break in my house will be added to your debt to me. Look, if you choose not to marry me, I can't force you, but you'll have to work for me for a long time to pay back three-hundred dollars."

Her head snapped up, and she stared at him. "You mean you'll allow me to work for you?" Before he could answer, she held her head high and her back straight. All her tears had disappeared. "You won't be disappointed. I'm an excellent cook."

****

Matt folded his arms across his chest and looked at her petite body. He would never have guessed that such a tiny young woman could have such a fierce temper. She surprised him, but he'd rather have a woman who would fight for what she wanted than a meek woman who was afraid of her own shadow. "As my wife, you wouldn't have to get up at 4:00 a.m. and work all day until dark. You would have a very nice life here, with me. If you had any sense, you'd realize that you're making the wrong choice, but I'm not a begging man."

"Listen, Mr. Campbell wrote my contract, and I didn't read it before I signed it. That was a big mistake that I brought on myself. I never intended to come here on false pretenses. Please believe me, I'm sorry if I have caused you a problem. If you like, I can leave here and go to work in town. I'll repay you a part of my wages each week."

"No, you aren't leaving here and don't even attempt moving back to town."

"Are you threatening me? Do you plan for me to be a prisoner on your ranch?" Before Matt could respond to these ridiculous questions, she screamed, "I won't stand for that. I'll leave when I get good and ready."

He met her eyes. "You just try to leave this ranch and you'll be sorry."

"Would you beat me?" Jocelyn asked. "Of course, Mr. Campbell said you had a fierce temper."

"I don't beat women, but don't make me show that side of myself, Miss Norwood." Matt turned and motioned for her to follow him. He strode to the large room off the kitchen, her footsteps letting him know she was following him.

"This is your living quarters. There's a key for your door on the dresser, so no one will invade your privacy." Matt opened the door for her to enter.

"My," Jocelyn said, glancing around the room. "I never dreamed that I would have wonderful quarters like this." She took a seat on the four-poster bed with a colorful quilt and many pillows near the headboard.

He could tell she was enchanted with the room, and rightly so. A stone fireplace stood against the wall along with a rocking chair, and small table. A large lantern on the mantel lent a warm glow to the room. Colorful rugs were scattered on the floor adding a warm feeling.

"This was my grandmother's room. She always did the cooking for the house, so she wanted to be near the kitchen." Matt turned and gave her a small salute. "Eight men will be ready for breakfast when the sun rises."

The next morning, after all the men were fed and back at work, Matt entered the dining room and wondered why Jocelyn wasn't clearing the table. He went into the kitchen and froze. His lovely cook was lying face down on the kitchen counter that was covered with flour. She was fast asleep. He stood, watched and listened to a soft snore coming from her rosy lips. When he touched her on the arm, she brushed his touch away. Then in a flash, her head shot up, and her eyes darted around the room. She leaped up from the stool. Matt stepped back and smiled at her.

Flour dusted her lovely hair that was hanging in her face and pressed against her forehead. She was a sight for sore eyes. It was all Matt could do not to laugh. "Are you all right?" Matt asked, hiding his laughter.

'Sorry, I just needed a few minutes of rest while the men drank their last cup of coffee. I'd better go check on them." Jocelyn jumped up, but Matt stopped her.

"The men are all gone. I came in to drink my coffee in peace."

"Again, I'm sorry. This won't happen again. What would you like for breakfast? I served the men flapjacks, bacon and ham. I still have some batter or I can make you whatever you wish."

Matt reached to move several strands of hair behind her ear. "Flapjacks will be fine with plenty of hot coffee, please."

Jocelyn nearly went to her knees from his hand's soft

touch. She followed Matt into the dining room and removed a stack of dirty dishes. She placed clean silverware and a napkin at the head of the table. Then rushing back into the kitchen, she came back with a cup of hot coffee before she started the flapjacks.

Matt watched his new cook fly out of the dining room. Jocelyn was dressed in a freshly ironed calico dress with a white apron tied with a large bow in the back. She might be covered with flour, but she was so darn cute. As Jocelyn placed a large stack of flapjacks in front of Matt, he asked, "Why were you so tired this morning? Is the cooking too much for you to do alone?"

"No, I didn't sleep very well in a strange bed, but I'm sure I'll get used to it."

****

Jocelyn had gone to bed, but tossed and turned for hours thinking about her new boss –the man she was supposed to marry. He was a man's man, for sure. She had heard that term said about a big, strong man, and Matt Colburn was undoubtedly that. He was a handsome cowboy, too. Mercy, it was hard to keep her eyes off of him.

"Come and sit down with me. First, we need to decide what we're going to call each other."

"Oh, I couldn't join you at the table. That wouldn't be proper for the boss and the maid."

"Bull. Grab a cup and come sit down with me, now. I'm the boss, and you will comply."

"Is that an order?"

"Yes, this is your first order from me." Smiling, he patted the table.

Chapter 6

Jocelyn poured herself a cup of coffee and sat down to his right. "You may call me Jocelyn," she smirked. "What do you suggest I call you? Mr. Colburn, boss or Mr. Matt?" She placed two teaspoons of sugar in her coffee.

"Well, Josh, you may call me Matt, not Mr. Matt, since you're older than six." Smiling, he sipped his hot coffee.

"My name is Jocelyn, not Josh," she said, bolting to her feet.

"Sit down, Missy," Matt demanded, taking her wrist.

Jocelyn was momentarily stunned into silence as she sat back down. Then, she lowered her face, her lower lip protruding.

"Oh, my goodness. Don't sit there pouting because I chose to shorten your name."

"I don't pout," she murmured. "And you will show me respect due a woman by calling me by my given name." Needing something to do, she took another sip of her coffee and wiped her mouth.

He rolled his eyes. "A bit of a testy filly, are we? Now that we have the names settled, is there anything you need from town? One of my men will go and pick up supplies for the house and kitchen. The pantry is probably depleted, so you'll need to take inventory. Make a list and I'll give it to one of the men. We have a smokehouse and milk is stored in the spring house by the well. My men like meat and potatoes with plenty of hot bread. You don't have to cook fancy dishes, just a lot of it."

"I'll prepare a list this morning," Jocelyn said. "Do you have a list of duties I need to do besides cooking three meals a day?"

"I have a wash lady who comes three times a week. Living alone, I don't need a housekeeper every day, but I have a woman who comes twice a week. Please tell me if you think I need more help keeping the ranch house clean and in good repair."

"What about a gardener?"

"A gardener? For what?"

"Well, for your flowers and the summer garden," she replied.

"I don't have many flowers and I don't have a vegetable garden."

"Well, you might need someone to plant roses and other flowering bushes for the front of the house. A few plants would look nice growing around the ranch."

"Did you have a gardener where you come from?" Matt asked, realizing he had a lot to learn about his bride-to-be.

Jocelyn didn't answer him, but she stood and began removing the dirty dishes.

****

Cassie winced as she stretched her arms after having slept in the parlor of a boarding house. Now, she was stiff and sore from sleeping in an oversized chair. After using the privy, she found the sweet lady who owned the boarding house on the verandah and asked where the Colburn ranch was located.

"It's about five miles north of Main Street. You can't miss it if you head straight down that road." She stood on the boardwalk and pointed toward a sandy road. "I'm so sorry, Miss, that I couldn't give you a room, but I have to have paying customers. This place is how I make a living,"

"I appreciate you letting me stay inside your parlor. You were the only person who would even look my way," Cassie said. "I have a friend working for Mr. Colburn. Maybe he will hire me too."

"Good luck to you," the older woman said. "He's a hard one. Don't know if he'd be the best to work for."

Even though it was late September, the weather was hot. Cassie had driven a wagon and fought with a team of mules across the country. Now, she wished she had walked more and gotten in better shape. She was already exhausted and sweating like a fat pig.

Finally, she sat down under a shade tree to rest. As soon as she got comfortable, she heard a wagon rattling toward her. Maybe the driver would offer her a ride. She stood in the road and waited for the driver to stop. "Hey, mister," Cassie said, as she hurried to the side of the wagon. "Do you have room for a very tired passenger?"

"How far have you walked? Are you coming from town?"

"Yep, I walked this far, but these old legs have given out on me." Cassie said, shaking her head and wiping her face with a hanky. "Are you heading anywhere near the Colburn ranch?"

"Sure am. That's where I'm headed." The man looked Cassie up and down. "Aren't you the bride that got rejected at the meeting house?"

Cassie dropped her head and studied her sandy boots. She wanted to die from embarrassment, but she didn't say anything. She guessed every man in town remembered her. She was a tall, large woman who would be easily recognized. "Yep, that's me."

The man jumped down from the wagon bench and offered his hand to Cassie. He spit a long stream of tobacco juice. "Well, all I can say is you're better off without that little snake in the grass. You'd have been his slave."

Cassie looked at the man in surprise and smiled. She allowed him to assist her on to the wagon. "Thank you so much. I have a friend working for Mr. Colburn. Maybe I can get a job working on the ranch, too."

"Well, his new bride arrived and she's a great cook. She's a beauty," the man said as he steadied the horse. "Most of the supplies I have in the wagon are for the kitchen. I missed breakfast, but the men bragged on his bride's cooking."

"That's my friend, for sure. But, I bet she ain't no bride," Cassie said.

****

By the time Cassie reached the ranch, she had already made a friend of Jim Watson. They had talked all the way and he told her about the ranch. But, he didn't give her any hope of getting a job, because it seemed the house had plenty of help already.

Once Jim stopped at the back door, he leaped down and helped Cassie onto the porch. Then he rapped on the back door.

The housekeeper opened the door and smiled broadly at him. "Who you got with you?" she asked, stepping back and allowing him in the kitchen with a big bag of potatoes over his shoulder.

"Where's the new bride?" he asked, teasing the housekeeper.

"Here I am, sir, but I'm just the cook. Please put those potatoes in the pantry."

"Hello Jocelyn," Cassie said, coming inside with her carpetbag.

"Cassie!' Jocelyn rushed over to Cassie and hugged her. Tears streamed down both of the girls' faces.

"Where did you come from?"

"Mr. Watson picked me up beside the road. I was walking here from town. I'm so grateful to him."

Cassie looked at the driver as he came out of the

pantry. "Thank you, Mr. Watson, for bringing me my best friend. I have missed her so much."

"Name is Jim, ma'am. Just plain Jim. We'll be working together a lot."

"Come into my private room, Cassie, and let's have a good long talk."

"My goodness, this is your room? It's the nicest room I've ever seen," she said as she inspected everything. "How is the boss man? Is he nice?"

"Yes, I guess. He was pretty upset with me for a while, but he finally agreed that I could work off my debt to him."

"Do you think he would hire me? I couldn't get a job in town, and I soon ran out of money. I have nowhere to go, but I don't want to make any trouble." Cassie sat down in the rocking chair and sighed. "I'm hungry. Unfortunately, I can't remember when I ate last." Cassie hung her head down and wiped tears from her eyes.

"Oh, my dear friend. There's the water closet. Go and wash your face and hands and come into the kitchen. I'll make you an early lunch."

Jim was leaving the kitchen. "Welcome to the ranch, ma'am. I hope you and Matt will be very happy."

"Mr. Watson, Jim," Jocelyn said. "I'm not Mr. Colburn's bride. All I am is the cook, not a wife. I'm sure he will tell the rest of the men."

"Yes, ma'am, whatever you say. I'll see you at supper tonight. Good day." He nodded and backed out of the door.

Once Jocelyn had made a plate of sandwiches for Cassie, she asked if she would like to take a nap."

"No, honey. I want to put on an apron and help you prepare the dinner meal. You tell me what you want me to do and let's get started."

"Oh, this will be so much fun now that you're here. First thing, I need to set about ten loaves of bread to rise. We have plenty of flour and there's a big jar of starter in the cooling box next to the door. Afterward, I'll put together three meatloaves and serve it with mashed potatoes and green beans that we have in the cellar. I'll make strawberry pies with the over-ripe strawberries, too."

"How many hands are you feeding?" Cassie asked.

"There will be about a dozen, total. Of course, we'll have to prepare a lot. Matt said that his men are big eaters."

"Are you prepared to cook for that many people without help? Golly, I'm sure glad I came along." The ladies laughed and poured out bowls of flour, lard, yeast, and milk.

"I hear someone coming, Cassie. Hurry into my room. I don't want my boss to see you yet."

Cassie quickly dusted her hands. "Jocelyn, I want to ask him for a job."

Matt entered the kitchen just as Cassie made it out of sight. "I could have sworn I heard you talking to someone."

"I'm the only one in here. Can I help you with something, Mr., I mean Matt?" She continued to roll the dough as he looked at the project she was working on.

"How many loaves of bread are you making at one time?" Matt circled the table with the two large bowls with flour and other items. "It looks like you could use some help."

"That's exactly what I told this stubborn gal. I'm here to offer her a hand," Cassie said as she swished into the kitchen.

Matt eyes widened as she grinned at him. Then he looked at Jocelyn and back at Cassie. "Who are you and where did you come from?"

Before Cassie could answer, he turned to Jocelyn. "I knew I heard you talking to someone." It seemed to anger him that Jocelyn hadn't been forthcoming.

"Yes, sir. She was talking to me about what we would prepare for all your men tonight. I love to cook, and I know how to cook for a crowd. I worked at a café before I joined the brides' wagon train." Cassie was rattling on. She was so excited to meet the handsomc boss.

"I'm sorry I didn't allow you to answer me. Who are you, and why are you on my ranch?"

"My name is Cassie Rowe, sir. I came from Midland on the brides' wagon train. But I came out here because I couldn't get a job in town and I knew my friend," she glanced at Jocelyn, "was working on a big ranch. I hoped that I could hire on." Cassie stopped talking and looked at Matt.

****

"Miss Rowe, please excuse Josh and me while we have a discussion."

"I can't leave what I'm doing. We'll need to talk later." Jocelyn continued rolling the bread dough, as if he hadn't spoken to her.

"Miss Norwood, you seem to have a problem following my orders. Now, get your fanny in my office." Matt stormed out of the kitchen and stood at the kitchen door.

Jocelyn took a clean dishrag and wiped her hands, not looking at Cassie. She marched to the door and went into the office. The room smelled like leather and beeswax. His oak desk was almost as large as a small dining room table. An oversized brown leather chair sat in front of wide, double windows without shades or drapes. He could look out over his ranch in one glance.

"My name is Jocelyn. Not Josh, sir. Please remember that in the future."

"Don't you *dare* stand there giving me orders. I'll call you whatever I wish. You remember I'm your boss." He took a seat in his big chair, never taking his eyes off of her.

"Take a seat," he said through gritted teeth. The man glared at her until she was forced to look down at her hands, twisting the dishrag into knots.

Matt sat at his desk and stared at her until she was forced to look down at her hands. She twisted the dishrag into knots while she waited for the storm to come.

"First, don't lie to me again. I hate a liar. It was a small thing, but small lies lead to big ones, understand?" Matt waited for Josh to give him a nod.

"Now, why couldn't you tell me that Miss Rowe was here looking for a job? I can see with my own eyes that you could use some help." Matt said, not waiting for an answer. "Why isn't she married, since she was one of the brides?"

"Her bridegroom rejected her in front of the whole town. The worm. I wanted to strangle him for hurting her feelings." She spoke through gritted teeth.

"Who was the man?"

"Willy Winters."

"Dang, she's better off without that little 'worm' as you called him. Do you want me to hire this woman to live here and work with you?"

"Oh, yes. Please do. We traveled together from Midland; She's hardworking and a wonderful cook. We can do a lot more for you besides cooking."

"Like what?" When she didn't say anything, he asked again. "What can you do besides cook?"

"Together, we could plant a summer garden and grow our own fresh fruit and vegetables, then we could can them to have for the winter."

"All right, Josh, I'll hire her, but you'll have to fire her if she doesn't work out. I'm not good at that thing."

"Oh, Matt, thank you. The men will love her as much as I do. She can share my room." Jocelyn said.

His eyes sparkled. The game was on. "There is another room down the hall from your room. It's not as nice as my grandmother's room, but I believe it will be satisfactory."

"May I go and tell her?"

"No, send her in to me. I need to go over the rules and discuss her wages. I'm still in charge." Matt opened the door and smiled as Jocelyn walked back to the kitchen.

Chapter 7

Why were all the men sitting on the corral fence, and what were they looking at? Carol Moore rode his horse over to the ranch hands and tossed his reins to a young boy, then turned to the group of rowdies. “What are you fellows looking at?”

One of the guys pointed toward the side of the house. “That little filly over there in denim with Jim Watson. She’s got a mighty fine backside.”

Carl glanced over his shoulder as the row of farm hands hooted at that new gal, who was just bending over to pull up a small tree. *Mercy me. It’s bad enough she isn’t married, but in a few days she’s managed to disrupt the whole ranch.* “Where’s Matt*?”*

“Here I am, Carl. What’s going on?” He strolled from the back of the corral.

The young hired hands leaped from the fence and rushed into the barn, leaving Carl alone with the boss man. Carl nodded his head toward Jocelyn and Jim.

****

Matt straightened, lost his smile, and marched toward the new space for the garden. He stomped around a few piles of dirt and weeds. Jim stopped hoeing as Matt strode by him to Jocelyn as she pulled up an angry weed.

“Man, I need an axe to get this bunch of weeds,” she said, wiping her dirty glove hand on her forehead.

“You’re going to need a pillow to sit on if you don’t

get your sassy behind in the house and get out of those . . . *britches."*

"What?" Jocelyn glanced up over at Jim as he was slowly sneaking toward the house. "What's wrong with working in my pants? It's better than fighting a dress tail in these weeds."

"First, you shouldn't be out here digging up this ground for the garden. I have a dozen men who can do this in a few hours. You are supposed to pick the garden's fruit."

"But, it was my idea to have the garden. I see no reason I can't help with it," Jocelyn said, her chin lifted.

"I don't know where you bought those things you're wearing, but I don't want to see them on you again."

"I brought these to wear on the wagon train under my skirts, but later, all the ladies were wearing them without skirts. They're great to work outside in."

"Do I have to remove them from your body?"

"Well, course not, you . . . "He could tell she was fighting to hold her tongue and not call him a terrible name.

"Careful, princess. I am still your boss." He waited for her to get control of her mouth. "Now, march in the house and remove those things, or I'll rip them off right here in front of my men."

"You wouldn't dare touch me like that." She narrowed her eyes and met his without blinking.

"Don't push me, Josh," he said softly, stepping toward her.

In a huff, Jocelyn tossed the hoe down and gave him a fierce look. Then she hurried from the garden, racing into the house.

. Matt watched his lovely cook disappear into the house. Jim was standing at the pump, washing his face and hands. He marched over to the man. "Jim, what were you thinking allowing that young woman to dig and pull weeds?"

Jim's ears and neck brightened with the flush of red. "I told her that I would get some help, but she wouldn't have any of it. She said she wanted to do it herself and later put the plants and seed in the ground. I did try, Matt, but she's a hard-headed young woman."

"Tomorrow morning, gather a few younger boys to prepare the ground for the summer garden. When it's completed, she can plant whatever she wants in it. You should have told her that she shouldn't wear those unlady-like pants."

"Believe me, I tried. She only laughed and said I was wearing them, so what was the difference?" He dried his face with a towel and grinned at Matt. "Who was I to argue with your bride-to-be?"

Matt shook his head, trying not to laugh at his old friend and went into his office.

****

Later, Matt put his feet on the desk and leafed through a farmer's magazine from Birmingham, Texas. Matt enjoyed his office. It was a symbol of his achievement on his ranch. He was proud to invite people into his domain to discuss business and make deals. A soft knock interrupted his reading. "Come in," he called.

Jocelyn stood in the doorway. She had bathed and dressed in a clean dress—the picture of freshness.

"Please come in and have a seat," Matt said.

"I wish to speak with you about this morning."

"What is there to discuss? In the morning, some of my young ranch hands will ready the garden for you, and after the grounds settles, you can ride into town with Jim and choose the plants and seeds."

"Thank you. I didn't mean to cause so much trouble. I hope you didn't punish Jim for helping me."

"Josh, I don't punish my men when they do something I don't like. I do have a temper, but I am not a brute. If a man continues to do things I don't like, I dismiss them and send them on their way. Besides, Jim is one of my oldest friends. He's more like family."

"Good, I feel better now. I only wanted to help, but I will talk to you before I take on another project." She stood and looked out of the window. Suddenly, she caught her breath. She leaned closer to the window. She stepped back, whirling around to confront Matt. "Do you know those men?"

Matt walked to his wide window and looked toward the men standing at the well. He could feel Jocelyn's body tremble. "No, I have no idea who those men are talking to Carl. Do you recognize them?" She was pale as a ghost.

"Yes, I have seen one of them before. I'm sure they are looking for me."

"What? Why?" Matt asked, puzzled.

"Please don't let them find me," Jocelyn said, pleading with Matt. She reached for the front of his leather vest with her two fists. "I must go away."

"Why are you hiding from those men?" Matt's heart was beating fast. He was suddenly afraid that he might lose this beautiful girl.

"Please, I'll tell you after they're gone. Don't worry, it's not the law that wants me, I promise you."

"Get into my gun closet. I'll have to let the men in the house, but they'll never scout around in here." Matt walked her to the closet and pushed the door shut. Then Matt hurried outside to greet the strangers. "Welcome to my ranch. How may I help you, fellows?" Before they answered, Matt asked, "Are you interested in one of my fine horses or some of my beef?"

"We are Pinkerton men. My name is Jeff Peterson, and this is James Williams. We're from Perryville, Texas. Mr. Willard Sullivan, the banker of Perryville First National Bank, has hired us to search for his son's bride.

"Now, Jeff, Miss Norwood is the banker's son's bride-to-be, not his bride."

"Of course, I'm sorry for that mistake. Anyway, we're looking for a girl."

"I'm afraid you men have wasted your time coming out here. I have a housekeeper, a washwoman, and a cook, none of whom would be your *runaway bride,"* Matt said. So that was why Josh didn't want to get married. She must have had a bad experience with a man before coming here.

"We have a search warrant to look everywhere on your property. May we look around in your house?"

"Please, come with me. I'll have my cook make you a cool drink and something sweet," Matt said, leading the men into the house. Take your time and come into the kitchen when you complete your search."

Once inside the kitchen, he called to the cook. "Cassie, please fix the Pinkerton men something to drink and cut them a slice of pie. We want them to feel welcome while searching for a runaway girl." Matt saw the scared look on Cassie's face. "I'm sure they won't find anyone like that here." Matt sat at the kitchen table and watched Cassie cut into a fresh apple pie. He gave her an assuring smile, which she returned with a wink.

A few minutes later, the men appeared at the door of the kitchen. "You were right, Mr. Colburn. Your foreman said that there wasn't a girl on your ranch. Although, I must admit you have a lovely home. The nicest place we've visited while traveling."

"Please sit and tell me about this runaway girl, in case she shows up here," Matt said. "Cassie has cut you some pie."

Immediately, Cassie set slices of pie before the two men which they each dug into.

"This is so good. Thank you." James Williams gobbled down the last bite.

"We don't have a picture of the girl we're looking for, but she's a beauty. She ran away from her father's house the day she was to marry."

"What does she look like?" Matt asked, very curious.

"She's this tall." He demonstrated by holding his hand shoulder high. "Her hair is very long. A pretty blonde, with blue eyes. We're told that she is educated, an excellent cook, speaks several languages and can ride a horse. One person said that she can ride like the wind, but you know how people talk."

"How did she escape the house? Did she ride away on a horse?" Matt asked.

"We're still determining how she traveled. She and her maid must have planned her escape. After examining the house, the banker discovered missing art paintings and expensive figurines. The maid said that the girl had sold those things to have money."

"What does her father think now that the girl has disappeared?"

"Oh, he died several weeks before the wedding date."

"Would you gentlemen like some more refreshment," Cassie asked.

Mr. Peterson stared at Cassie. He was sure he had seen her before. "You know, I remember seeing you on the wagon train. There were some young ladies with you. Where are they now?"

"All the ladies took husbands after we arrived in Amarillo. I haven't seen them since their weddings."

"Did you marry?" the other man asked.

"No, I got a better offer. Mr. Matt needed a cook." Cassie walked over to the dry sink and began cleaning carrots.

"Thank you for your hospitality. Unfortunately, we have a lot of ground to cover before we head back to Perryville," Jeff Peterson said.

Matt walked the men to the front door and saw Carl leading their horses from the barn. The men had fed and watered the two animals. He saluted Carl and hurried back to his office, where he had hidden Jocelyn.

Chapter 8

While still hiding in the back of the dark closet, Jocelyn heard Matt open the door. She blinked at the bright light and waited for him to invite her to come out. Instead, the handsome young man with short brown hair, green eyes and a short, mustache barely covering his top lip blocked her passage.

She thought she might start weeping. Her eyes were misty. She shifted from one foot to the other as he stood in front of her. She thought he might be trying to get his thoughts under control. Or his temper. A blush rushed to her neck and face, and she shifted from one foot to the other. He placed his hand on her shoulder and guided her over to a chair in front of his big oak desk. He could feel her trembling.

"Sit Josh."

Matt was a very handsome man, regardless of whether he was angry or gentle. She couldn't look away from him as he moved to take a seat in his leather chair. He was ordering her around as if she were a dog, but two could play that game. She knew how to break a horse as well as he did.

His voice was cold when he spoke. "I believe you owe me an explanation as to why those men were here searching my home."

She swallowed, ready to take on an angry boss man. She had not realized how much she admired him. He seemed so sure of himself. Matt had an air of quiet authority about him. She witnessed how he didn't demand respect from his men; he earned it and their trust. She had never heard him raise his voice to anyone, except her. She smiled to herself as remembering he had raised his voice to her several times. He wasn't disciplined around her and she wondered why he couldn't control his temper in her presence?

For a few minutes, she thought about what and how much she should tell him about her past. Then, squirming around in the oak chair, she was determined to keep her mouth shut. She needed time to think about what she wanted him to know about why she'd run away from Perryville.

****

Matt waited patiently for Jocelyn to tell him what he wanted to know about her. She was delightful. *Lord help me, I love this girl.* This petite gal, strong-willed, courageous, but tenderhearted, had captured his heart. All he wanted to do was put his arms around her and pull her close. How he longed to tell her that he cared deeply for her, and she would never have to be afraid of anybody again. She belonged to him, and he would protect her with his own life. But now was not the time. Instead, he said, Josh, we can sit here all morning, but you have a big lunch to prepare for my men. Tell me why those men are hunting you like a criminal."

Matt's words had the power to make her feel so vulnerable. She burst into tears and heart-wrenching sobs overflowed.

As fast as lightning, Matt hurried around his desk and pulled Jocelyn into his arms. "It's all right. We can talk later. Now, stop crying," he said, rubbing his hand up and down her back. "Come, let me walk you to your room. Pull yourself together, wash your face and have some tea." Matt led her to the bedroom and motioned for Cassie to follow.

Tingling chills raced up and down her spine. She didn't know why her body responded this way whenever he touched her.

Once Jocelyn walked into the water closet, he told Cassie to take care of her. "Pamper her a little and give her something to do to get her mind off what happened. Those Pinkerton men frightened her." Matt ran his hand through his hair, sighing. "The men will be in shortly for lunch."

"I have lunch well on the way. Now, you go on, and I'll take care of my friend." As he turned to leave, Cassie asked, "Did she tell you anything about why those men were here?"

"No, she didn't, but one of the men told me about her running away from home. I wanted her to tell me herself, but she broke down crying. We'll talk later," he said as he left the bedroom.

****

Jocelyn helped Cassie prepare a big lunch for the ranch hands and later supper. In addition, she helped make several apple pies. The two ladies cleaned the kitchen and prepared the bread, setting it to rise for the next day. Once done cleaning the kitchen, Jocelyn excused herself. She knew Matt would be waiting to talk with her in his office. He had requested coffee and a piece of pie. Jocelyn had made plans to leave as soon as the sun set after the men had completed their evening chores and were settled into the bunkhouse. She quickly dressed in her denim britches and packed her smallest carpetbag.

****

Cassie knocked on her door to tell her that the boss man was waiting for her in his office. She repeated the knock. When Jocelyn didn't answer, she opened the door to find an empty room. She searched the house and went outside scouting around for her. Sometimes the two of them would sit on the back porch steps for a breath of fresh air.

"Cassie, did you tell Josh that I was waiting for her in

my office?"

"Yes sir, I mean no sir. She's not in her room and I just came in from outside looking for her," she said, twisting her hands in her apron.

****

"Come with me," he said. Matt marched over to Josh's bedroom door and knocked. With no answer, he opened the door. Lying on the neat bed were the dress and apron she had worn that day. He glanced in the water closet, looked at the pegs on the wall where she hung most of her clothes, and noticed that her men's britches were missing.

"Cassie, did she say anything to you about leaving or possibly running away from the ranch?" he asked as he continued to search the room.

"No, sir. Why would she run away and from whom?"

"Me, most likely, but if she has, she's going to be sorry." He stormed out of the house and ran into Carl as he leaped upon the porch.

"Matt, your new stallion is missing. I put him in his stall myself, not an hour ago and he's gone."

"Damn her spoiled, rotten hide!" he yelled as Carl looked at him dumbfounded. "Come with me and tell the men to saddle up for a search party. My new cook has run off. I pray she doesn't get thrown from that wild horse and he doesn't get hurt running loose. He cost me two thousand dollars."

Within fifteen minutes, all the men had split up and rode in different directions looking for the runaway cook.

****

Jocelyn had no idea if she was headed in the right direction to town. She had chosen a beautiful horse from the barn. Having ridden many times at home, she knew how to handle an animal full of energy, and she loved how he cantered away from the ranch. With her hair blowing away from her face, she felt wonderful and stress-free for the first time in months.

At home, she'd had a horse similar to the one she was riding. Her horse was a big stallion that was headstrong and hard to handle, but this horse wasn't dangerous or unpredictable. This stallion was a well- trained animal.

As she rode on the trail through the dark forest, she heard growls and cries coming from a wild animal, probably a cougar. She had to be careful as she coaxed the horse to move forward. The cries of the wild animal echoed through the woods. Listening and watching for the wild creature that was possibly trailing them, she hated to pull her horse to a stop. A fallen pine tree with green branches was lying across the path. She would have to turn around or attempt to walk into the thick forest to stay close to the trail.

As she was deciding which path to take, the stallion got skittish. He reared up on his hind legs, causing her to slide out of the saddle onto the soft edge of an embankment. She had just jumped up to grab its reins, when a rifle fired near her ear, and a yellow and black cougar fell from a tall pine tree at her feet.

Screaming as she turned the horse loose, then felt herself sliding face-downward on the slippery, wet ground. Jocelyn clawed at the wet earth attempting to slow her descent through the tall weeds, over tree roots and toward the murky water. She was terrified that she was slipping into a deep ravine. She screamed again as she slid down into the marsh.

****

Matt leaped off his horse, waving a lantern toward the gully, and scooted on his backside down the incline until he reached her. He grabbed at her tangled hair that floated on the surface of the water, covered with wet leaves and mud. He lifted her out of the water and carried her to the bank. Her body was covered with filthy water. Was she dead? "Josh, speak to me!"

She started coughing, retching on the bilge she's

swallowed. Her eyes fluttered open.

"Thank you, Jesus." He gently laid her on the muddy slope. "Are you hurt?" he barked.

"Don't think so. Just cold," she said, shivering." Did you find my horse?"

"My horse, you mean," he yelled, feeling disgusted with himself. She was more concerned about the horse than her own life.

Several of the men rode into the clearing and watched as Matt practically dragged Jocelyn up the slope. One of the men was holding the reins of her horse.

Matt balanced Jocelyn's shivering body on her feet and said through clenched teeth, "Don't move." Then he turned to one of his men. "Johnny, climb on the back of Jimbo's horse and give me yours. My horse is probably back at the ranch. When I fired my rifle, killing the wild cat, my horse got skittish and took off. Take my stallion home, rub him down good and make sure he doesn't have a scratch on him."

"Yes, sir. I'll take good care of him," he said, as all the men left Jocelyn and Matt alone in the deep forest.

****

Jocelyn was watching Matt as he sent his men on their way. Finally, he turned to her, and his stare was hot enough to turn water into steam. "You scare me when you look at me like that," Jocelyn said.

"You need to be afraid of me," he said, not smiling.

What she wanted to do was put him in his place. She had to leave with or without his permission.

"Are you sure you aren't hurt?" He began running his large, rough hands over her body. She was soaked to the skin and shivering.

"I'm fine," she said, attempting to step away from his rough treatment.

"Look at me, Josh. Something's going on between us, and we both know it." He took her chin in his rough, wet hands.

"How can you say that when I don't even know you?" All she wanted to do was return to the ranch and get into a hot bath and dry clothes.

"But I know you." When Jocelyn's eyes showed her disbelief, he confirmed his statement. "You're a loyal employee. The men trust that you'll take care of their meals, but you're scared of your past." He stared at her without blinking. "I'm here to protect you, but right this minute I would like to beat some sense into you. A smart gal wouldn't have run away after dark, much less jumped on a strange horse and rode out into the forest heading to heaven knows where." He nodded his head and sighed, "I hope you haven't damaged my prize stallion."

Matt placed both his hands on her shoulders and turned her around. We are going home, and you'll tell me what I want to know. There'll be no more half-truths or lies between us."

Jocelyn didn't move a muscle. She felt like an animal caught in a net. Her bottom lip quivered as she fought back the tears.

"If you continue to look at me like that, we won't be going anywhere," Matt remarked. Moving quickly, Matt removed his jacket and wrapped it around Josh's shoulders. He pushed her forward as he untied the horse's reins from a tree limb. After getting on Jimbo's horse, he reached for Jocelyn's hand and pulled her on to his lap. "Sit still, and this animal will behave."

****

Early the following day, Jocelyn woke up to a very quiet house. She tiptoed from her bed and opened her door. Poking her head out, she saw a clean kitchen. Jocelyn called to Cassie but received no answer. She slipped over to Cassie's room but it was empty. Everything was as neat as if no one had slept in the room.

"Are you all right?" the near voice caused her to jump.

Matt stood so close that she felt his breath on her ear. She glanced at Matt as she ran a hand over her long, blonde braid and pushed the loose hair that had escaped. "I'm so embarrassed. I never oversleep. It won't happen again."

He hooked a loose strand of hair that she had missed behind her ear. "Cassie took care of the men."

A wild rush of goose bumps raced up her arms, causing her to shiver. She realized that she was only dressed in a thin cotton gown. "Why didn't Cassie wake me?" she said, crossing her arms to cover her breasts.

"I told her that I would check on you. You'd had a rough evening and I feared you might be hurt. Besides, you looked so peaceful. I didn't have the heart to disturb you."

Oh, he'd been in her bedroom. She bit her lower lip and started around him. At that moment, her stomach growled. He raised his eyebrows as if to say, 'I know you're hungry.'

Hurrying, she skirted around him and entered her room, leaning against the door as she closed it behind herself. She knew it was time to confide in Matt and tell him the truth. He wasn't going to listen to any excuses after last night. Did she need to tell him everything or just the reason she ran away from her wedding? Would he want to know all about her plan to travel on the wagon train with no intention of becoming a bride? Knowing this man so little, she was sure he would want the whole truth.

Chapter 9

In Perryville, Texas, Luther Sullivan sat in front of the desk of his father's lawyer. He wanted to kill the arrogant man as he listened to the disgusting words he was reading. He called them Father's Wishes. His father was making demands from where he lay in his fresh, six-foot deep grave.

It was still hard for Luther to believe his father had died. One day, he was demanding that he marry a girl like Jocelyn Norwood, and the next, he was robbed and left for dead on the road where he'd been to see a client five miles from town. Luther was disappointed his father had been killed, but he was happy he didn't have to listen to his father ridicule him because he wasn't a manly man.

"Mr. Sullivan, do you understand what I've read to you?"

The young man just stared at the lawyer. He was so angry he couldn't form a word to respond. But, his father was determined to have the last word about how he lived his life.

"Mr. Sullivan, would you like for me to read your father's wishes to you again?"

"Why don't you just spell it out, Mr. Taylor? You and I both know that if the Pinkerton men can't find my runaway fiancée, how do you think I'll be able to discover her whereabouts in less than ninety days?" He looked straight into the lawyer's eyes. "If I don't find my bride-to-be and marry her, this bank will be granted all my father's properties and my inheritance. A tidy sum of money for you since you're one of the bank's silent partners."

"It's never been a secret Mac and I were your father's business partners. Your father wanted us to remain behind the scenes, so to speak. When times were bad, we helped keep the bank afloat, but your father was a shrewd businessman."

"Well, I can be shrewd myself." He leaned forward and glared into the lawyer's eyes. "I will find Miss Jocelyn Norwood. She will honor her word and marry me." He stood, giving the man a nod and marched out of the office.

****

Mac hurried into his partner's office as the young man practically waltzed out of the bank. "Wheeze, how did the prissy young man take to the reading of Willard's wishes?"

"He was stunned into silence. Then he became angry. He said he could be as strewed as his father, and he would find his run-away bride." The lawyer leaned back in his desk chair and smiled. "You might as well start looking for buyers for the property on Water Street. I'm willing to bet some of my stock that he won't find that gal; within the ninety days' time limit."

****

Boomer, Luther's footman, was parked at the curb in front of the bank waiting for his boss. When he saw Luther marching toward the carriage, he leaped down onto the ground and immediately opened the door.

"Take me to the Norwood estate, and don't spare the rod. That maid knows where my bride is, and she will tell me or else." Luther was practically foaming at the mouth.

Boomer had worked for the Sullivan's for many years, and he knew that the son could be very mean. He prayed that Maria, the maid, would tell his boss man what he wanted to know. But if needed, Boomer would never allow the young man to harm the older woman.

Luther didn't wait for Boomer to get down and open the carriage door. Instead, he jumped down, opened the wrought-iron gate and rushed to the front door. Using the end of his walking stick, he knocked on the door. Within two seconds, he used the cane and banged again.

After a few minutes, a tearful Maria, Jocelyn's personal maid and nanny, answered the door as she kicked a carpetbag out of the entrance. She recognized the angry man standing at her door. She wrapped her arms around her chest. "What do you want?"

Luther didn't answer her right away. He pushed his way into the foyer and surveyed the room before turning back to Maria. "I want answers and I know you can provide them. First, I want to know where your mistress, my bride-to-be is hiding?"

"Why should I tell you? Since your father died, your bank has put me out on the street. My husband and I have lived in this house for over twenty years. I helped bring Miss Jocelyn into the world and raised her like my very own after her poor mama died. Because of you, I have to leave my home. Yes, my home. Now, we're penniless with only poor relatives to take us in."

****

Luther suddenly had an idea. If the older woman needed money, now was his chance to get information out of her. He circled the room and noticed that pieces of the art on the walls had been removed and most of the furniture was covered with white sheeting.

"I tell you what, Maria? Your name is Maria, am I correct?"

"Yes, that's what I'm called."

"I will give you five-hundred-dollars for information about Jocelyn's whereabouts. The money's right here in my vest pocket."

"Why should I help you? I know how you hurt my

baby. You're lucky she didn't have you arrested. My friends wanted to hunt you down but Jocelyn begged them not to. It took me several hours to calm them down. So why should I tell you anything about her?"

"Money. I'm ready to give you this five-hundred-dollars for any information about her." He patted his vest pocket.

"I don't know where she went. I found her wedding dress on the floor and an open window. I haven't heard a word from her."

"You're lying. I know you know something that will help me locate her."

****

Maria wiped away tears. She could use the five hundred dollars, but she couldn't betray the dear, sweet child. Besides, she was telling him the truth. She had no idea where she had run off to. Marie wasn't surprised she'd escaped, but she wouldn't tell him. She kept praying for a letter but she knew Jocelyn was too smart to write her a note so soon. The five hundred dollars would help Maria and her husband get settled somewhere else. She hated having to move in with her relatives. So, Maria made a snap decision. "Give me the money now, and I'll tell you what I know. That's how desperate I am."

Luther fumbled with his wallet in his vest pocket and counted out the money. He lingered for a moment, just to let her know who was boss before giving her the money.

Maria immediately stuffed the bills down the front of her bosom.

"Talk. I don't have all day," he barked.

"Miss Jocelyn left here with very little money. I saw her place a handful of paper money in her personal bridal bag. She carried it with her as she went into the bathroom to change into her wedding dress." Maria looked at the little man, who strutted around like a rooster.

"Continue. What did she tell you?"

"Nothing. I went to get her something to drink and when I returned, she'd gone out the window. I was going to hook up the back of her gown, but I found it on the bathroom floor."

"Where was she going and who helped her escape?"

"I told you all that I know."

"That is not five hundred dollars' worth of information. Tell me everything or so help me I'll strangle you with my bare hands." He stepped toward Maria. His eyes were glazed over, and his shaking hands were set to do her harm.

Suddenly Maria flashed a small derringer in his face. "Step away from me or this little gun will blast that nose off your pretty face. I told you I had no information. Probably I said more than I should have. Now you leave before I call the men. They like you even less than I do."

Luther stormed to the foyer. He jerked the door wide open then whipped around, his lips curling into a scowl. "You will be sorry for stealing my money."

****

Boomer was waiting at the gate and quickly opened the carriage door. "Take me to my office." Maybe the older woman didn't tell him where his fiancée was, but the fact that Jocelyn only had a small amount of money was a big help. Now, he knew that she couldn't get far away from Perryville. She may have taken the train or a stagecoach to a very near town. Once he reached his office, he would spread the big map out and make a plan to travel to a few towns within a hundred or so miles away. He and Boomer would make the trip this time; it was useless to send more dumb Pinkerton men.

Chapter 10

After returning late to the ranch with Jocelyn in tow, Matt sent her to bed. After his long, hot bath and settling in bed, he relaxed his stiff muscles and listened to the katydids and crickets. Matt had decided to let Jocelyn come to him and tell her story. He figured if he stopped badgering her, she might relax and start trusting him.

Later that evening. Matt entered the dining room. The men were laughing and enjoying a big dinner Cassie and Jocelyn had prepared. He was pleased that Jocelyn felt well enough to get up and move around. He was sure her body was bruised from her head to her toes from falling off the horse and tumbling down into the nasty ravine, but he wasn't going to ask her how she was.

As Jocelyn nervously refilled his coffee cup, he smelled a vanilla scent surrounding her and the smell of fresh starch. She was wearing one of the two dresses she owned, looking fresh as a daisy with a white apron wrapped around her small waist tied with a crisp bow across her backside.

After all the men had left the table and gone out to do their daily chores, Matt asked Jocelyn to sit and have some tea or coffee with him.

Hesitating, she said that she had too much work to do.

He ignored her rejection. "I'm going into town after

lunch tomorrow and want you to go with me. I don't want to embarrass you, but you need a new wardrobe. Now, don't get your feathers ruffled, but I am your employer, and I furnish certain items for all my hired hands." He watched as her face flamed bright red. "I want you to pick out several new dresses and other personal items. You can pick out a few things for Cassie too, while we're in the dry goods store." He waited for her to make an excuse, but she remained quiet. "Be ready to leave after you've helped Cassie with lunch. We'll take my small black carriage." He stood, pushed his chair into the table and smiled at her as he strolled out of the room.

****

The next afternoon, Matt stopped in front of the large dry goods store, owned by Ben and Gloria Crocker. As Matt helped Jocelyn down, he heard a soft groan as she stepped to the ground. "Are you all right?"

"Yes, I believe you hit every bump and rock in the road," she said with a small chuckle.

As the bell above the door announced their arrival at the store, Mrs. Crocker smiled at them. "Good morning, Matt. My gracious, it's about time you brought in your new bride. We've all been waiting to get a better look at her." Gloria wiped her hands on the front of her apron and held out her palm to shake hands with Jocelyn.

"I'm sorry, madam. I'm not Mr. Colburn's wife."

"Josh, sweetheart, you don't need to discuss our personal relationship." Matt glared at her and reached for her hand. "Come, my dear. There are plenty of nice dresses in the back of the store."

Jocelyn shook his hand loose from hers and hurried away. "Gloria, will you help her choose some nice day dresses in her size and a larger size for one of my cooks."

"Be happy to help. She's a perfect size and I'm sure I have something she'll like."

As Matt strolled around in the store, he picked up a

pair of ladies pantaloons and held them in front of his pants. Whistling, he tossed them over his shoulder.

When Jocelyn noticed what he was doing, she hurried over to him with fire in her eyes. "You've embarrassed me enough," she said, jerking the underwear off his shoulder. "I'm going home."

Matt watched Jocelyn march out the front door. "Well, damn," he muttered. "Gloria, gather me several dresses that you think will fit Jocelyn and other ladies' personal items, shifts and nightgowns. I also need things for my cook, who is about my size." He chuckled at the surprised expression on her face. "Will your boy bring my order out to my ranch this afternoon?"

"Sure enough. But, Matt, you haven't married that gal yet?"

"Now, don't start any gossip. We'll marry as soon as we get to know each other."

"Don't mess around too long. Once the single men learn that she ain't hitched, they'll be coming to court her. She's a beauty for sure."

Jocelyn was sitting in the carriage when Matt came out of the store. Without a glance at her, he untied the reins from the hitching post and climbed into the small carriage. He wished he'd brought the larger carriage because Josh was practically rolled into a ball, not daring to touch him. From the look in her eyes, she might explode and knock him into the middle of next week. "Why did you run out of the store? Now Gloria is going to select new items for you and Cassie without your approval."

"Don't you dare . . . pretend that you don't know how much you embarrassed me in front of your friend? My word, why didn't you go outside with those ladies' personal items draped around your head? Let everyone know you're picking out my underclothes. And another thing, you allowed your friend to believe I'm your bride. How could you?"

He could feel her anger. Turning toward her, he said, "First of all, woman, I was trying to help you choose a few things and I did set Gloria, my friend as you called her, straight. I told her that we aren't married. But, you listen to me, lady. I can't help what my friends think." The more he talked, the madder he got and the faster he drove the carriage. The two horses were racing down the rough road, swaying and bumping up and down.

"Slow down, you fool. You're going to get us killed," Jocelyn screamed.

"Fool? Now I'm a fool? You probably have that right. I should have tossed you out on your sassy fanny when you refused to marry me."

Suddenly, the two horses turned sharply in the curve of the road. One of the carriage's wheels flew off the rig, and the carriage flipped over on its side, tossing Matt onto the hard ground.

****

Jocelyn's body rammed against the front of the carriage, and the next thing she knew she was lying on the floor, suspended sideways. Everything came to a stop, except the two horses reared up several times. Both were covered with white foam on their mouths and chest. They were trying to pull free of the bridle. Jocelyn struggled to a sitting position and saw that the whole carriage had toppled onto its side. Where was Matt? She placed her hands over her mouth and cried. "Oh, my goodness," she murmured a prayer. "Please, God, don't let him be dead."

She pushed open the door and slowly climbed out. Every bone in her body hurt, but nothing seemed to be broken. She couldn't think of herself. Matt?" she called out. No answer. Then she saw him and raced over to him. He lay on his stomach with his face turned sideways, his eyes closed. He was knocked unconscious, but he was breathing.

Jocelyn knew she had to get help. They weren't very far from the ranch, so she started limping down the road.

Several cramps made her grab her lower stomach and her side ached. The small of her back felt like it was broken. After what seemed like forever, she saw one of the ranch hands working cattle in a pasture. "Help," she screamed, then leaned over to catch her breath.

Fortunately, the young man heard her and rode over to the fence.

"I need your help. Matt is hurt. Our carriage turned over. Please go get some of the men. We're a little ways down the road. Please hurry." Jocelyn turned and began walking back to Matt as she watched the young man ride toward the ranch house. She'd almost reach the carriage when Jim and a few men rode past her. Suddenly, she dropped to her knees and doubled over with a sharp pain between her thighs.

Blood flowed down her legs and onto the ground. Jocelyn nearly screamed with joy, but she didn't have time to question what had taken place within her body. She removed her under-shift and wiped the blood off her legs and feet. Something must have torn inside her with the tumble off the horse and the carriage accident hadn't helped.

The young rider stopped, jumped off his horse and asked if she was hurt. "Only a scratch on my leg, but I'm fine. I've stopped the bleeding."

The young man's eyes reflected concern at the sight of blood on her.

"Don't move. You can sit on the ground while I go to the ranch and get another carriage to take you home."

"Please, don't worry about me. Let's get Mr. Colburn back to the ranch."

"Let me pick you up and place you on my horse." With so much blood on the ground, covering her bare legs and in her shoes, he was sure she was hurt more than she was admitting.

Her lower body ached as he lifted her to sit behind

him. He rode the animal around the curve toward the ranch hands.

The men were lifting Matt to a standing position, his head lolling to the side.

She couldn't believe what she was seeing. "What are you doing? Can't you see that he's unconscious? Go fix the carriage so we can place him in it. He can't ride a horse."

When one the men slapped Matt in the face to awaken him, she lost it. "Don't you dare touch him again? Then, grabbing a gun from one of the men's hostler, she yelled, "I'll shoot the next man who goes near him." Her hand was shaking so bad the men stepped away from her.

One of the men waved a dismissive hand at her. "Come on now, Miss Jocelyn. Matt's a tough bird. He's going to be fine."

"Yes, he is and I'm going to see to it. Send for the doctor immediately."

"I don't think he needs . . ."

"Find the doctor and get him out here as quick as he can come or all of you'd better be afraid to eat at my table." Holding the revolver with both hands, she whirled and pointed the gun at each man.

"The wheel is back on the carriage, and the horses are ready," one of the men said.

She pointed the gun in the direction of Matt. "Two of you men gently pick him up and place him in the carriage with me." Jocelyn slowly climbed into the carriage. She felt like she might faint, but she took several deep breaths. "I'll hold him while one of you ride beside the horses. Drive slowly and for goodness' sake, try not to hit every hole and rock in the road."

After arriving at the ranch house, Cassie rushed outside. "Oh, Cassie, Mr. Coburn is hurt badly Tell two of the men to move his bed downstairs into the kitchen where we can tend to him."

"Sure thing. Right away. You two come with me."

Cassie motioned toward the two ranch hands who were chatting near the barn, then she turned and rushed back into the house. In mere minutes, they placed Matt's bed in the kitchen corner. Cassie prepared hot water to clean his cuts and bruises. He still had not awakened, which had Jocelyn very concerned.

Just then Cassie looked at her with a frown and grabbed her around the waist. "Where is all that blood coming from that is down in your shoes? Where are you hurt?"

"Please Cassie, I'm fine now. Really. Please don't let those men touch Matt until I go into my room and clean up. I'm bleeding, but I can take care of myself. Give me a few minutes of privacy. Don't say anything about me being injured."

"All right, if you're sure."

****

In a short while, Jocelyn was cleaned and had taken care of her personal problem. She pinched her cheeks attempting to bring some color to her face. She placed a little vanilla behind her ears and plaited her long hair. She felt better now and hopefully no one would be the wiser that she had a personal problem.

The doctor had arrived and examined Matt. He was pleased that Matt didn't have any broken bones. However, he did have a few badly bruised ribs and a large knot on his forehead. The main concerned was that his patient had not woken up.

Matt kept his eyes opened just a sliver and his breathing even. He didn't want Josh to know he was awake. He'd awakened as she explained to the doctor how she caused his injury. Only she would assume something so illogical. She believed it, though. Even when he was the one driving the wagon too fast because he was angry.

Doctor Murclock must have heard Matt moving around because he stood from his chair. "You're going to have to stay in bed, son."

He stared at the doc like he'd lost his senses. The doctor knew that Matt didn't like that comment at all.

"Listen, you can't even make it from the bed to the door. You must rest. I'm concerned about that knot on your head. You could have a concussion."

"How long do I have to stay in bed?" Matt finally asked.

"At least a week or more."

"No, that's impossible." Just then Jocelyn's pale face appeared in his line of vision.

The doctor glanced at Jocelyn and smiled. "I can see you'll have your hands full with this one."

"Were you hurt in the accident?" Matt reached for Jocelyn's hand but she pulled it back from him. He glared at the doctor. "She's very pale. Have you examined her?"

The doctor placed two pills in his rough hand and told him to take them. He gave Matt a glass of cool water to drink. "No, Miss Norwood said she was fine."

When Matt fell asleep in a matter of minutes. Jocelyn stood beside him and moved his hair away from the large swollen area on his forehead. "Shouldn't he stay awake if he might have a concussion?"

"I'm more worried about his ribs than his head. I don't think he has punched a hole in his lungs, but his ribs are damaged. Sleep and lying still will help him. The head wound is not as bad as it looks. He's going to hurt like the dickens when he tries to move around, but he does need to get up a little every day. I don't want blood clots to form from lying too long."

After a few hours, Matt awakened and insisted on sitting up when the men came to visit. He nearly cried out when he first tried to sit up, but he held himself in check.

The men ate a hearty meal while Jocelyn served Matt a small bowl of chicken soup. He complained that there wasn't anything wrong with his stomach, but later he calmed down. Jocelyn suspected that Jim had given him a piece or two of pork chop when she wasn't looking.

After Jocelyn finished washing the dishes, Cassie stacked them on the open shelf. Meanwhile, several of the men lingered at the table and spoke about the accident which entertained the doctor and a few of the ranch hands.

Jocelyn wasn't listening to them as she reflected on what Doc had told her earlier. Well, she wasn't God, and she couldn't control an angry man. The accident wasn't her fault according to the men. Matt got hurt when the wagon rolled over. A big weight was lifted from her shoulders, but she did feel guilty for making him angry.

People make their own choices. Papa had chosen to gamble. She had lied to him about why she didn't want to marry the banker's son, and she'd misled Matt about why she had run away from her wedding and joined the wagon train.

Later after Cassie set loaves of bread to rise, Jocelyn insisted that Cassie retire for the evening. "Don't you want me to help you with Mr. Matt? Besides, I'm worried about you. You seem so weak and you're awful pale. Are you sure you weren't hurt more than you are saying?"

"Please Cassie, I'm fine. Please retire and don't fret over me. Jim will help me with Matt's personal needs, and I'll give him some medicine to help him rest. You have to be dead on your feet. Please go on to bed."

Cassie waved her hand at Jocelyn. "No. I've warmed some water for the big tub in your room. You come with me and have a nice bath. I'll feel better knowing that your body will feel better after a nice soothing bath. Come with me while I pour the hot water in the tub. I'll watch after Mr. Matt while you relax in that warm water."

"Oh, Cassie, that sounds like a dream come true. I'll take a nice bath if you promise to go to bed when I get my night clothes on."

"I promise, but you take your time. Mr. Matt ain't

going nowhere."

****

"Josh . . ."

Very late into the night, Jocelyn awakened and shivered. She had been sitting in a chair next to Matt's bed. Was she dreaming as she'd heard someone calling her by that nickname?

"Josh. . ." he murmured louder.

Realizing that Matt was calling out to her, she immediately asked, "What's wrong, Matt? I'm here."

"I can't breathe. My ribs hurt so badly. I need to sit up. Please untie this choke hold on me. That crazy doctor is trying to squeeze the life out of me."

Jocelyn stood and moved her neck back and forth. It was stiff and hurting from hours resting in the chair. Looking around the room, she found a pair of scissors and cut the tape.

"Oh, that feels so much better," he said as he took in a big breath. Easing back on his pillow, he fell back to sleep.

Jocelyn rubbed his arms, and forehead as she pulled up the covers and watched him sleep. He was taking over her heart.

****

. Almost morning, Matt awoke feeling something heavy lying beside his legs. He reached for it and discovered a handful of silky hair. Lifting his head, he looked down at his hand to see Jocelyn asleep with her mouth opened just a little. She looked very seductive for such an innocent young woman. If his ribs didn't hurt so badly, he would have pulled her into his arms. But, he just lay with his right hand tangled in her hair. He'd slept most of the day and night, but now, he was wide awake.

Feeling her silky, soft hair, he wondered how he was going to convince Josh to tell him about her past. He was sure she wasn't in trouble with the law, but she was running from a man. The Pinkerton man said she was a run-away bride. Why would she refuse to marry a man she was engaged to? Maybe he should just ask Cassie, but in the past days, he wanted Josh to tell him.

He thought about his actions in the dry goods store and chuckled to himself. Throwing the ladies underwear over his shoulder wasn't a good idea, but he wasn't thinking. He knew she had a right to be mad, but he didn't know she would be so embarrassed. Matt was so sorry he had embarrassed her to the point that she stormed out of the store without any of the things that she really needed. Josh hadn't asked for anything. It was his idea to buy her a new wardrobe. When she woke up, he'd apologize for his actions.

Chapter 11

After leaving the First Bank of Perryville and speaking with Mr. Taylor, his father's silent partner and lawyer, Luther Sullivan was almost too angry to think of anything but Jocelyn Norwood. He must find that gal and make her marry him or he'd lose everything his father had wanted him to inherit. Add to that he wanted to stop the rumors about him been a sissy. His father was embarrassed that he wasn't a big, strong brute like so many others.

He laid his head back on the carriage seat and remembered the last time he spent time with his bride-to-be. Memories came back of the time he went to see her alone in her father's beautiful library. The reason he sneaked into her house was to present the idea that once married, they wouldn't have to share a bed until they got to know each other better or never.

All the household staff and her grandfather were all settled in for the night, so it was easy for him to enter the house. Jocelyn had been sitting in a rocking chair reading when he opened the door and slipped in unannounced. She leaped out of her chair and demanded that he leave, but he had other plans. His father wanted him to stop the rumors about him not being a real man. "If you get married, the gossip will stop. So, I demand that you do something to convince that Norwood girl to marry you."

Well, Little Miss Goodie Two Shoes got her proposal and when she refused, she got an early honeymoon night. He still felt the claw marks on his neck, shoulder, and back. She almost ruined him from making love when she kicked him in the groin. After hitting her hard, she was unconscious for the rest of the evening while he had his way with her. Grinning, he would have loved to inform his father about the night of lovemaking with Jocelyn, but he wouldn't have approved, especially about the pain he had to inflict on her. Had his seed taken hold? It was really too early to be sure one way or the other.

Little Miss Goodie Two Shoes wouldn't get away from him this time. He'd break her arm if she tried to defy him. Next time she wouldn't get a chance to scratch or kick him again. "*Maybe when Miss Norwood meets up with me again, if my seed took, she'll be willing and ready to marry him.*" He murmured out loud.

"Did you say something Mr. Luther? Can I do something for you before we arrive at your house?" Boomer shifted around in the driver's bench waiting for an answer from his boss. When Luther didn't answer, Boomer continued on his way.

Once the two arrived at Luther's father's mansion, he instructed Boomer to pack his bags for a weeklong trip to Texas. They were going on a hunt.

"A hunt? Do you want your father's rifle and ammunition?" Boomer quizzed.

"It's not that kind of hunt, my man. We're going after my bride-to-be." He pranced around in the living room and smiled. "I'm sure she'll be glad to see me." He fiddled with a sharp bowie knife his father kept on the mantel. A gift from a great outdoorsman.

"Yes sir. When do you want to go on this trip?" Boomer asked.

"At first light. Be sure to pack me some nice things to wear in town. Pack clothes for yourself, too, and maybe an extra blanket and pillow for the carriage. May as well be comfortable while I travel. I'll get the cook to prepare plenty of food for us to eat, and also some supplies we need to make a campfire if we're too far from civilization to get anything. She will know what we need."

****

Early the following day, Boomer and the three horses, stood in the front of the stables waiting for Luther's appearance. The groomsman eased beside Boomer and whispered that the young scaly wag was late as usual. "He makes appointments with people to ride and he's always the last one to arrive. Most of the time, somebody has to go and get him out of bed," he snickered.

After the sun was up, Luther came staggering out the back door. "Why didn't you wake me? You know I wanted to get an early start on our trip. The next time you let me oversleep, I'll use my buggy whip on your hide."

Boomer and the groomer stared at the young man half dressed in his new western gear; jeans, plaid shirt, belt and brand new shiny cowboy boots. Boomer jumped to attention and helped his boss into the carriage. As he rushed to untie the lead horse, the groomsman moved close to Boomer. "He's going to die wearing those new boots after the first day. You'd better watch over that tenderfoot for sure."

Good advice. Boomer hurriedly climbed in the driver's seat of the carriage. "Mr. Luther, I hope you don't mind, but I saddled another horse and tied him to the rear. I thought you would want your own animal to ride in town or elsewhere, without the carriage.

"Good thinking, Boomer. Just for that I'll forgive you for not waking me. Now let's hit the trail."

Luther slept the rest of the morning away, leaving Boomer to decide which direction they should travel. Thankfully, he had an idea where his master wanted to look first. Midland, Texas would be the first big town to scout

out someone on the run, since there was a train that carried people in all directions.

Once Luther woke up, he ordered Boomer to pull over so he could take a leak, then he rummaged through the basket of food and grabbed a sandwich and an apple. Never once did Luther ask Boomer if he wanted something to eat until the spoiled man told him to help himself to some grub. Boomer rearranged the basket and selected a sandwich for himself. He also chose two small apples and fed them to the team.

Once back on the road, Luther wanted to know where Boomer was taking him. "We're headed to Midland, Texas, sir. It's the first big town we'll come to. A person can catch a train and go just about anywhere. But, maybe, your lady didn't have any money, so she might be somewhere in Midland."

"So, now, you're playing detective?" Luther smirked.

"No sir. I had heard there's a train that travels in and out of that city. I'm sorry to get into your business. It won't happen again."

Chapter 12

Early the next morning, Cassie discovered Jocelyn asleep with her head next to Matt's thighs. She touched her lightly to wake her, not wanting to disturb Matt.

Jocelyn stood and nearly fell into Cassie's arms. "I'm sorry," she whispered, stumbling a little. "I was so tired I don't remember falling asleep."

"I've started the stove and put the coffee on to boil. "Go into your room and take care of yourself. I'll be just fine."

"Oh Cassie, you're too kind to me. Thank you, dear friend. I'll make it up to you for all the good care you've given me, I promise."

"Shucks, gal, get on with yourself. You'd do the same for me."

Jocelyn hurried into her bedroom. As she glanced at the mirror, she caught her breath. She had never seen such a sorry sight. The night had taken its toll on her. Her eyes were blood red, her cheeks were pale, and her blonde curls were a tangled mess. She studied herself in the mirror and thought she looked very old indeed.

After she washed her face and brushed her teeth, she dressed in one of the two-day dresses that she owned and coiled her hair into a soft bun at the back of her head. On impulse, she applied a small amount of vanilla on her wrists. Feeling human again she hurried into the kitchen to help Cassie.

****

As Cassie hummed a Christian hymn, Matt lay awake on his bed, listening for Jocelyn. He'd enjoyed having Jocelyn so near him last night. She was a good nurse, ensuring he wasn't in any pain and could rest. A rustling nearby got his attention. He opened his eyes. Thank you, Lord.

"I see you're awake. How do you feel?" Before Matt had time to answer, she asked if he was hungry.

"I could eat a bear, and I feel like one," he said as he ran his hand across his rough face.

"Well, let me fix you some strong broth, and I'll gather your shaving gear. I can shave you if you like?"

"I want some hot biscuits and scrambled eggs."

"Doc Murclock said until the swelling on your forehead goes down, you must eat very light. He doesn't want you heaving up your food and hurting your ribs more than they are already."

Once he'd swallowed a cup of chicken broth, Jocelyn brought out the shaving gear and set out to clean him up. She wasn't sure how to go about shaving him, but she had watched her father do it many times.

Jocelyn placed a towel under his jaw and then lathered him up. She seemed to enjoy making swirls on his cheeks.

His head hurt, and this was taking much too long. "Get on with it and stop playing with that damn brush."

She took the blade in her hand and twisted it back and forward.

He closed his eyes as she quickly made a slice right under his nose.

He grabbed her hand and looked at the hairy blade. "Did you just cut my mustache off?"

"Well . . . "

"Cassie, bring me a hand mirror," Matt bellowed.

Cassie took the mirror off the wall near the dry sink

and handed it to Matt. He cut a glance at Jocelyn and growled, "Woman, have you lost all your senses? It's taken me three months to grow this mustache and only five seconds for you to cut it off."

Jocelyn stepped away from the bed and looked at him in surprise. "I'm sorry. I've seen my father always cut under his nose first while shaving. I didn't think."

"Of course, you weren't thinking. Give me that blade and get away from me."

As he wiped away the lather, Jocelyn hung her head. "You're right. The mustache really belongs on you, just like your thick brown eyebrows. How in the world will I ever make it up to you?" When he didn't answer, she said, "Please, let me complete your shave. I know your ribs are killing you as you hold your arms up."

"Stand back and keep away from me, my beard, and what's left of my mustache. I can manage without your help."

"Oh, you're such a brute. You're lucky I didn't shave you bald." She crossed her arms and lifted her chin.

As she watched, he shaved the other half of his mustache off and uttered an exaggerated sigh for her benefit. Shaving had become more complicated than he thought. She was right. His ribs hurt like the devil as he shaved his face from one side to the other. He should let her complete the job for him. A few minutes before, he wanted to throttle her, but to be truthful, all he wanted now was to pull her into his arms and whisper in her neck that it was all right. He knew she was only trying to help him.

She whirled around, looked out the kitchen window, and wiped her eyes with the tail of her apron. Why the heck would she be crying over him? Maybe, this was a sign that she really did care.

She hurried over to the kitchen and mixed a concoction for him to drink.

He looked at it. Was she trying to poison him?

"It's only soda water." She pressed a cloth under his chin and the glass touched his lips. "Ewe. Salty."

"Keep it in your mouth and allow it to bubble around." He was actually too weak to argue as she brought a bowl for him to spit into. She reached toward him to wipe the soda water off his chin, but he leaned away from her.

She burst out laughing. "Surely you didn't think I was going to hurt you with this soft cloth."

"Go cook me something to eat. I want meat, woman, none of that slimy chicken broth."

"I need to take care of a few of my personal needs, and I'll talk it over with Cassie. We can compromise on something that won't harm your stomach."

****

Jocelyn hurried into the bedroom and went to the water closet to make sure she'd stopped bleeding. She was thankful that she was almost completely well from her mishap, but she was still very pale. Nevertheless, she was pleased that Matt had not questioned her about the accident. When Jocelyn returned to the kitchen, Cassie was arguing with Matt.

"What are you doing up?"

He stood near the kitchen archway, bending over and holding his sides. His hairy chest, calves and feet were sticking out from the sheet he'd placed around himself.

"I called, but no one answered. I've got to pee, and I can make it to the privy by myself. Just then he swooned, mumbling that he felt light-headed.

"Don't you dare fall, you big over-bearing . . . oh, help me, Cassie," Jocelyn called.

Cassie hoisted one of his long arms across her shoulders while Jocelyn wrapped her arm around his waist and led him to the bed.

He groaned. "If you spent more time caring for me than standing there calling me names, I might have made it to the water closet. Now, get me that awful pee-can and remove your sassy-butt out of my sight for a few minutes.

Cassie brought Matt the chamber pot while Jocelyn stood guard over the big man. "Quickly, take care of business," Jocelyn demanded while both ladies left him alone.

In a few minutes, Jocelyn returned to his bedside with a bottle and spoon. He'd placed the used pot beside his bed and was lying down with his eyes closed. Perspiration beaded his forehead. She realized he was in pain. "Open your mouth and take this medicine. It will help you rest."

As he swallowed the liquid, she couldn't stop herself from scolding him. "I'll thank you to use your brain from now on, unless you damaged it when you were thrown from the carriage. You cannot parade around the house without clothes. If you insist on getting up, please dress in your pajamas and robe."

"I don't wear pajamas, woman. There's a robe in my closet. Get it. I'll be using the water closet from now on."

As Jocelyn straightened his bedcovers and adjusted the pillows, he took one of her hands and held it close to his side. She stood looking down at the handsome young man's clean-shaven face and noticed his even breathing. He was fast asleep.

****

Late into the night, he awoke, and his ribs and side didn't hurt as bad. He thought about the afternoon and puzzled over Josh. How in the world did she get under his shin? There was the obvious things –slicing off his mustache, and making him wait to use the water closet. Then, nearly starving him, but to tell the truth, these weren't the real reasons for his anger. He knew that in the morning he would have to apologize, which went against his grain. What other reason could it be that made him want to shake her? As he thought about it, he came to the gist of the matter. She would not confide in him. He needed her to trust him and confess the truth about her past.

****

In the early morning, Jocelyn tiptoed into the kitchen to put on a pot of coffee to serve the men. Was Matt groaning? Tiptoeing over to the side of his bed, she watched his restless movements with his right foot dangling off the mattress. Hurrying, she grabbed the bottle of medicine and a clean spoon and rushed back to him. "Matt, open your mouth and swallow this medicine. It will relieve the pain."

He raised his head and grabbed her shoulders, pulling her down onto his chest.

"Please, Matt, turn me loose. You're going to hurt your ribs and me," she whispered. The moonlight shone through the kitchen window, and they could see each other's faces.

Matt held her tight and, using his right hand, pulled her face toward his and kissed her so hard she didn't dare fight against him. He buried his face in her hair. "You smell so good," he whispered.

She had never felt a man's lips over hers. This was her first real kiss. She melted into his body and groaned with delight.

Placing more kisses against her lips, he whispered, "You like that, sweetheart?" Before she could reply, he placed sweet kisses to her eyes, cheeks, and her neck. His left hand moved close to her soft breasts.

Suddenly, light flooded the room. "What the hell?" Jim, the older foreman, stood in the doorway of the kitchen.

Coming to her senses, Jocelyn realized that she was lying across Matt's bruised body. "Oh my, please turn me loose." Jocelyn scooted on to the floor.

Matt was holding onto her arm to keep her steady. "Please, turn me loose," she whispered. "I don't want you to touch me."

"It's a little late for that," he said, looking around her trembling form to see Jim.

"Hey, look at me," but she only starred at the floor, wishing she could disappear.

"Nothing that happened here is your fault."

Cassie came up behind her. "Go and get yourself together. I'll take care of Jim."

Chapter 13

"What a morning," Jocelyn sighed as she rushed to the wall mirror to look at herself. Oh dear, she thought, feeling her cheeks flush. Thank goodness she didn't look different as she twisted her face from side to side. But she did feel different. She had experienced her first real kiss from the man who made her heart quiver whenever he touched her.

She threw herself on her bed and punched the pillow with her fist and muffled her cry. She wanted Matt, and she would have allowed him to have his way with her if not for Jim coming into the house. Rolling onto her stomach, she hugged the big pillow.

Crying until she started to hiccup, she flopped onto her back and stared at the ceiling. She had to pull herself together. Life must go on, and Cassie would need her help with cooking for the men. With determination, she would make herself get over Matt. Rising from the bed, she went into the water closet and told herself to be sensible. Since she wasn't getting married, she wouldn't allow Matt to touch her again.

As she dressed, raised voices came from the kitchen. Jim was demanding to know what Matt thought he was doing. "That girl is as innocent as they come. If you aren't going to marry her, keep your hands to yourself." Jim stomped around in the kitchen.

"By the way, what in the world happened to you? You look like a sickle mower ran over your face."

Jocelyn placed her ear to the door to try to hear the men's conversation. She could only hear mumbling coming from Matt. Hopefully, Cassie would tell her what he said.

Just as she opened the door to the kitchen, Cassie stood at her door. "I was worried about you. Are your all right now?"

"Yes, just embarrassed." She gave her sweet friend a little smile.

"Come and help me whip up biscuits. I have the coffee ready, and the oven is hot. The men will be in soon." Cassie tied the apron around Jocelyn's waist.

Jim walked over to the kitchen table and picked up two coffee cups. "Can we have a cup of fresh coffee? It sure smells good."

Jocelyn hadn't looked over at Matt, but she knew he had propped himself up on the bed. She handed the coffee to Jim, then returned to the counter to knead the dough.

The one time she looked up, Matt's eyes contacted with hers. She quickly looked down and continued punching and rolling the biscuit dough. Feeling sorry for herself, she rolled out the biscuits and placed them on a greased pan. Quickly, she scooped up the bowl of two dozen eggs, and began cracking them to be scrambled.

****

Matt watched as the men came in and gathered around the dining room table. They were a bunch of lonely men who worked together each day, but lately they'd appeared happier than they had in a long time. With Josh and Cassie cooking delicious meals, they smiled and laughed daily. At least he'd done one thing right. Allowing Josh to live and work on the ranch as his cook instead of his 'new bride' was better than sending her back to town.

Jim adjusted the cover on Matt's bed and then positioned a small table beside him for his plate and coffee. "Now, you listen to me, you *'randy'* man. Leave that gal alone. I mean it. I'd better not hear of you touching her again before you marry her. And I hope that will be soon."

"Have you forgotten I'm your boss, not the other way around?" Matt growled low.

"I feel somewhat responsible for that pretty, young miss. I brought her out here to you." Jim smiled at the girls, got up and took a plate of food from Cassie. "I believe he can feed himself."

"I agree. After witnessing that wrestling match, he's back to his old ornery self, to my way of thinking." Cassie smiled at Jim and both of them laughed with their heads together.

"What are you and Cassie laughing about?" Matt asked. "It looks like you two might have something going on between you?"

"If we do, she don't need your permission. She's a grown woman who can take care of herself."

****

Late into the afternoon, after Jim and Cassie drove into town to get supplies for the kitchen and feed for the animals, the house was very quiet. Matt wondered what Jocelyn was doing besides trying to avoid him.

Just as he started to get out of bed to go and relief himself, Jocelyn entered the room. "Well, I 'm glad to see that you haven't run off again," he said.

"What are you doing?" She looked at him as he sat on the edge of the bed.

"I need to go to the water closet. Since, I was alone, I figured I'd have to go by myself."

"Let me give you a shoulder to lean upon. Your forehead is still swollen, and you shouldn't walk alone. You could easily fall." Hurrying across the room, Jocelyn placed his arm across her shoulders, and they inched to the water closet. Once at the door, he told her to get lost. He would call when he was ready to return to bed.

In a few minutes, he stood in the doorway wearing his pajama bottoms with a towel draped across his neck. He wrapped his arm around her thin shoulder as she led him back to the bed, but he didn't lie down.

"Listen, I need to apologize to you. I didn't mean to embarrass you in front of Jim and Cassie, but I only wanted to pull you down next to me. Gracious, woman, all I wanted to do was touch you, but instead I got carried away and kissed you. You liked it, too. A man can tell."

"I didn't have a chance to get away from you. You grabbed me and caused me to fall over you." Furrows formed between her eyes.

"Ever since you've lived under my roof, I've been living like a . . . monk. Don't you know a man like me needs a woman in his life, once in a while?"

Her eyes grew narrow, and her voice was taunting. "So, what will I be? A notch in your belt. Another conquest?"

"That's not what I mean and you know it. I want you to marry me, and the sooner the better. I've begged you to tell me about your past, but instead of talking to me, you cry or run away. Well, lady, I don't care how you came to be here. I know for a fact you aren't wanted by the law, and you're not married. I paid for your passage here, and I was expecting a bride. But, no. I got a cold-hearted cook."

"Why you insufferable . . . goat. You said I could work for you as your cook. You said I didn't have to marry you. Have you forgotten that already?" But instead of answering her, he studied the way she stood toe-to-toe with him. She should be afraid of him, but she stood with challenging eyes as she stared him down, unsmiling.

Matt thought to himself, *I can surely control myself . . . but why should I*? Surprising himself, he took three quick steps toward her, dying from pain, but never taking his eyes off hers. He pulled her into his chest. Before she could move away, he kissed her hard.

Jocelyn's lips fell open, and she gasped.

He met her eyes. "Think about what I said. I want you to marry me . . . soon."

Chapter 14

"How far do you think we are from Midland?" Luther asked Boomer.

"I believe we're about ten miles or a little less. We need to cross a small river about a mile from here. I ain't sure how deep it is."

"Well, let's get a move on."

Less than an hour later, Boomer steered the horses close to the edge of the water. The animals were pulling to get a drink, but he held the reins tight and moved back from the water.

"The water looks real calm. Get in the water and wade out a far piece, and gauge how deep it is," Luther demanded.

"Will do." After Boomer tied the horses to a tree limb. He removed his worn brown boots and rolled his breeches to his knees. He touched the water with his big toe and shook it. "Man, that water is cold."

"Get your big self in the water before I fill your behind with buckshot. I'm in a hurry to get to Midland."

Boomer slowly took one step after another into the murky water until he was up to his knees. He kept walking until he was about halfway across.

A growl came from the riverbank. "Ouch, I'm getting eaten up by mosquitos. Come on back and let's drive across. The water isn't that deep. This carriage can make it

"Sir, you cannot sell me. I'm a free man, and I only work for you."

"So . . . now you're a lawyer. I can do whatever I want with you, and don't you forget it."

Boomer kept his mouth shut. Just as soon as he got to Midland, he'd part ways with this lazy, mean man. Neither, Mr. Sullivan or his son owned him, and he wasn't going to allow this crazy man to continue mistreating him.

Once the coffee was ready, he poured Luther a tin cup of the strong brew. He handed him a plate of eggs and beans and poured himself a cup of coffee. Boomer blew on the hot liquid as he studied his boss who stood shivering near the fire. His thin body was covered with the dry horse blanket that had been under the saddle of the spare horse.

Boomer wanted to laugh at the sight. What would his rich friends think of him if they could see him now? Boomer also had no dry clothes to put on, so he tossed more logs on the fire.

Luther sat down on a log and wrapped his arms around his knees. He laid his head down and soon was asleep. Boomer was a light sleeper, so he lay close to the fire. If it became too low, he'd keep it burning all night.

The sunrise came early. Boomer built up the fire and made a fresh pot of coffee. Luther woke up in a bad mood. His clothes were still damp, but he was ready to get moving. He could buy clean clothes and hot meals when they arrived in Midland.

Boomer hitched the horses to the carriage and saddled the spare horse. He gathered all the damp clothes and placed them in the food basket since the carpet bags were still wet on the inside.

After traveling several miles, the town of Midland came into view. "You fool, look how close we were to town. We could have driven on and spent the night in a hotel. You are the dumbest man I know." Luther spewed out a wad of spit with his words.

Boomer drove the carriage around the back side of town to the stables. A young man about twelve came running out and asked if they wanted to board their animals. “It will be a dollar a day for three horses and for an extract helping of feed, it will be twenty-five cents more.”

“Can I leave my carriage here, too?” Luther stepped in front of Boomer and questioned the young man.

“Yes, sir. You can park it in the back of the barn, but I can’t promise it won’t get stolen." The boy shook his head. “Now for an extra fifty cents a day, I can guard it for you.”

Luther walked up to the young boy and stood so close to him he was practically spitting in the boy’s face. “You got a racket going on here, but you aren’t going to rob me. Come on, Boomer, we’ll find another stable.”

“There ain’t another one. You don’t have much choice unless you want to go outside of town and camp.” The young boy grinned at Luther.

Luther reached into his pocket and pulled out five dollars. “This should cover a few days. We won’t be here long.” Luther turned and stomped out of the barn and up the street. Boomer watched until he turned into the doorway of a big hotel.

Boomer stared all around the stable. *Man, it smells to high heavens in here, but with a little work, this could be a nice place to board animals.* “Do you think I could sleep in one of the empty stalls? I can help you clean this place for a meal a day.”

“Sure, but what about your *master?* Don’t he pay for a place for you to sleep and feed you?”

“He might. I ain’t sure. This is our first trip together. Besides, I like to take care of myself. Once I find out what he’s planning to do, I’ll be getting away from him. He’s my boss, not my master. I’m my own man.”

“If you’re sure you can help me out, I’ll let you stay. Customers will be coming in to get their horses and others will be bringing them to board. I can use the help, but for now, I've got to go home for breakfast. See you in a while."

Boomer watched the young man leave by the double back doors. He walked over to the wide barn doors and opened them. Outside was a large corral where several horses walked around. Some were drinking water from the troughs. Boomer picked up a rope and tied the two doors open to the corral fence. He moved over to the stalls and noticed the animals had been fed their morning oats, so he led the animals outside.

Once all the horses were outside, he took a shovel and mucked out the stalls. He placed the horse manure in a wheelbarrow and emptied it at the back of the corral. After all the stalls were cleaned, he poured buckets of water on each stall floor and raked them smooth. Once the water was dried, he filled each stall floor with fresh hay.

After finishing the last stall, Boomer opened the two front double doors to the livery stable. He was washing his face and arms when the young boy returned. "Mercy. I almost didn't recognize my place. It ain't never been so clean and it smells nice and fresh in here."

"A little work is all that was needed to clean this place. What you got in that sack that smells mighty good?"

"Oh, I told my mama that you were working for me so she sent you some hot breakfast. Hope you like it." The young boy carried the sack over to a small table at the rear of the barn and placed the food on it for Boomer.

"Be sure to thank your mama for me. I could eat a horse."

"Sure glad you didn't eat one of our customers' animals," he said laughing. "Oh, by the way, what did you do with the manure?"

"I carried it to the back of the corral. Someone needs to dig a trench alongside the back fence and bury the droppings. Cover it and plant grass seed on top. Soon you'll have a nice row of green grass for the animals to eat, and the awful smell will be gone too, along with those nasty green horse flies."

"Sounds to me like you've worked around animals before."

"Mr. Sullivan, Luther's papa, has a nice spread with plenty of animals. When I worked for him, his foreman taught me how to care for a place. I worked at several large plantations too and I learned that if a man keeps his place clean, his animals won't get sick, and things always look better, too."

"My pa never taught me anything. Of course, I was real young when he died and Ma finally had to stop working here. She's too old to handle horses."

"Well, I don't know how long I'll be here, but I'll teach you how to care for the animals that are left in your care. People appreciate their animals being well- looked after," Boomer said. "That was a mighty fine breakfast. Now if I could just clean myself with some dry clothes, I'd be on top of the world."

"I forgot. Mama sent over some of my Pa's things for you. I told her how your carriage turned over in the river and you had on wet clothes. There are a bunch of overalls and a couple of flannel shirts. My Pa was a large man, just like you. Let me get them off the back of my horse."

****

Later that afternoon, Luther came walking into the livery stable, clean shaven, with a fresh haircut and wearing new duds, from top to bottom. He looked like a new man. "Well, look at you, Boomer, all decked out in new clothes yourself. I'm glad to see you got cleaned up."

The young boy circled Luther and laughed. "Mercy, you look as pretty as a young gal that hangs out on Broad Street."

"Keep away from me, young man, before I have my man beat you into a pulp." Using his new cane, he pushed the young boy's shoulder. "Boomer, I discovered that just maybe *our prey* may have joined a wagon train that was headed to Amarillo, Texas. It was a train filled with women who wanted to be brides. Sounds like a good way to escape without being noticed."

"Didn't the Pickerton men search that city?" Boomer asked. He remembered Luther's father explaining their report after returning.

"They did, but I am nearly one-hundred percent sure that she's hiding somewhere in Amarillo. We'll depart in two days on the ten am train. Be ready and have my carriage and the horses at the train depot early that morning, so they can be put in a box car." He didn't give Boomer a chance to reply, but turned and strode out of the stable.

"So, it seems he is sure you're going to travel with him as his servant," the young boy said.

"Yes, it seems so. I'd better go with him, if only to protect the young lady he's searching for. He's a mean man and he wants the young lady to marry him, even if he has to use force, but I won't allow him to hurt her."

"No gal would want to marry man," sneered the young boy. "She'd have to be desperate."

"He's desperate for money and property," Boomer replied.

Chapter 15

Jocelyn had to do something to make Matt understand that she could not marry him. If she could get on his good side, he might listen to her and understand why she wouldn't tie herself to a loveless marriage. Her gaze turned to the outside window. Watching the men train the horses was a sight to see. Given herself a shake, she had to focus on the matter at hand—to tell him. "Matt, I can't thank you enough for all you've done for me, and I apologize if you think I was trying to rile you." She thought she sounded real sincere, but he was smiling when she looked at him. "So, you were really only trying to make me mad?" He asked.

"I was," she admitted, "but I'm sorry. You embarrassed me and my temper got the best of me."

Matt reached and took a long blond curl in his fingers. "I didn't mean for us to get caught. I thought we were alone." He couldn't believe he'd said those words until he'd uttered them. Never before had he been sorry for any of his actions, especially toward a woman.

Tears filled her eyes. Thankfully, just as Cassie entered the room, she did an about-face and left the kitchen faster than she entered. Cassie must have sensed immediately that something was taking place between her boss and best friend.

Jocelyn walked away from Matt and placed the kitchen counter between them. "Look, I know you said you wanted to marry me, but I can't and will not marry a man who doesn't love me."

Matt ambled over to the back door and opened it to allow fresh air to flow through the room. The air felt good even though it had a chill in the breeze. "I can understand how you feel about a loveless marriage. Never-the–less, we must marry. The men are already talking about us and soon the whole town will be gossiping. We can learn to care for each other after we're married. I know you have feelings for me, so don't stand there on your high horse and try to deny it."

Jocelyn jerked her head up and glared at Matt as he propped his leg against the back door. "What about the feelings you have for me . . . beside the *lust* in your lower abdomen?"

Matt slammed the wooden door and strode within inches of her. "You'd better watch that nasty temper of yours before I turn you over my knee and blister your sassy backside. No woman of mine will talk like that."

"You just try to beat me, and you'll never have a good night sleep again." Jocelyn raised her chin high and backed away from him.

"You will marry me, tomorrow, or I'll carry out my threat right in front of the minister and my men. You got that woman?" Matt whipped around and stormed straight out to the front porch.

****

Cassie peeked around her bedroom door and saw Jocelyn was alone in the kitchen. "Wow that was some argument you two had. I'm sorry, but I couldn't help but overhear most of what you both said. I hope the men weren't close to the house."

"Me, too. That man can make a saint lose his or her religion."

"Well, are you going to marry him, tomorrow, like he threatened?"

"Oh, Cassie, I don't want to marry like this. He's right. I do have feelings for him, but I was hoping that in time he would grow to care for me, too."

"Honey, that man already cares deeply for you. When you ran off, he was nearly out of his head. He was deathly afraid you would be found hurt or even dead when you rode off on that wild stallion."

"If I thought I could get away and have a place to hide until those Pinkerton men stopped looking for me, I would pack a bag and leave now. But, I Matt has the house guarded. He knows that I don't want to get married so he won't take a chance and allow me to run away again."

****

"You're right about that, Miss Jocelyn," Jim said as he entered the back door. "I heard you saying that you would leave if you could. If I were you, I wouldn't even try. There's no telling what Matt might do when he found you and believe me, he wouldn't leave a rock unturned until he did. That boy is determined to marry you, so you'd better go along with it. But he'll never harm a hair on your head, I can promise you that."

"That's what you say, but he did threaten to beat me," she said.

"I wouldn't be surprised if he gave you a well-deserved paddling, but that's not the same as a *beating*."

"My Papa never laid a hand on me, and I will never allow a man to hurt me again." Suddenly, she placed her hand over her mouth. She realized that she had spoken out loud about something she never intended to tell anyone.

"What man hurt you, Miss Jocelyn? I can assure you no one will ever harm you again and I will personally take care of any man that abused you."

Rushing over to Jim, Jocelyn pleaded. "Please don't repeat what I just said. I've never spoken about it to anyone." She glanced back to see Cassie nodding to the man.

"I promise, child, Jim and I will never repeat what you just told us." Cassie looked at Jim. "For now, anyway." Slowly, he nodded his head in agreement.

"Jim, I got in trouble in my past, and I don't want to bring it here. It's my problem, not Matt's. As long as I'm not discovered, things can go along like normal."

"Listen to me, child. You couldn't have a better champion on your side than Matt. He can and will take care of you. You have nothing to fear as long as you are at his side. As his wife, he'll move heaven and earth to take care of any problem you might have."

"My problem is my problem. I will take care of it if I'm discovered."

"So, you do have another man in your past? Is he the reason you are hiding on my ranch?" Matt growled.

All three of the little group spun around to see Matt standing in the back doorway. They had not heard him open the door and enter the room.

When Jocelyn didn't make a response, Matt spoke and didn't brook an argument. "Jim, I believe you have work in the barn and Cassie, I noticed the wash lady on the back porch. Please go give her some instructions while Josh and I have a private discussion."

Jocelyn wished Matt would say something as he looked at her. His expression didn't give her any idea what he was thinking. She began to feel very nervous. Maybe it was because he was such a big man, and he seemed to swallow up all the space around her. Standing so near him, caused her a great discomfort. She wanted to run from the room and escape, but he would only follow. Tears filled her eyes. She dropped her face so he couldn't see her sad expression.

"Josh, I don't like making you cry, and I 'm not angry."

He sounded angry to her. She eased away, but he reached for her and pulled her close to his chest. "Don't fight me, Josh. My ribs hurt like the dickens, and I can't wrestle with you."

His mouth came down over hers, stopping any protest she might have. And goodness, how he kissed her. His mouth was hot, hungry and he thrust his tongue into her mouth. She nearly fell down because she remembered another tongue that caused her to gag. She went weak in the knees and held tight to his side, causing him to gasp from pain. Just then she kissed him with every bit of passion she could muster.

****

Bryan, Matt's foreman, opened the door and laughed at the sight he was witnessing. Matt tried to ignore the young man. Josh's lips still begged for more. As he pushed Josh behind him, he noticed her lips were swollen were rosy, and her eyes were still damp from tears. He wanted to throttle his foreman for not knocking on the door before barging inside. "Get out, and don't come back in here until I call you," Matt growled, then he turned to face Josh. Go help Cassie while I can still control myself.

She didn't look like she understood what he meant. She didn't understand his frown either.

"If you dislike kissing me, why do you continue to do so?" She gave him a disgruntled look when he laughed.

She took exception to his reaction. "Please let me go now."

"I already have."

Jocelyn immediately stepped back from him, pushed her long hair back behind her shoulders and turned to leave when she froze at seeing several men standing on the front porch. Her face heated to a full blush, and she raced out of the room.

****

Cassie jumped off the bed and hurried over to Jocelyn. "Did you decide to get married tomorrow?"

"No. No decisions were made. We need to get the

lunch meal on the table. The men are gathering on the porch."

"Did he kiss you again?"

"Yes," twice, I think."

"Did you kiss him back . . . twice?" Cassie asked, wondering how far things went between them.

"Yes."

"I see," Cassie smiled.

"No, you don't see. We're attracted to each other, that's all. I'm not sure why we are. He doesn't act like he even likes me most of the time."

"I know one reason he's attracted to you, Jocelyn. Don't you ever look in the in the mirror? You're a beautiful girl."

"That's not true, Cassie. Oh, people have said that I'm pretty, but no way," she replied. "Besides, I can't marry while I'm caring this awful secret."

Cassie placed her arms across her friend's shoulder. "Maybe if you told me why you're running away from your past, it would be easier to tell Matt. Think about confiding in me while we prepare lunch."

Chapter 16

After strolling away from that wicked young boy and Boomer, Luther wandered down the boardwalk without a care in the world. He wasn't afraid of being in a strange city and even enjoyed the raucous and boastful men gathered in large groups. They were his kind of people. Loud piano music came from the batwing doors of the many saloons lining the street.

Luther felt good in his new clothes and shiny shoes as he saw his reflection in the front windows. He needed more clothes, but he wanted lunch before shopping. As he headed to the café on the next corner, he thought about his future marriage with Jocelyn Norwood. Once they said their vows before a judge, his life would be good. He'd have a thriving banking business, successful friends, and a beautiful mansion.

He twirled his cane, but it stopped in mid-air when two sets of nasty, scuffed boots stood in front of him. He looked to see who they belonged to. Sensing something was about to alter his plans for the day, he attempted to sidestep the two burly men.

"Good day, my pretty little gringo. We want you to come with us."

Luther nearly gagged from the man's drunken, stinking breath. He reached into his pocket and pulled out his new handkerchief to cover his nose. Glancing around he searched for a way to escape these awful intruders.

The two men grabbed Luther's arms and lifted him off the ground hurling insults and sneers about his dandy dress and appearance. As they carried him into a nearby, rat infested alley, he almost vomited form the smell of their nasty, uncleaned bodies.

"Let's get to it," one of the men shouted to his partner.

As the men dropped Luther onto the wet, muddy, ground. Luther reached into his vest and pulled out his small derringer and pointed it at their noses.

"Now, is that any way to treat your new friends? That little thing might hurt one of us." One of the men glanced at his partner with devilment in his eyes.

"Yes, we never planned on hurting you. We only want your money, then we'll go on our merry way."

"No, I'm not giving you anything. I can shoot one of you, if you dare make a move. Which one wants to get a bullet right between the eyes?"

The two men laughed and smacked each other's backs. Luther's hands were shaking, but he tried to hold them steady.

"Now Joe, let him shoot you." one man said as Luther made the mistake of looking at one of them. The boasting man grabbed the small gun out of Luther's hand and held it in the air.

"Now, look. . .ee what I have?" You, my friend, are out of dumb luck."

The two men undressed Luther while searching for his wallet. They took his new clothes as he fought to hold on to them. As he fell to the ground, they hit him on top of the head, and kicked him in his sides. The last thing he heard was piano music pounding, men shouting and women's laughter, then he faded into oblivion.

Later, as rain fell on Luther's body, he felt something heavy on his forehead. He opened his eyes and saw a thin dark tail swishing across his nose. He bolted up screaming and slapping himself in the face. He couldn't believe a giant rat had been sitting on his face as he lay on the wet muddy ground. "Oh Lord, help me!" he cried as he looked down and saw he was wearing only his white drawers. *I need help.* As he tried to stand, he knew of only one person who would help him. . . . Boomer. Crawling to a stand, he slid against the alley's back walls leading to the stable. He didn't want to be seen even though he needed to report the abuse to the constable. The men had taken his money and destroyed his clothing. They needed to be punished.

It was dark inside the barn except for a light from a lantern. He pounded on the wide doors. Luther prayed that his slave was still working there.

****

Boomer eased over and glanced out the back window to see who needed to get inside. Once he recognized Luther, he opened the door and stared at the man he called Boss. Boomer was shocked to see the pitiful creature standing in front of him.

"Don't just stand there. Could you get me a blanket, you fool? I'm soaked to the skin and freezing."

Boomer rushed into the storage room, snatched a fresh horse blanket hanging on a stall wall and wrapped it around the scrawny, naked man who was caked with mud and had red marks all over his body. "Let me heat some water so you can take a hot bath. Who in the world beat you to a pulp?"

"I was carried to an alley, robbed and beaten hours ago. They left me for dead, but the rain and rats woke me. So, I crept through the back alley to reach here without being seen."

"I'm sorry this happened to you, Boss." Boomer hurried and built a fire and heated a large tub of water. He helped Luther into the tub and left him to take care of himself.

"You'll have to stay wrapped in the blanket until I can ask the boy to bring you something to wear." Boomer smiled thinking about Luther wearing hand-me- downs from a young country boy.

After Luther completed his hot bath, Boomer stretched out several wool blankets over a pile of hay in a clean stall. "You can sleep right there for tonight. I will ask the boy and his ma for help in the morning. Don't know what they can or will do for you."

"What do you mean? Surely, they'll assist me?"

"They don't have a lot. I think you'll need to telegram your banker partner and tell him you need more funds, since you've been robbed."

Luther stared at Boomer and grinned really big. "Finally, you do have a brain in that head. Yes, that is what I'll do. I'll tell my lawyer, Mr. Jordon, to contact the Midland banker and have him give me a line of credit." Luther wobbled over to the stall and peered down on it with a disgusted expression. Obviously, he had never slept in such poor conditions, but for now, beggars couldn't be choosy.

****

Earlier the next morning, the boy stood with Boomer looking down on Luther as he slept, rolled into a knot like a baby. "He ain't got no clothes?"

"Afraid not. Those men took all his money and stripped him and destroyed his clothes. I guess they were attempting to be funny. They beat him and left him for dead in a dark alley. He said the rats and rain woke him up. I sure would have liked to be there when he saw all those rats," Boomer chuckled as he looked down on the ugly little weasel.

"Man, that gives me chills just thinking about that," the young boy said.

"Listen, young man, I can't continue to call you boy. What's your name?"

"Butch, you can call me Butch."

"Please to meet you, Butch. Do you think you have

some pants he could wear until he can buy new clothes?"

"I guess I can fix him with some of my Sunday duds. Can't let him run around looking like that. He'd scare the customers and their animals," he said chuckling. "I'll go and get them and have mama advance him a few dollars so he can go and get something to eat. I ain't asking her to cook extra for him. He can pay her back when he gets some cash."

****

After a few customers came to get their horses, Luther woke up but stayed hidden in the back stall. He couldn't parade around near naked. Boomer told him that the boy called Butch had gone to fetch him some clothes.

Butch stood at the stall gate, peering down at the scrawny man. "Here's all I got that's decent. Be real careful with them or you'll be replacing them with new ones." Butch tossed Luther a pair of gray trousers and a clean, ironed white shirt. He also brought a pair of scuffed boots that were too big for him. "My ma said I could make you a loan of this here five dollars until you get your own money, but she'll take it out of your hide if you don't pay her back in a few days."

Luther took the money and stuffed the coins in his fresh pants. When he didn't acknowledge the boy's gift of money, Boomer said, "Ain't you going to thank him for all his trouble, Boss?"

"He doesn't have any trouble. And don't you start trying to tell me what to do. I'll take that horse whip to your hide."

"No, you won't, mister. You'd best finish dressing and get to the bank so you can be on your way. My name is Butch, and this is my stable and barn, and if you don't change your manners, you might be back in that alley you came dragging yourself out of." Butch picked up a pitchfork and stuck it in the center of the stall that Luther had been using.

"Whcrc's a placc I can rclicvc mysclf?" Luther demanded.

Butch nodded his head to the two back doors. "Out that way to the left."

After Luther had left the livery, Butch placed a basket of food on a small table. "Ma sent you some breakfast and both of us some sandwiches for lunch. She don't have time to cook a hot mid-day meal today."

"That's mighty fine of her. I 'm starved," Boomer said as he peeked into the basket.

****

Luther wandered down the street and saw the sheriff's office. Finally, a place where he'd receive justice and get some help. It was time to report the two men that had robbed and beaten him. Luther entered the small office that had an old oak desk and two straight-back chairs sitting in the middle of the room. From where he stood, he could see several windows across the front and two jail cells in the back with single cots. A tall cowboy, wearing a badge on his vest, welcomed him, peering down at his outgrown clothes. He stood next to a young man who also wore a star and was busy whittling a block of wood.

"My name is Sheriff Wagner, and this is my deputy, Tory. How can we help you?"

"My name is Luther Sullivan from Perryville, Texas and I'm part owner of the First Bank of Perryville. I'm traveling to Amarillo. Last night two ruthless men accosted me. They stole my money and clothes and left me for dead in an alley two streets over. The rain woke me and I managed to get to the livery stable where I stayed the night in a horse stall. The owner, Butch somebody, loaned me these duds and a few dollars until I can contact my bank for more funds, so I can continue on my journey to Amarillo."

"Well, I must say you do look a little roughed up," the sheriff said as his eyes darted over him from head to toe. He winked at his deputy who stood leaning against the cell door.

"What did these men look like that took advantage of you, Sir?"

"What do you mean?"

"I mean were they young or old. Tall or short?"

"Yes, they were middle aged, tall and filthy. They were liquored up and smelled like a pig pen. One of them grabbed my gun, and they hit me in the head and knocked me to the ground. I woke up almost naked, and all my money was gone. I did find my empty wallet near where I lay.

"All right, Mr. Sullivan. My deputy will get right on your case. Do you mind telling me why you're traveling to Amarillo and how you're traveling?"

"Of course, I don't mind telling you. In fact, I have a few questions to ask you about a certain young lady that might have come to your town." When the sheriff continued to stare at him, Luther replied. "My man servant and I were traveling by carriage. We had an accident crossing the river, so we were staying overnight here to have the carriage repaired. I left my man at the livery stable, and I went to the hotel and had a nice supper. After I left there, well, the men followed men and accosted me in the alley."

"Who's the lady you're searching for in Midland and why?"

"Sir, it's not any of your business why I am looking for someone."

"It is my business if you want me to give you any information." The sheriff cocked his head.

"Well, all right, but you must keep this confidential. Your deputy, too."

"Certainly. Now who are you looking for and why?"

"The young lady is my fiancée, or was to be my bride, but she left before the ceremony. I'm looking for her."

"And her name?"

"Miss Jocelyn Norwood."

"What does this young lady look like?"

"Beautiful, of course."

"Of course?" the sheriff replied with a grin.

"Very attractive, long blonde hair, blue eyes, petite figure and very intelligent. You would remember her if you saw her."

"I believe I would for sure," the deputy said.

"I was told that a wagon train of brides left bound for Amarillo. If I can't find her here, she might have joined the train of ladies to escape Midland without being seen. She would have changed her name, if she did join up with them. I have sent Pinkerton men to look for her, but they didn't find a trace of her whereabouts. I believe I can find her."

"Why do you think you can find her if detectives couldn't?"

"Because I am smarter than she is," Luther commented.

"Well, Mr. Sullivan, I'm sorry, but I can't say that I've seen this young lady in Midland, but I'll keep my eyes open for such a lovely creature. My deputy will start a search for the two men that robbed you. How long will you be in town?"

"Right now, I'm going to the bank and then to the telegraph office to wire my lawyer. I know your bank will give me funds so I can be on my way after they hear from my lawyer. You see, I'm a very important person in Perryville."

"If we find the two men or the young lady, where can we locate you?"

"I'll check back with you in the morning. Good day, gentlemen." Luther almost clicked his heels together as he nodded goodbye.

The two men shook their heads and laughed. "I'll be right back," the sheriff said to his deputy. "I'm going to the telegraph office and send a wire to the sheriff in Perryville.

We need more information about the *fugitive bride."*

Chapter 17

After Jocelyn served the men breakfast, she watched Matt as he lay on his side. She carried him a cup of coffee. "Would you like a plate of food now?'

"No, I'll wait and eat with you. I've noticed Cassie eats before the men and you eat afterward. Why is that?"

Shrugging, she said, "I'm never hungry early in the morning. I'd rather eat later and take my time, but I'll be glad to have breakfast with you. Maybe we can talk about private things."

"I'm ready to listen to whatever you tell me, as long as it's the truth." Matt set his coffee cup down on the side table.

She gave Matt a shy smile as she headed back into the kitchen to start cleaning and planning the men's lunch. Food was the priority of the day.

After she placed a pot of dried field peas on the stove to simmer, she asked Cassie to go to the hen house and gather fresh eggs. She had already requested six fresh chickens for the evening meal. For lunch the next day they'd serve a large chicken pot pie made from the left-over chicken.

Jocelyn prepared a plate of ham and eggs with large butter biscuits for Matt's breakfast and two scrambled eggs and buttered bread for herself. She carried a tray over to Matt's bed while Matt sat up with a blanket covering his lower body. After pouring two fresh cups of coffee, she sat beside his bed.

As they ate the delicious food, Jocelyn's mind was racing. How much was she going to tell Matt about her background? Would he understand why she ran away from her fiancé and fancy wedding?

Jocelyn took their dirty dishes to the kitchen, put them in the sink and filled it with soapy water. Matt looked extremely tired. While she was putting the plates on the shelf, she practically dropped a dish when she turned and saw him standing there barefoot, dress in a clean shirt and a pair of soft buckskin breeches.

With a shy grin, he said, "You'll have to excuse my feet. I had a hard time getting these pants on, so I knew I'd never be able to pull on my boots."

She smiled and pointed to the chair. Maybe this was a good time to tell him. "I've something to tell you. Do you know that since I arrived in Amarillo, my every conviction has been turned inside out? I feel like I'm hanging upside down. I really believed that one day I would return to Perryville, but now I have no home to return to. And after meeting you, even realizing how arrogant and overbearing you are, I really like it here."

****

Matt gave her an exasperated look because he really wanted her to tell him about the man who was trying to find her. He rubbed his sides and ran a hand through his hair. Maybe this was a good time to have that talk. She offered him coffee, but he refused.

How about you tell me why you left home on your wedding day."

Jocelyn nodded. She closed her eyes and took a deep breath. Folding her hands in her lap, she ignored Matt and stared straight ahead.

Matt covered her soft hand with his large, firm one. She tried to shrug it loose, but he held it tighter. "Come on, Josh. Tell me your story."

She knew from his expression that he wanted her to begin. Sighing with exasperation she started by telling him about her father.

"I always felt my papa was a perfect man. He was a good father and a sweet loving man to my mama. After she died, he and I grew closer. Papa was a giant of a man, at least to me. He stood over six feet tall and had wide shoulders. Although, he looked intimidating, he was as gentle as a lamb. He'd never harm anyone. Also, he was a smart businessman, but he did have one weakness. Papa enjoyed gambling and often held a card game in our library. He gave me everything a young girl desired, and sent me to the best school back east, and hired smart tutors to come to the house when I wanted to come home. And he dressed me like royalty. I never wanted for anything. But, one night he held a card game with high stakes. I wasn't there, but Papa later told me he had a great hand. He had already lost most of his funds, so he signed an IOU, putting up our home and all the surrounding property. Unfortunately for him and me, another man held the winning hand. Later, Mr. Sullivan, a banker in Perryville, purchased the IOU.

****

Jocelyn stopped talking and looked at Matt. She could still remember the day he told her. "As he struggled to tell me what he'd done, he grabbed his chest and fell over onto the floor. Once the doctor came, he told me my father had been suffering from heart failure for a long time. The stress weighing on his mind and heart was almost too much for his body to handle. He lay in bed several weeks. One day the banker came to visit my papa. He told my father that if I would marry his son, Luther, he would tear up the IOU, and all the debt would be forgiven."

Matt's head tilted to the side. "What did you think of that idea? Did you know the banker's son?"

"Yes, I knew him." Jocelyn knew that very minute that

she would have to tell Matt everything, things she had never shared with anyone. "Later that evening he told me that I had to marry Luther Sullivan."

"One day, when my papa was very weak, I sat next to him for hours. Later that evening, he told me that I had to marry Luther Sullivan. "This young man is rich and he'll provide for you in the same lifestyle you're accustomed," Papa said.

"I begged papa not to make me promise, but he was so weak. He kept pleading with me to promise and when it became clear he was dying, I promised. I cried and cried as he rubbed my hair. Later than evening, he did pass."

"So, you promised your father that you would marry this man, but when the time came, you reneged on your promise and ran away?"

Jocelyn held her head down, looking at Matt's bare feet. "At first, I asked Luther's father if we could wait a year to marry. It is the custom to have a year to mourn one's loved ones. Mr. Sullivan denied my request and said I had two weeks to prepare for our wedding, and if I didn't marry his son, he would toss me out in the street. My papa had left me no funds, property, or any of his investments. I would be a pauper."

"The marriage was to take place in two weeks?" Matt asked, "Why did the banker want you to marry so soon?"

She shrugged. "I had no other choice. I had never worked outside of my home. But, with no funds, I had to do something." Releasing an anguished sigh, she continued. "I went through the motions of planning a big wedding. My dressmaker worked night and day to make me a beautiful dress, which I do regret. My maid, Maria, helped me sell some of my mother's jewelry and a few items from the house that wouldn't be missed. As I planned my wedding day, I was also planning my escape. I didn't tell anyone, not even Maria, even though I was sure she knew." Jocelyn looked at Matt's pale face. "Would you like to lie down?"

Matt didn't answer but continued to rub his side, obviously aching from the top of his head to his toes. "No, I don't want you to stop. I want to know everything."

Jocelyn leaped up from the kitchen table and hurried to the small table to retrieve Matt's medicine. When she returned with the bottle, he refused to take any of it.

"Get me some coffee. I'm not taking any more of that stuff. It makes me sleepy, and I don't want to take a nap. I'll rest later."

Jocelyn poured two cups of coffee and they both sat quietly for a few minutes. Then he said, "Please, continue. How did you escape from the wedding?"

"Well, the only salvation to my horror, was no one had seen me crawl through the window and race to the stables. I'd already packed a small carpetbag with some of Maria's old dresses and sewn most of my money into the hem of my shift. My sweet maid had to deal with Luther and his father."

"Mr. Sullivan, the banker, was the man who hired the Pinkerton men who came searching for you? Why would he force you into marriage with his son?"

"I don't know, but he's a very hard man. His word is the law, and once he decides, he won't change his mind even a little. I experienced his attitude about my papa's death. He didn't threaten me with harm, but his eyes said a lot. The man scared me."

"How did you get away from Perryville without being seen?"

"I dressed in Maria's clothes and plaited my long hair into a rope. My head was covered when I hurried to the train station. I gave a small boy some money to go and purchase me a ticket to Midland. Once I boarded the train, I sat in the back and looked out the window the whole time. No one seemed to notice me. Once I reached Midland, I rented a room at a boarding house. The next day, I saw a notice on the boardwalk about the brides' wagon train going to Amarillo.

As I sat in the café, I overheard some ladies talking about traveling with the train, and then I met Cassie. She asked me if I was going to join the wagon train and I thought it was a way to leave the area. Cassie wanted to get away from working in the hot kitchen, so she and I made a pack to stay together, so we went to talk to the wagon train's owner. I wouldn't sign a contract unless it read that I could travel to Amarillo, without agreeing to be a bride. At first, Mr. Campbell said I couldn't travel on his wagon train, but he changed his mind when I told him I would like to be a cook or housekeeper for a ranch. He told me you were willing to pay the passage fee for a new cook for your ranch. If you didn't want me, then I could work off my three hundred dollars."

"So, you came to me under fault pretenses. You never intended to be my bride."

"Now, that's not true. Mr. Campbell knew that I wasn't going to be a bride. It was in my contract."

"But, you didn't read the contract before you signed it," Matt countered.

"That was my mistake, but I trusted the man."

"I hope that is a lesson well learned. Never trust a stranger," Matt said with a grin. "How did you learn that Mr. Sullivan was trying to find you to marry his son?"

"As Mr. Campbell and the men were preparing the wagons and ladies to move out, I saw the sheriff with some men. They wanted to search the wagon train for someone. I knew it was me, so Cassie hid me in the bottom of our covered wagon." She drew in a deep sigh.

"When I saw the men here on your ranch, I knew it was the same ones that had searched the wagon train."

When Matt shifted around and winced every time he moved, it was clear his ribs were hurting. "Come and lie down for a while. Later, I'll walk with you outside. You're getting better daily, but please don't rush and harm yourself."

He grimaced but nodded. Since I now know about your past, it is imperative that we marry. The sooner the better. This way, you no longer have to fear this man, Mr. Sullivan and his son. You'll belong to me, and no man will ever harm anything or person that's mine."

"I can believe that, but you may change your mind once I tell you something I'm so ashamed I haven't told anyone." Wiping her tears with the tail of her apron, she couldn't meet Matt's eyes. "I'm sorry, Matt but I can't marry any man."

Matt reached for her hand and squeezed it tight. "I can't believe you did anything shameful. But, even if you did, I'm sure you had a good reason. Now tell me."

"No, not now. Please let me pull myself together. I promise I'll try to tell you after lunch."

****

After all the lunch dishes were cleaned and put away, Jocelyn told Cassie they would have fried chicken, mashed potatoes and hot biscuits to go with the field peas for supper. "There's a barrel of fresh apples in the cellar if you want to make several apple pies while I'm gone."

"Where are you going?" Cassie asked. "I notice you'd been crying.

"Matt and I will go on a short stroll around the ranch. He needs to build up his strength again. I hope his ribs get better soon."

"Hey, Josh, I'm ready to go, if you are," Matt said.

Jocelyn and Matt walked out into the sunshine. The fresh air felt good on Jocelyn's face. Several of the men were sitting on the corral fence, watching one of the hands walk Matt's large stallion around in the fenced area. He seemed as gentle as a new baby, but that was because no one was attempting to ride him.

"What a beauty," Jocelyn said. "I loved riding him."

His eyes grew large. "I would have never let you ride

him if I had known. I'm just thankful that you're a trained rider. If not, he would have thrown you over his head and probably stomped you in the ground. He's one dangerous animal."

"Watching him now, that's hard to believe. I'm glad that I didn't know he was your new, expensive horse." Realizing that she had touched his arm, she jumped back and said she was sorry.

Grinning, Matt took her hand and continued to amble around the property. They passed the corral, the new winter garden, then headed toward the pasture. Under a shade tree was a wooden double swing. "Let sit here and talk," he said as he waited for her to sit down. "I enjoy watching the calves and cows gaze," Matt said. "This is a quiet place where my mama would come and read when she had the time."

"This is a lovely spot I never noticed the swing before."

"It had been broken. Jim repaired the chain, painted it, and hung it up a few days ago."

"I'll have to remember it is out here. I love to read." Jocelyn said as she sat on the swing and smoothed her skirt around her legs.

"Now, Josh, please tell me why you can't marry me. I can't imagine any reason that would keep us apart. I don't want to give the Sullivan's any reason to take you back to Perryville."

She blew out a breath. "All right. I'll tell you my secret. As I said before, I never told anyone what had happened to me. Maria found me, but I didn't tell her what had caused me to be unconscious."

"Go on, but start at the beginning."

"It was a known fact that Mr. Sullivan wasn't happy with his son. You see, Luther isn't built like other men his age. He's tall, thin and very pale. He is what you might call a delicate man. He doesn't care to work on a ranch or even ride a horse. His actions are more girlish than manly. So, his father was after him to marry, and he figured Luther could marry any young girl he wanted because he was a very wealthy young man. Mr. Sullivan had told many young ladies' fathers that his son was ready to marry, including my papa."

Jocelyn put her foot down on the ground and stopped the swing. They sat still and gazed off into the distance. "One night, after my papa and the servants had retired for the evening, Luther sneaked into our home unnoticed. I was in the library reading. Luther opened the door and entered the room. I was surprised to see him and asked what he wanted. He said that he wanted to talk to me about getting married. I wanted no part of marriage and certainly not to him. I demanded that he leave, but he only laughed. Then he jerked me out of my rocking chair and started kissing me. He said his father was demanding that he marry, and I was the perfect girl he wanted to court and marry. He told me that his father ordered him to do anything to make me change my mind and agree to marry. When I refused and called him ugly names, and he slapped me. I kicked him hard and clawed his face. Then he punched me and knocked me out. While I was unconscious, he had his way with me."

"Damn! Surely, he didn't think you would have anything to do with him after that." Matt huffed. "How long did you lie on the floor until you were discovered?"

"I woke up, bloody and practically undressed. I tried to make it upstairs when Maria heard me crying out from the pain. She carried me to my room and helped me bathe. She wanted to wake my father and then get the constable. I wouldn't let her."

Why didn't you let her tell your father?"

"Because he would have made me marry the young fool. I would have died if I had to marry him."

"But, you agreed to marry him later."

“Yes, but that was different. I would have done anything to make my papa happy before he died. But, I hoped that I would have a year to convince Luther to change his mind about marrying me.”

“Yes, I can see that now.”

“After arriving here, I discovered that I might be with child.—a chilling fact that I was going to have to face. But, when I fell off your horse, my lower abdomen started hurting and the pain lasted for several days. After we had the accident in the carriage, as I was running to get help for you, I started bleeding badly, but I knew in my heart it was a blessing. Though I was in pain, I screamed with joy. Never would I have to think about that horrible night again.

Matt turned in the swing, took her shoulders and shifted her to face him. “Oh, my Lord, Josh, I could have killed you when I turned the carriage over. I did great harm to you, but you never said anything. I’m so sorry.”

“Please, don’t be sorry. I know the fall off the horse and sliding down into that awful gully did damage to my body. It just took a few days. Besides, that man hurt me, not you. I’m well now, but don’t you see. I’m not a pure, clean young girl anymore. I can’t ever marry.”

“Josh, I hate what happened to you. I’ll beat that young man to a pulp if I ever get to meet him. What he did to you is unforgivable but it doesn’t change how I feel about you. I care deeply for you, and I want us to marry.

She held her face down in her hands and cried. “No, we can’t.”

“I know you insist there is nothing between us. You avoid looking into my eyes, and yet your body trembles when you’re in my arms. Your body contradicts your words of protest.”

“I know,” she murmured.

Her admission pleased him. He took her shoulders and pulled her face toward his. His mouth gently brushed hers.

When she smiled and he kissed her again, applying

more pressure. He wanted more, but he'd wait for her to make the next move.

She pressed against his chest, but her eyes sent a different message. When he leaned into her again, she didn't refuse, so he demanded a deeper kiss. He wanted her with a burning desire that he had never felt with another woman.

****

The intensity of what was happening between them scared her. The way she was acting, he must think she was a loose woman.

They separated on the swing but continued to talk for a little while longer, until Matt finally announced that he better go back inside and rest. She prayed that his ribs would soon heal. He was so tired of hurting.

Matt stood and surveyed the cattle. "We can come to an agreement about marrying. I want to send for the minister to come out and talk about us getting married quietly. Most of the town believes that you're already my bride, so we can have a small ceremony with close friends and the ranch hands."

"Now listen to me for a minute, Matt. I know that Luther is pursuing me. He wants to take me back to Perrysville, and you know that I will never go home with him. It's funny. I know all about him, but I know very little about you. All I know is you're wealthy and well respected, just like my papa was. You have been good to me."

Matt grimaced as he turned too quickly to peer at her. "We don't have time to learn about each other's dreams for the future, but we'll do that after we are man and wife. I can promise you that I will never mistreat you and I'll be faithful. Now," he sighed and frowned at her, "I need to take some of that awful pain medicine."

Chapter 18

After a few days of waiting, Luther's lawyer sent a telegram to the bank in Midland requesting that five hundred dollars be given to his client, Luther Sullivan. Once Luther received the money, he went straight to the livery and informed Boomer that while they were in this town, he was always to be with him. He wouldn't allow those nasty men to accost or waylay him again. Boomer's size was enough to intimidate any man or at least think twice about robbing him again.

"Yes, sir, I'll stick to you like a bee on honey. I won't let no man hurt you again." Boomer declared, then sighed wearily.

"Just follow along behind me. I need to purchase some new clothes and afterward, I will buy two tickets to Amarillo. Tomorrow morning you'll have to take our carriage and horses to the train depot and put them in a stock car."

Before they walked out of the shop, Boomer pointed at several large packages for Boomer to carry. "Let's get a room at the hotel so I can have a nice hot bath and change into my new things. I'm sick of being dirty," he said as he brushed at his sleeves, "and I'm ready for a warm meal. Come on now. Be quick about it, and let's get this show on the road. I'm ready to catch up with my bride-to-be."

Boomer followed Luther to his hotel room with the parcels, then returned downstairs and asked the young clerk to bring several hot buckets of water to the room. The young man rushed downstairs and about thirty minutes later, Boomer helped Luther into his bath. "Boomer, get in here and scrub my back. After sleeping on that pile of hay for two nights, I feel like I have fleas on me."

Boomer sighed but knelt down and scrubbed Luther's pale body. Luther was so thin that it unnerved him sometimes. He had never had to be his valet before because he was the groomsman. His duty was to only drive Luther back and forth to places. He also worked around the barn and helped take care of the horses, cows and sometimes gathered eggs for the lady who cooked for the Sullivan's. Boomer had already decided that he would disappear from Luther's life once they found Miss Norwood.

Luther's father was a stern man, but he wasn't unkind to his house or field servants. Many of the people who worked for him were slaves working off their indenture contracts. But Boomer had never belonged to anyone. His parents died when he was a small child and he survived by wandering from town to town and worked for people for a place to sleep and a hot meal. Boomer had worked for many people who were very good to him, but he stayed only a short time. No one ever asked to see his papers or questioned him about his master. He was a free man, and he intended to stay that way. He wasn't afraid of Luther, but he didn't trust him not to try to sell him to a rich white man.

"Boomer, here's some money. Take this and those rags with you to that boy at the livery. Settle up with them and prepare the carriage and horses for our train trip. The train leaves at 9:00 a.m. so get back here to the hotel around 8:00 a.m. to pick up my carpetbags. I'll see you at the train depot."

"You don't want me to walk you to the train?"

"I can manage the short walk without being harmed. But don't you dare be late."

Boomer walked back to the livery stable. He hated to leave Butch. The young man had been good to him. He had never met his mama, but she had been very kind, too. Boomer was glad that he had helped clean the stable and helped with the horses. He felt he had paid for his food and sleeping quarters there. Luther had never offered to put him up at the hotel. He didn't care anyway. Most hotels didn't allow black folks to stay in their fancy rooms.

Butch looked like he might cry when he heard they were leaving. "Man, I sure hate to see you move on. Sure wish I could afford to pay you a decent wage so you could stay on with me. All my customers like you and the way you care for their animals. I appreciate all you did for me while you was here."

"Now, boy, just try to keep this place clean and you'll keep a good business. I'm going to miss you, too. I brought the clothes back that you loaned Luther. I'm sorry they're dirty. He got some money from his lawyer back in Perryville. Luther paid you in advance for boarding the animals, but I brought the five dollars your mama loaned him. Sure, appreciate everything."

****

It was several hours before the train pulled in Amarillo. Boomer jumped off the train and helped one of the men open the stock-car doors to allow the animals to walk down a plank to the ground. After thanking the man for his help, Boomer tied his three horses to a hitching post while two men guided the small carriage down the plank. He hitched two horses to the carriage and tied the spare horse to the rear. After gathering all of Luther's new carpetbags, he drove the carriage to the front of the train. Luther climbed into the carriage and sat like a crown prince in the back.

"Boomer, stop somewhere near a nice café. I'm

starving," Luther hollered.

Boomer was also hungry, but he would take care of himself. He was well aware, by now, that Luther only thought about his own needs and comforts. It was imperative for him to find himself a job and get away from Luther. He had wanted to stay with him until he discovered the whereabouts of Miss Norwood, to make sure she was safe. Boomer was a patient man, but his patience was wearing thin. He didn't want to hurt Luther, but he was tired of being treated like a purchased slave.

****

After Matt's long nap, he told Jocelyn that he had arranged for Bryan, the foreman, to take her into town so she could purchase a bride's trousseau or something similar. Once things were settled with Luther Sullivan and his ribs were healed, they would take a real honeymoon and shopping trip. He wanted her to have everything her heart desired, but Amarillo shops' inventories were limited.

"I don't want to hear any complaints. Bryan is going to meet with a cattleman for me, and later he can stop by the church to speak to the minister. When he says he can come out, please have Cassie make something sweet to eat. That man does have a sweet tooth." Matt laughed as he walked outside.

****

Early the next morning, after helping with breakfast and cleaning the kitchen, Jocelyn changed into a more appropriate dress for the trip to town. This was the first time she'd been back to town since the accident on the way home. Bryan stopped the carriage in front of the store and told her that he would return after finishing his business and speaking with the minister. As Jocelyn stepped onto the boardwalk, she had a funny feeling that she was being watched. She stood and glanced all around as many ladies smiled at her and men tipped their hats. She smiled back, shaking off that awful feeling, and entered the store.

Immediately, she was greeted by the store owner, Gladys Crocker.

"Good day to you, Mrs. Colburn. I'm so happy to see you again."

Jocelyn smiled and shook her head. "I told you before that I'm not Matt's bride."

"I know," she whispered, "but with you living on his ranch, I like for others to believe you two are hitched. You did come here to be his wife."

"Have it your way," Jocelyn said, laughing.

"I see the dresses fit that I sent out to you. You're wearing one of them."

"Yes, everything you delivered was perfect. Thank you so much."

"So," Mrs. Crocker took Jocelyn's hands in hers, "what can I do for you today?"

"Well, Matt, Mr. Colburn and I will be getting married soon, and he insists that I buy some new clothes. He's one man you cannot argue with, so I want to choose a few things that you have in stock. I'll go to the back of the store and look around. Please don't say anything about us getting married."

"Oh, I won't since I let everyone think you're already hitched." Both ladies laughed.

****

As his carriage moved down Main Street, Luther searched for a nice café when suddenly he yelled for Boomer to pull over. "Stop, Boomer. I want to get out here." He saw a young blond girl enter the dry goods store. Although, he didn't see the girl's face, she reminded him of his prey. "I'll check in at the hotel and have a hot meal while you take care of the animals. In a little while, I'll come for you, so settle in at the stable like you did in Midland."

Luther headed to the store's big display window. He pretended to be admiring the items for sale, but he wanted to get a good look at the pretty girl who had entered the store. One look at her, and he pulled down his hat, straightened his vest and went inside.

****

As Jocelyn rifled through a rack of dresses, she felt someone's breath on the back of her neck.

"Hello, my dear runaway bride," a voice whispered.

Jocelyn whirled around and attempted to move away from the tall, slight man she knew was Luther. "Get away from me," she screamed loud enough for Gladys Crocker to hear. Jocelyn paled and looked for a way to escape.

"Now, my dear, you don't have anything to fear from me," Luther said as he gripped her upper arm. "We have a lot of things to talk over."

"Is this man bothering you, Jocelyn?"

"Yes," she said at the same time he said, "No."

"I believe the lady wants you to leave, sir," Mrs. Crocker said.

Luther turned to face Mrs. Crocker, then poked his cane at her shoulder. "Why don't you go mind the store and leave my bride-to-be and me alone? We have things to discuss." He continued to hold Jocelyn tight.

As Mrs. Crocker turned and left, Jocelyn yelled, "Go get Matt," but she disappeared around the corner.

Luther was jerking her toward the door demanding that she come with him when he stopped, almost knocking her over. She glanced back to see Mr. Crocker jabbing a double-barrel shotgun into Luther's back.

"I believe the lady would like for you to leave this store," Mr. Crocker said, as he poked him harder.

Luther turned around surprised to see a man taller than himself holding a shotgun. Trying not to appear intimidated, he moved the gun away from his body. "This lady will soon be my bride, and we're leaving together. Now point that gun somewhere else."

The shopkeeper joined her husband. "She can't be

your bride. Jocelyn is married to Matt Colburn. And whoever you are, she ain't going anywhere with you. Now, sir, my husband will arrest you if you don't leave our store."

"You can't be married," Luther turned to Jocelyn. "You'll have to have the marriage annulled."

The woman turned to her husband. "Ben, hold that gun on him. I'm going to get the sheriff. Jocelyn is scared to death of this man. I can see her trembling."

"No, that won't be necessary. I will leave." Luther turned Jocelyn loose and headed to the door. "We'll meet again soon, my dear."

Jocelyn watched as Luther left the store. She nearly fell into Mr. Crocker's arms. "Thank you so much for your help--both of you. I can't believe he found me so quickly."

"Who is that man? He said that you're going to marry him?" Mr. Crocker questioned. "I have never seen such a handsome man before. He almost looked like a young woman in the face."

"I'm so sorry I brought my troubles here. I never intended for him to find me, but I knew that he and his father were searching for me. The Pinkerton men followed me to Midland and then here, but I was able to hide from them."

"But who is he?" Mr. Crocker asked. "I haven't had to get my rusty shotgun out from behind the counter in years."

"I was promised to him . . . in marriage before my papa died, but I never wanted to marry him and after my papa passed, I thought I would have a year to mourn his death. But Mr. Sullivan made demands on me and set the wedding date. On the day of the wedding, I ran away."

"Why would he insist you get your marriage annulled?" Mrs. Crocker asked.

"I don't know the answer to that. I'm sure Matt will find out the answer," Jocelyn said.

"So Matt knows about these men?" Mr. Crocker asked.

"Yes, he seems to think that if we marry, that will be the end of Luther trying to make me return to Perryville with him."

"I don't think marriage will end your problem with that man," Mrs. Crocker said. "Come into the back room with me and let's have a cup of tea so you can pull yourself together. You still need to purchase some new clothes."

Chapter 19

When Jim entered the house, he could hear Cassie in the kitchen humming and the smell of pies she was baking. He found her in the kitchen all alone.

Cassie looked up and wiped her hands on a dishtowel. "Now, Mr. Watson, I've instructed you not to call me Miss. My name is Cassie."

"The old man ambled over to the kitchen counter, wearing a silly grin. "Let's make a deal. I'll call you Cassie if you call me Jim."

Cassie felt a blush spread over her cheeks. "That's a deal, Jim. How would you like to sit and have a cup of coffee with me? I just finished making four apple pies and they are in the oven for dinner tonight. I need to take a load off my poor feet."

"I believe I'll take you up on that offer. There was a reason for coming into the house, but I can't remember what it was."

After pouring the coffee, Cassie asked Jim what he had been doing all morning. "Oh, this and that. Mostly, I like to let the new colts out in the corral one at a time, lasso a rope on them and walk them around. They need to get used to the rope and let people lead them. So many of them like to try nip at their leader, but they have to learn not to do that."

"Golly, the mules would try to do that on the wagon train, too, but I quickly had to break them of that."

"What did you do when one of them tried to bite you?"

"I'd hit them in the nose with my fist." Cassie made a fist and showed Jim. Both of them laughed.

"Woman, you're something else," Jim chuckled.

"The men on the trip didn't help hitch the wagons so we had to learn to do many things for ourselves. Caring for those stubborn mules was the hardest job."

"I just bet you were a big help to the ladies on that long trip. When you arrived, I'm glad you decided not to marry that Willy fellow," Jim smiled sheepishly at Cassie.

Cassie looked down at her hands. "To tell you the truth, Jim, he rejected me, but I think he did me a big favor. I'm glad that I had the chance to come here and work on this ranch with Jocelyn. We've become as close as sisters."

"I can tell that she's happy to have you here. She needed help, but she was too proud to tell Matt. He can be an ornery cuss and he wasn't happy that she wouldn't go into town and marry him." Jim looked toward the door to make sure they were still alone.

"Both of us decided before we left Midland that we wouldn't be brides, but I kinda changed my mind. I think the good Lord was watching out for me. I'm happy now, and I believe Jocelyn and Matt will marry soon."

Jim stood and walked to the front door. He removed his hat from the hat rack and held it before him. "Cassie, I was just wondering if you would like to attend the service with me Sunday. We could ride down by the lake and picnic after the preaching."

"Well, I declare," Cassie stood and walked over to Jim. "I would like that very much, and I'll fix us a nice lunch to share."

"There you are, Jim," Matt ambled into the kitchen. "The men have been wondering where you got off too," Matt said.

He held up his coffee cup. "I took a little break and had a nice hot cup of coffee. Is that a crime?"

"No, of course not," Matt smiled and walked over to

his bed. "I believe I'm ready to move back upstairs. Get a couple of the boys to come and take this bed apart and carry it up to my bedroom."

"Sure thing. I'll be back with them in a few minutes. Cassie, you'd better take those covers off the bed if you want to keep them clean." Jim eyes lingered on her then he hurried out to the corral.

****

Bryan and Jocelyn arrived back at the ranch just as the men came out of the house. Bryan, the foreman, stopped the carriage in front of the house and jumped down to help Jocelyn. Offering his hand, he said softly, "You have to tell Matt about that man in town. If you don't, I will. "

"I know he has to know, but please give me a little time before I tell him."

He inclined his head toward her, his face somber. "Today. You have to tell him when you get your things put away. I like my job and I don't want him to hear this gossip from someone else." He turned and lifted several packages out of the boot of the carriage.

Jocelyn took a deep breath and walked slowly to the porch. Matt was standing in the doorway smiling as Bryan carried in a bundle of packages.

"I see you did as I asked and purchased some things."

"Yes, Mrs. Crocker helped me select some nice dresses. I am afraid I ran your bill up pretty high at the store." Jocelyn removed her hat and hung her wrap on the hat rack by the door.

"Don't you fret about the expense? I look forward to seeing you in different attire." Matt winked, then moseyed over to the kitchen table and sat down.

"My goodness, I see your bed has been removed. Did you have it taken to your room upstairs?"

"Yes, I can walk up and down the stairs now and I don't need assistance anymore," Matt said, taking a cup of coffee from Cassie.

Bryan had placed all the packages on the end of the dining room table. “I am going now, Miss Jocelyn. Please . . . remember what I said.” He smiled and said that he would see everyone at supper.

Matt sat at the kitchen table and watched Bryan go out the door. He waited for a few minutes. Jocelyn hurrying over to the dining room table to get a package for Cassie. “Look Cassie, I purchased you a few things. I know Matt will agree that you needed these.”

Before Cassie could respond, Matt said, “Jocelyn, what did Bryan mean? Do you have something to tell me?”

“Matt, please. Let me show Cassie her gifts. And, yes, I do have something to tell you.”

“Cassie can wait and whatever you have to tell me, she can hear it too. I’m sure you’ll tell her later anyway.”

Jocelyn placed the wrapped package on the kitchen table and cried. “Oh, Matt, it was awful. Luther was in town, and he came into the store. He demanded that I leave with him. Mr. Crocker got his shotgun and chased him out of the store.” Cassie brought her a soft white towel to wipe her face from tears.

“Josh,” Matt said, “start from the beginning. I know you were scared, especially if Ben had to get his old shotgun out from under the counter.”

Words spewed out as Jocelyn sat next to him and relived the story from when she got down from the carriage in front of the store. “I felt as if someone was watching me. Mrs. Crocker told Luther we were already married, but he didn’t care. He said we could get the marriage annulled.” Tears pooled down her face. “He scared me, but Mr. and Mrs. Crocker gave him a good scare. He left the store, but said he would see me again.”

Matt stood and pulled Jocelyn out of her chair. He pushed her hair away from her face and then wrapped his arms around her.

She rested her head against his chest and tried to relax.

"I feel safe now. You and your men will take care of me."

Matt realized that they couldn't wait any longer to get married. "Now dry those tears because I want you to go and put on one of your new dresses. Jim will go over to his little church and get his pastor. He's a nice, quiet man and he'll marry us. This *Luther* fellow will never know when we were married."

Jocelyn walked away from Matt. "This is either a nightmare or you have completely lost your mind. You don't love me, and I'm confused as to how I feel about you. We can't just marry to keep Luther away from me."

Matt was surprised that she wasn't screaming at him. Yes, he had treated her poorly, but lately, they had become friends. She'd confided in him about her father and how the Sullivan men, father and son, had mistreated her.

****

Jocelyn continued to stare at Matt. Many thoughts flooded her mind. For the first time in her life, she was completely overwhelmed as to what to do.

Matt took her hand and led her toward her bedroom. He said over his shoulder to Cassie that he and Josh needed a few minutes of privacy. A few moments later, he pulled Jocelyn into her room, and she heard the door click.

"We should not be in here together." Her lip quivered. "It isn't proper."

He dabbed at a tear on her cheek. "You should know by now that I'm never proper."

Jocelyn stepped back out of his reach. "Please open the door and leave."

"Josh, we're going to be married in a few hours. I've never been in love before, but I feel that I'm very close to falling head over heels in love with you. You care for me, too. I want us to have a wonderful future together, and I'll protect you from your past."

"Oh, Matt, I want to believe you." Jocelyn sat down on the bed and then leaped back up. She didn't need to be near a bed in a locked room with this handsome knight in jeans.

"Believe it or not, we will be married. I'm going to take care of some business. While I'm gone, Cassie will help you get ready. A light supper of sandwiches and apple pie will be just fine."

Matt left Jocelyn alone in the bedroom that used to be his grandmother's. She sighed, turned, and surveyed the room for the first time. Touching the back of the rocking chair, she realized that from this day forth, Matt would most likely demand that he sleep in this room since they would be married. "Oh, Lord, please help me."

Chapter 20

After giving Jim instructions to have the minister come over in the afternoon to perform a wedding ceremony, he slipped on his boots and grabbed his Stetson. He went to the barn and signaled for Bryan. “Go into town with me. I need to settle things with that man who is bothering Jocelyn. Did you see him?”

“No, he was already gone when I picked up Miss Jocelyn from the dry goods store. She couldn’t get in the carriage fast enough. Her head was on a swivel as I drove down Main Street and left town.”

“I assured her that I had my gun, and nobody would bother her again in my presence. She seemed to relax on the way home.”

“Mr. and Mrs. Crocker can give me a description of him and maybe where he’s staying. I’m going to make sure he leaves town.”

“How are you going to make him leave?”

“If I have to, I’ll have the sheriff arrest him for something?”

On the way into town, Matt wished they had taken the carriage. Riding his frisky horse was almost too much for his injured ribs. He’d thought he‘d healed up, but he hadn’t been on a horse since he got hurt.

“Are you all right, boss? You’re sweating like crazy, and your face is as white as cotton.” Bryan asked. “We can stop for a minute to rest if you need to.”

"I'm fine. It's just been a while since I've been on the back of a horse. I guess I'm just getting soft."

As they rode into town, they passed an alley filled with men. Some were sprawled out on the ground while others were on bended knees. They were playing some kind of gambling game with dice. Continuing down Main Street, they stopped in front of the dry goods store. A young boy was sitting on the boardwalk.

Matt glanced down at the sad-looking youngster and asked if he had seen a new city dude hanging around town.

"Yep, he's been standing in front of the Lady Luck saloon. I've been watching him. He was scared to go inside for a long time because there are lot of rowdy cowboys inside. They're laughing and fighting with each other. Several have come flying out the batwing doors onto the street. I guess he finally got the nerve to go inside."

"Thanks, fellow. If you see him come out, please come in the store and get me."

"What will you give me if I tell you I saw him again?"

Matt laughed and rubbed the little boy's head, "How about a bag of candy?"

"Gee, mister. I'd like that. When I get a coin from somebody, I have to give it to my mama. She works real hard and can use the money."

As Matt turned to walk in the dry goods store, he called to the kid. "Hey son, take this money to your mama now, and get busy watching for my man." He pushed several dollars in the boy's shirt pocket and smiled.

As Matt entered the store, Mrs. Crocker smiled broadly as she looked up from sorting canned goods. "Thank goodness you came into town, Matt," she said, walking toward him. "I guess your wife made it home safe?"

"Yes, she told me what happened here with that Sullivan fellow, but I'd like to hear from you and Mr. Crocker about the man."

Mrs. Crocker told Matt about how the man was trying to force Jocelyn to go with him, and how she hurried to tell her husband, who made him leave the store."

"What did this man look like?" Matt asked as he unconsciously rubbed his side.

"You still hurt from your accident?" Mrs. Crocker asked.

"I'm better, thank you, but I haven't been on a horse. I came to town to have a talk with that man who followed Jocelyn from Perryville."

"I don't know where he went after he left, but he said that he would see her again. He made me so mad, I would have slapped that pretty face of his."

"Bryan and I are searching for him. I'm headed to the livery stable to see if he left town. Thank you so much for your help earlier." Matt and Bryan left the store and headed down the boardwalk toward the livery.

"Hey, mister," the young boy called to Matt from the boardwalk. "That man is not in the saloon. I peeked under the batwing doors and looked all around. He ain't in there."

"Thanks, son. Appreciate the information." Matt entered the livery and saw two men standing near a stall. A big man had his back up against the wall while a tall, thin man dressed in a fancy, colorful vest was shouting at him.

When the shouting man noticed him and Bryan entering the livery, he immediately got quiet and stepped behind the big man he'd been belittling.

Matt knew immediately that he'd found Luther Sullivan. He strode close to the two men, placed his arm on the black guy's shoulder and motioned for him to move away.

"Who are you? Can't you see I have business with my slave?" The wisp of a man swelled up like a rooster.

"I done told you that I ain't your slave!" The big man's fists clenched and unclenched.

"You better shut your trap before I hit you." Luther

shook his fist at the man who was twice his size.

Matt looked at Luther. So this was the creature who had scared Josh. He would make sure this man left town and never bothered her again.

"Look at me, pretty boy. My name is Matt Colburn, and if you come near my wife again, you'll be sorry. Another thing, you aren't going to hit anyone. I'll wipe that smug expression off your face if you don't get on your horse and leave town." Before he knew it, he grabbed Luther under the armpits and picked him off the floor to meet his eyes. He shook the man hard to make a point.

Suddenly, Luther butt-headed Matt in the face. Blood shot out of Matt's nose, and he dropped the man onto his feet. His hands went to protect his face. Luther stepped backwards and kicked Matt in his knees and then jabbed his fists into his hurt side.

Matt lost his breath but he grabbed a post to pull to his feet. He wanted to scream from pain, but he kept his composure. With as much force as he could muster, he hit Luther in the jaw, knocking him across the room. The man landed in one of the empty horse stalls unconscious.

Matt gripped his side and wiped his hand down his face. Breathing fast and hard, he told the big man to take his boss and get out of town. "Tell him if I ever see him again, he'll be one sorry man." Matt was having difficulty breathing. His face, shirt, and hands were covered with blood from his nose.

"Yes, sir, I'll sure tell him. I'll put him in his carriage and head back to Perryville as soon as I hitch up the horses. Yes, sir, we'll leave town. "Boomer lifted Luther from the floor and walked to the back of the livery.

Matt and Bryan returned to the dry goods store to get their horses. Before returning to the ranch, Matt asked Mrs. Crocker to let him clean up. He didn't want Jocelyn to see him all bloody.

"My goodness, Matt. What does the other fellow look

like?" Mr. Crocker asked.

"Better than I do because he got the best of me. He used his head to butt me, causing my bloody nose. I'm lucky he didn't break it." Matt tried to make a joke out of it. "Can I use your back room and wash my face? Oh, and I'll need to buy a new shirt."

"Certainly, let me tell Gloria to get you a hot pan of water, and a nice clean cloth. Bryan, go and choose a shirt for Matt while he's washing up."

"I have one more favor, Ben. Can I borrow your supply wagon to ride home in? My sides are killing me. I thought that Bryan could drive the wagon while I lie in the back. I can't ride my horse home."

"Of course, you can have anything I have. Looks like you were in a pretty good brawl with that fellow. Sure, wish I could have seen it."

"No, it was over quick, but he did do damage to my injured side," Matt said, rubbing his body. He lowered his voice and said, "Jocelyn and I are getting married at the ranch as soon we return. Sorry. We aren't having a celebration. We're keeping this marriage date a secret from that Sullivan fellow. He already believes we're married."

"I know that much. Gloria told that fellow you were already hitched. Boy, that woman of mine is still madder than a hornet. That fellow better not cross her path again anytime soon," he said, laughing.

After cleaning up and changing into a new shirt, Bryan helped Matt into the back of the wagon that Mr. Crocker for his deliveries. Mr. Crocker tied their two horses to the back of the wagon.

Chapter 21

Less than an hour later, Luther sat up in the carriage. His jaw felt like it was broken, but he was thankful that he hadn't lost any teeth. He scowled at Boomer as he sat staring at him, waiting for instructions. "Boomer, we're going to the Colburn's ranch and get that gal. I am getting tired of this chase."

"That man said if he ever saw you again, he'd kill you. I'm sure he meant it, too."

"You fool! We aren't going to be seen. I said when the time was right, I'll nab her. Get this carriage moving to the Colburn's Ranch. I was told it was about five miles from town, and a person couldn't miss it."

"After we get there, what are you going to do?"

"We'll hide out in the woods. I'll watch and see which bedroom that witch is in. I have a gut feeling they're lying about being married."

In a short while, Luther and Boomer sat in the woods and watched the back of the house. It wasn't long until Jocelyn came onto the back porch and then hurried back inside. Someone lit a lantern in a back bedroom. He was sure it was his fiancée.

Sneaking close to the wall of the house, he peeked in the window. It was his lucky day. Standing near a mirror was his beautiful prey. He watched her put a brush down and then hurry into the water closet. This was his chance to sneak inside without her seeing him. Luther raised the window, and crawled over the ledge, and slid onto the floor. He stood, slipped over to blow out the lantern and hid behind the water-closet door. Jocelyn came out, her face registering surprise that her lamp had gone out.

"If you scream, or make any noise, I'll cut your throat." He held the cold blade next to her neck. She nodded to let him know she wouldn't make any sound.

"Now, move over to the window," he whispered. "We're going on a trip. Boomer has my carriage at the edge of the woods. Be a good girl and follow my instructions and I won't hurt you, otherwise . . ."

Jocelyn lifted her pretty new dress to her knees and crawled out the window. Boomer took her hands and helped her stand. Luther stood close to her, flashing the sharp knife, then, took her hand and pulled her along until they reached the carriage. Grabbing her around the waist, he flopped her on the seat, and jumped in. "Let's get out of here, Boomer. Be as quiet as you were coming here."

"Yes, sir." He mumbled something she couldn't hear.

****

Jim returned with his minister and Cassie was busy preparing sandwiches to serve after the wedding service. The ceremony would start as soon as Matt returned from town. Cassie turned to Jim and wiped her hands on her apron. "What will the men be doing during the wedding and when will they eat supper?"

Jim smiled at the woman who was taking hold of his heart. "The boss said the men will attend the wedding and have their meal later. They're all anxious to see their boss married to their beautiful cook. Several have commented that she's the best cook that ever worked on the ranch, and you're the best baker."

Matt and Bryan returned to the ranch after resting a while in Mrs. Crocker's kitchen. He was having a hard time breathing. After lying in the back of Mr. Crocker's supply wagon on the way home, he was feeling better.

Bryan parked Mr. Crocker's supply wagon behind the barn. He didn't want the men asking questions. "Don't mention the fight, and I won't let on that I'm hurting. You do remember that this is my wedding night."

"Of course," he replied. "You sure you don't want me to stand in for you? I know how to treat a real lady." He said, lifting his eyebrows up and down.

"That's not funny, my man. I'll be able to do my duty with my bride."

Jim hurried over to them when they entered the house. "Where in the devil have you two been? My pastor has several sick people waiting for him to visit them. So, I had to beg him to stay to preform your ceremony."

"Look, Jim, I appreciate that he came. Be sure to give him some extra money from me."

"I will, but for now, I'll tell Cassie to go get Jocelyn, and let's get on with it." He did a slow turn. "How do I look? I ain't ever been a best man before."

"You look just fine," he grinned and then requested that Bryan gather all the men while he went into the bedroom and washed up."

****

Cassie knocked on Jocelyn's bedroom door and waited. When she didn't answer, she knocked again. When no answer came, she opened the door and found the room dark. A breeze was blowing the curtains at the side window. "Oh, my goodness," Cassie said out loud.

Jim came to the door. "I am supposed to escort Jocelyn to Matt. She asked me to give her away," he said to Cassie.

"Jim, she ain't here. I'm afraid she ran away again from her wedding."

"No way. Jocelyn was eager to marry Matt. She would never do that."

"What's the problem?" Matt asked. "Where's Josh?"

"We aren't sure. That window is open, and she's gone." Cassie said, tears streaming down her cheeks.

****

Matt was dumbfounded for a second. Surely, the girl he had fallen in love with, revealed her past to him, and finally agreed to be his wife couldn't be another runaway bride. She wouldn't do such a thing to him.

Bryan rushed outside to the open window. "Matt, come outside," he yelled through the open window. "Hurry, there's something for you to see."

Matt emerged from his deep thoughts and raced to the back of the house. Bryan was down on his hands and knees in the dirt.

"There are three sets of footprints in this dry dirt and sand. She may have crawled out the window but she wasn't alone." The two men followed the prints to the edge of the woods and saw carriage wheel tracks.

"My Lord that crazy Luther must have recovered fast. After my threats to him, I never dreamed he would try something like this. He's one determined man or just plain crazy to come here and take her by force. Let's get some men and follow those tracks before it's too dark to see."

As they headed to the barn, Matt instructed Bryan to send one of the men to town and alert the sheriff that Luther Sullivan has kidnapped Jocelyn. "He can't do much tonight, but they can watch the train station."

Then he turned to Jim. "Go ahead and pay your preacher and thank him. We'll use his service as soon as we find Jocelyn. Tell Cassie to feed the men who remain behind, but pack a basket of food for the other men. We'll be gone for hours."

Chapter 22

After Luther was sure that no one could hear the carriage, he told Boomer to hurry and get away from the ranch as fast as possible. "Where're we going, boss?" Boomer yelled back at the wild man.

"Just away from town. I don't know this area, but we should be traveling toward Midland. Once we get there, we can catch the train."

"Boomer," Jocelyn screamed, "please slow down. You're going to turn this carriage over driving so fast."

"Don't you dare slow down? Keep those horses moving as fast as you can," Luther yelled at Boomer. They had hitched the spare horse to the rear, with the other two pulling the carriage. The spare animal was not used to running so fast behind the carriage and one had been limping. Boomer had to fight to control the horses.

After traveling several miles, Boomer flew around a curve, and one horse pulled one way while the other horse went another. The carriage was sliding from one side of the road to the other. Jocelyn screamed again for Boomer to slow down, but he fought with the reins. Suddenly, the carriage tilted and turned over. The team kept running until they couldn't pull the carriage any longer. The spare horse had gotten loose and ran into the woods.

****

Jocelyn was holding on for dear life, but Luther wasn't. He'd been thrown out into the dark. Boomer had jumped off the carriage just as it began to turn over. Jocelyn was hanging onto the seat for dear life while lying on the carriage floor. Once the horses stopped, she was shaken but wasn't hurt.

"Are you all right, Miss?" Boomer rushed over to Jocelyn and hoisted the carriage back upright. He helped Jocelyn get down to the ground.

"Yes, but what about him?" She pointed to Luther, sprawled out on his stomach. He looked like he was taking a sweet nap. Jocelyn prayed that Luther wasn't dead, but she wouldn't touch him. "See if he's breathing," she said to Boomer.

He touched his neck. "Yep, he is still alive."

"I'm glad he isn't dead but I'm getting out of here while he's unconscious. You can stay with him, if you like, but I'll find my way home."

"Wait, Miss. Can I go with you? I've wanted to escape that crazy man for a while, but I feared he was going to hurt you. That's the only reason I have stayed with him.

"Thank you for telling me. You may call me Jocelyn if I can call you Boomer?"

"Please, Miss Jocelyn. I'll search Luther's clothes and take the money he owes me."

"Take all his money so he can't travel on the train. I want to have him arrested for kidnapping me."

Boomer turned Luther onto his back and found his wallet in his vest. He only counted out the bills that Luther owed him. He didn't won't to be arrested for theft."

He glanced at the ground with a sad expression. "I did help him, Miss. Will I be arrested, too?"

"Never, my new friend. Let's get out of here before he wakes up."

"You know, I'd better unhitch the horses. One is limping badly, but Luther won't care when he wakes up. Maybe they will run off, and he'll have to walk."

Jocelyn and Boomer turned and went in the opposite

direction. "Luther had you heading straight to town. We will walk back to the ranch."

After walking for a mile or so, sounds came from around the curve of the dusty road. "Hurry and get in the woods. Someone's coming fast." Boomer pulled Jocelyn beside him, and both stooped down in the brush.

"My goodness, it's Luther. He recovered fast," Jocelyn said. He was driving the damaged carriage with only one horse.

"You know, Miss, you need to hide out somewhere until your man has Luther put behind bars. You aren't safe with him running loose."

"But, I don't have any place to go except the ranch. I'll hide out there."

"There're too many people, and people talk. You can't trust everyone, and if someone finds out that Luther will pay them for information, then they'll tell him where you are," Boomer said, as he pulled Jocelyn back down. "Someone else is coming but they're walking."

As the person approached their hiding place, Jocelyn whispered, "Boomer, that lady is the ranch's washwoman. She comes twice a week to do our laundry. Maybe she lives somewhere near here."

Jocelyn stepped out onto the road and waited for Mabel to come closer to her. Surprised and a little nervous, Mabel gasped, "Miss Jocelyn, what in the world? I heard them say you were getting married this afternoon."

"How did you know about the wedding? It was supposed to be a small quiet service with only the men on the ranch."

"Well, with me coming and going, I heard the men talking about how you and Mr. Colburn were getting hitched for real. So many people, even me, thought you were already married."

"You see what I mean about people talking, Miss Jocelyn?" Boomer said.

Shaking her head, she turned to Mabel. "Do you live nearby? Does Matt or anyone on the ranch know where you live? I was kidnapped today, but we escaped when the carriage overturned.

Mabel eyes grew like saucers. "You did? Are you all right. I don't think they know where I live. I always walk to and from the ranch or I walk into town to do other people's laundry. Why do you care where I live?"

"I'm in trouble, and I need a place to hide for a few days. Could I stay at your place? I can pay you extra if you let me, and you don't tell anyone where I am."

"I ain't got a fancy house. It's only a shack where my son and I live. Of course, you're welcome for a day or two. I mean until you find something nicer."

"Thank you. Oh, this is my friend. He's big but harmless," Jocelyn said smiling. "Boomer will be a big help around your place while we hide."

"Let's get going. My son will be hungry. I just live around the bend, down a long trail that is hard to see even in the daylight.

Boomer reached and took the heavy basket of laundry from Mabel and placed it over his shoulder.

"Oh my, thank you."

Jocelyn was in a state of shock to see how Mabel lived. As she walked into the small one-room shack, she glanced from the floor to the ceiling. Her little boy was sitting on the dirt floor rolling a small round stone across the floor to hit another stone. A poor boy's version of marbles.

The walls were made of gray wood with daylight showing through the cracks. Two windows had pretty printed curtains, but cardboard covered several of the window planes. A curtain hung on the back wall with a small bed hidden behind it and another bed was in the kitchen area. There was a small table in the center of the room with two straight-backed chairs with soft cushions covering the bottom of the seats. A large fireplace was on the side wall, probably used for cooking and heating the shack. All in all, the little house was quaint and tidy.

Jocelyn's heart broke for this tiny woman and her little boy. She had always lived in a lovely home with many luxuries. Her heart never desired anything, but looking around at Mabel's shack made her want to cry. How long had Mabel lived like this? Turning around, she smiled at Mabel and thanked her again for taking her in to her home. "

"I don't know how safe you'll be in this rundown shack, but as long as no one knows you're here, I guess your man, Boomer, will protect you."

"Boomer is not an employee of Mr. Colburn's. He worked for the man that adducted me. He needed to escape from him, so he came with me."

"I see," Mabel replied, looking at the big black man.

"Please, "Jocelyn said, as she took Mabel's hand. "You don't have to be afraid of him. He is one of the biggest men I've ever seen, but he is a gentle giant."

"If you say so. You probably would like to wash up a bit. I can see you have been in those woods." Mabel walked over to a small table next to the fireplace and poured water in a big pot to warm it. "Sonny, take the bucket and go get some fresh water from the well."

"Here, let me do that." Boomer took the bucket and went out to the well with the little boy on his heels.

Chapter 23

The following day, Boomer walked to town, entered through the back alleys and watched as customers left the dry goods store. When he was sure no one was inside shopping, he entered the back door. Mr. Crocker was surprised to see the enormous giant coming in the store's back door.

"I hope you don't mind, sir, but I didn't want to be seen by a certain tall, thin man. He quickly picked up an empty box on the floor and filled it with flour, sugar, lard, and fresh baked bread. Next, he requested canned goods, eggs, and fresh butter. He selected several peppermint sticks and waited for Mr. Crocker to total his bill. While waiting, he explained to Mr. Crocker that he was hiding from Luther Sullivan who had threatened to sell him. Assuring Mr. Crocker that he was a free Black man, Mr. Crocker promised to keep his secret that he was hiding in a cave.

Struggling with the supplies on his back, Boomer made good time in returning to the shack in the woods.

"Oh, Boomer, how did you get these supplies without Mr. Crocker seeing you?" Jocelyn asked as Mabel and her son stood staring at the bounty.

"He waited on me. I told him Luther was trying to sell me, and I ran away from him. He promised not to say anything about me. As I started out the door, he asked where I was staying. I lied. I told him that I'd found a cave in the woods to live."

"Well, if Mr. Crocker promised he wouldn't say anything, you're safe." Peering down into the box, Jocelyn told him he had chosen good food. "I can cook us something to eat."

After they finished eating a hot meal, which Sonny gobbled down, Mabel said that she had to go to Matt's ranch to take clean laundry and get the dirty clothes."

"Oh, Mabel, while you're there, will you seek Cassie out and tell her I'm all right. Don't tell her anymore, but make her promise to keep quiet about me being safe. Just listen to what Matt and the men are doing about finding Luther and me. I can't come out of hiding until I know that man is in jail or on a train back to Perryville," Jocelyn said.

Boomer looked up. "I'll go with you and hide in the woods near the ranch. I can carry the clean laundry for you and help bring the dirty things back here."

"That's awfully nice of you, Mr. Boomer, I mean, Boomer, but Sonny can help me."

"I know, but let your young man stay and protect Miss Jocelyn. Those baskets are heavy."

"While you two are gone, I'll cook lunch and prepare the wash water for the dirty clothes."

"How do you know so much about doing laundry?" Mabel asked.

"My mama made me help around the house when I was young. She said a young lady needed to know how to do every job in a household. So, I played in the wash water and helped hang clothes on the line. So you see, I am not helpless."

After Mabel and Boomer had been gone for a couple of hours, Sonny rushed into the house. "Hide, lady! I hear horses coming down the trail."

Jocelyn looked around the small shack that had no hiding places. The only place was under the bed. Once she slid under, she pulled the cover down to the floor.

****

Sonny stood on the front porch stirring the two tubs of wash water. He looked at the six men on horseback. "Howdy, son," a man with a star on his chest said, while two others barged onto the porch and inside the house.

"Hey, they can't go inside my house." Tossing his stirring stick down, he shouted at the deputy. "My mama ain't here, and she wouldn't like it if I let strangers go inside."

"I'm sorry, young man. I guess we should have introduced ourselves. I'm Deputy Parsons. We are a posse looking for a young woman who was kidnapped by a city slicker. Have you seen any strangers out this way?"

"No sir. When I was in town, I did see a stranger dressed in fancy duds. He kinda reminded me of a girl in the face."

"You did? When was this?" The deputy questioned, his eyes darting in all directions.

"A couple of days ago. I was sitting on the boardwalk, and he went into the Lady Luck saloon. Is that the man ya'll are looking for?"

"Yep, that's him." The deputy settled back in his saddle. "Have you seen him since?"

"No sir, I was in town with Ma waiting for her to collect some wash from the Crocker's."

The two men who had barged in came back out in less than three minutes. "Nothing in there, sir. Too small to hide in."

"Thanks, young man." The deputy touched his hat and rode away with the other men.

Sonny watched until the men were out of sight of the shack before telling Jocelyn that all was clear.

"Where did you hide?" Sonny asked, his tiny forehead furrowed.

"I was under your mama's bed."

"That was a close call. I'm sure glad I heard them coming." Sonny moved close to her.

"Me too," Jocelyn said, hugging Sonny's small shoulders.

Chapter24

Matt along with the posse, arrived back at his ranch. They had searched every inch of Amarillo and the men needed rest, fresh horses, and food. "Go home, get some sleep, and meet back at the sheriff's office at first light. He waved at them. "See you tomorrow." Matt watched as the men rode away from his ranch. They'd been eager and faithful in their search for Jocelyn and Luther. He would always remember their effort today. "Lord, please let my men find the woman I love soon. Please protect her while she is held captive by a man that is not well, amen."

Jim and Cassie met Matt at the front door. "Did you find any sign of them?" Jim asked, while Cassie next to him.

"No, I'm sorry to say. He didn't catch the train so he's traveling by horseback or in his carriage. Luther has to be hiding out somewhere. Several of the men in the search party caught the late train headed to Midland. They'll search the town, and if he arrived there, they'll telegraph me and, of course, get help from the sheriff."

"That was smart having the men travel to Midland. They should arrive before Luther can get there. Do you know if that Black man who came with him is still traveling with them?"

"We aren't sure, but he hasn't been seen anywhere in town. I hope he's with them because he appeared to be a good man. Maybe if he is with them, he will protect Josh from that crazy fiancé of hers."

"I'll draw you a hot bath, and put it in your new room, Mr. Matt. While you clean up I'll prepare you something hot to eat. You need to rest for sure," Cassie said as she hurried.

Later, Matt sat at the kitchen table gobbling down a big bowl of chicken and dumplings with fresh cornbread. "Cassie, did Josh every talk about Luther to you?"

"No, I'm afraid not. She didn't talk about her past or why she wanted to join the bridal train, except to get away from her home. Jocelyn made it clear that she wanted to travel here, but she would not be a bride. I wish I could tell you more," Cassie said trying to hold her tears at bay.

"That's all right. Jocelyn shared her past with me. I know why she ran away from that crazy man, but I thought maybe she may have told you something that would help me locate their whereabouts." Matt wiped his mouth and stood. "I'd better try to get a few hours of sleep."

****

Once Sonny assured Jocelyn that the posse was gone, she collapsed on the bed. She cried until the pillow was soaked. Poor Sonny stood at the end of the bed watching her. He didn't know what to do because he had never seen his mama break down.

Sonny touched her shoulder. Even though he was small, his grip felt like Herculean. "Miss, I'm here. I'll take care of you. Please don't cry."

Jocelyn sat up on the bed and pulled her little protector into her arms. "Oh, Sonny, I never cry but I guess I was afraid that the men would find me. I'm not ready to go back to Mr. Colburn's ranch until that crazy man who abducted me is caught."

"You're safe here . . . with me. I won't let anyone take you away until you're ready to leave. Mama and Boomer will be back soon."

"Thank you so much. I feel better already." She stood

and wiped tears from her eyes. "I'd better get busy and fix some lunch. They'll be hungry from that long walk." Jocelyn climbed to her feet and hurried over to the box of food.

****

Cassie looked at Matt and could tell that he didn't get any rest. She wanted to run to him and tell him she'd learned that Jocelyn was safe, but she promised Mabel she wouldn't say anything. Besides, if she did, Matt would race to Mabel and make her tell him where she got that information. She carried the bags of food she had prepared for Matt out onto the front porch.

Jim was ready to ride with the posse today. He stood next to the porch waiting for Matt. Cassie liked the way he looked. For an older man, he looked extremely fit, and she found herself smiling at him. His buckskin breeches were as snug as they were the first time she saw him, and his dark brown coat made him look wider than he actually was. Cassie realized that Jim was staring at her as she looked at him from head to toe.

"Well, woman, what's wrong?"

"Nothing is wrong, you old fool. Just take care of yourself." Cassie had been surprised to learn that Jim was going on the hunt for Jocelyn. She gave him two white bags that contained apples and several meat sandwiches. "Maybe this will knock off the hunger while you're searching."

"I'm hoping we'll locate their whereabouts today. Hopefully, that fellow won't hurt her because he needs for her to return with him to Perryville," Jim said as he tied the food onto his saddle horn.

"I pray you're right. Be careful. That man is a city slicker so he probably don't know how to shoot a gun. Someone like that is dangerous with a pistol."

"You're right. Don't fret too much." He looked over his shoulder. "I overheard Mabel talking to you." Jim gave her a wink and a reassuring smile.

Cassie mouth dropped open, but she shrugged at her new friend.

****

Once Luther woke up on the ground, he discovered he was alone. Jocelyn and Boomer were both gone. One of the two horses was standing in an open field eating dried wheat while his carriage sat off the road. He stood and was pleased to find he wasn't hurt. Dusting off his clothes, he took out his wallet and looked inside. Some of his money had disappeared, but he still had money. "Boomer," he said out loud. The fool should have taken all the money, but the amount of money gone was the sum he owed him. "Smarter than I thought," he muttered to himself. Boomer knew he would have him arrested for stealing his money. He laughed. *I would never have paid him anything. He's my slave, whether he admits it or not.*

He headed out into the field and coaxed the horse to be still while he grabbed the bridle and walked him back to the carriage. With the help of the horse, he managed to push the carriage upright. All the wheels looked to be intact. He hitched the horse to the carriage and headed into town. Once there, he'd listen for any news as to what was being done about finding Jocelyn.

Luther removed his fancy vest and jacket and wore only his white shirt and blue denims. Maybe he wouldn't be recognized if someone saw him. When he arrived in town, he kept to the back alley until he reached the Lady Luck saloon. Someone there would know what was going on. A few bucks would loosen their tongues. When he entered the silent saloon, he was surprised to find it almost empty of drinking customers.

The barkeep was busy drying glasses when he looked up. "Can I help you?"

"Sure, I'll have a beer." Once the barkeep put the drink in front of him, Luther tried to look nonchalant. "Where is everyone?"

"Most all the men are with the posse looking for a young lady that was kidnapped by a city slicker from Perryville. I feel sorry for the man once he's caught. If he's hurt that girl, the sheriff won't be able to keep the men from hanging him to the nearest tree."

"Who is the girl that got kidnapped, and why was she taken?" Luther knew he was staying too long, but he needed to hear what was being said about Jocelyn.

"She married one of the richest men in the state, and he is well thought of too. His wife came on the bridal wagon train from some town up north. She's a beauty. Her husband has a fierce temper, and I wouldn't want to be in that guy's shoes when they catch him."

"What makes you think he'll be found?"

"You're kidding, aren't you? He'll be found and soon if I know this posse. They always get their man."

Luther downed his beer, like he had seen rowdy cowboys do, and thanked the bartender. "See you later," he said as he strolled out the bat-wing door. He looked both ways and headed to the nearest alley that would take him out of town without being seen. Once he retrieved his horse and carriage, he kept to a dirt trail that was off the main road. What he needed was an abandoned shack to stay hidden in without the posse finding him while he traced the whereabouts of Jocelyn. One thing he knew, she didn't go back to the Colburn man.

After traveling a couple miles from town, he pulled off the trail and sat still in his carriage. He was trying to decide where to go when he heard voices coming upon the trail. Peeking out, he saw a shack in the distance and an old couple in front of it washing clothes. Just maybe they never went into town so they wouldn't know anything about him. Lady Luck was on him. Just maybe this was the place to hide out in.

As he drove closer to where a little shack stood, he veered to the right to hide in the woods and survey the shack and the people who lived there. As he watched the house, a young boy came out with an empty bucket to pump water from the well.

After the youngster went back inside, Luther snuck up to the side window and peeked inside. He caught his breath. This was his lucky day. Inside was his fiancée and Boomer. Another woman was sitting in front of the fireplace while the two adults sat around the small table. The child sat on the hearth.

As quite as a mouse, Luther stepped on the porch and entered the front door. He slammed the door closed, causing the women to scream with fright. "Well, do I get a welcome?" He said, as he waved his small pistol toward the occupants.

Jocelyn and Boomer both leaped out of their chairs.

"Of course, you aren't welcome here. I don't allow strangers to enter my house," Mabel said as she stormed to face Luther.

"You have to be a sad woman if you call this place your home. It's a pitiful shack, barely good enough for field rats to hibernate in."

Jocelyn finally spoke. "Luther there's no need for you to hurt this family with your cruel words about their home. These are good people."

"Yes, I can see how good they are. You and Boomer look mighty cozy sitting at the table while the whole town is busy searching for you. What would they think if they knew you weren't being held captive, and you could have gone back to your so-called husband at any time?"

"Every one of those men knows that it isn't safe for Jocelyn as long as you're running around free. They know you kidnapped her," Boomer said.

"I see," Luther said as he strolled inside the shack. "So, no one knows that you two got away from me. How funny is that?" He laughed.

"You two sit back down, and you woman, fix me

something to eat. I am starving and don't try to harm me with your food. If I feel sick, I'll shoot that little boy of yours. I don't like kids anyway."

Mabel grabbed Sonny and told him to sit on her bed. "Stay out of his way while I cook him something to eat. Please don't do anything to anger him."

"Boomer, go out and take care of my horse and carriage. Move it out of sight in case someone comes here unexpected." Luther pointed to the door. "Jocelyn and this other woman will stay with me."

****

"What's your name," Luther asked Mabel as she placed ham, eggs and hominy on a plate.

"My name is Mabel Ritter."

"What's this stuff?" Luther took his fork and moved the hominy around on his plate.

"It's a dish made from corn. It's very good for you."

He pushed his plate away from him. "Take it off. It makes me sick just looking at it."

After scraping the hominy off Luther's plate, she replaced it with another piece of ham. "Now, that's better," he mumbled.

'Anything to please you, sir," Mabel said, sarcastically.

Luther glanced at Jocelyn and told her to go sit in the rocking chair. "In the morning we'll be traveling to Perryville. I'm taking you to my lawyer's office where we can marry. Once we're wed, I'll be able to get my inheritance."

Jocelyn eyes narrowed in his direction. "What will happen after we are married?"

"After we leave the lawyer, you and I can part ways. I don't care what you do."

"You mean that?" Jocelyn eyes lit up.

"Well, first, we'll need to travel far enough away from the lawyer's office. If you want to get on the stagecoach and travel to Midland and then travel back here on the train, I don't care. I only want what my father left to me."

"That's the only reason you wanted to find me? To get married so you could inherit what your father left you in his will?"

"Yes, what did you think? I never wanted to marry you or any other gal. All I ever wanted to do was get away from Perryville and travel, but my father wouldn't let me do anything."

"I'm sorry, Luther, but I can't marry you."

"Look, Jocelyn, you *will* marry me and there will be no arguing about it," Luther stated. "I've lost my patience's with you. If you don't come with me and do as I have requested, I'll kill Boomer. I mean it. I'll shoot him right in front of you."

"Why would you do that? Boomer is such a gentle, good man. He's been devoted to you, and you know it. Don't you have a conscience?"

"No, I don't anymore. I want and need my inheritance, and I will have it. My father's lawyers won't give it to me if all the requirements of my father's will haven't been met. You see, they don't want me to marry because they'll get everything."

"I can't believe that. Most lawyers are good, trustworthy men."

"My father's lawyers are silent partners of the bank. They've kept the bank in good standing. If I refuse or fail to marry, they'll inherit my money." He waited for a response but she didn't reply. "Now, you see? You don't have a choice. I want my money, and I mean what I said about Boomer. So, you see my dear, his life is in your hands."

"At least let me go back to the ranch and talk with Matt. I'm sure he will understand that after we marry, we can have it annulled. He's a reasonable man."

"Absolutely not. No man who loves his woman would

allow her to go with me and marry. He'd never let you travel to Perryville with me. Colburn will follow you back here and have me arrested. So, forget your plan. We'll travel to Midland tonight. I'll take that woman and her little boy with us. When we get far away from here, I'll put them out of the carriage. They won't be hurt if you behave yourself. If not, I'll beat the woman and shoot the boy."

Jocelyn was in total shock. She knew that Luther was a mean man, but she never would have thought he would hurt an innocent woman and her child. She didn't have a choice now but to go with him.

Chapter 25

Late into the night, Boomer had packed the carriage with the blankets and a basket of food to cook over a campfire. It was at least fifty miles to Midland, and it would take two to three days of hard traveling.

Jocelyn and Mabel took turns holding Sonny in their lap while they traveled. He was a smart boy. He had a bag of marbles and as they traveled, he dropped one over the side of the carriage. He hoped that if they were followed a person would recognize the trail. He sure hated to have to give up his prize toy, but he had to help save his mama and his new friends.

After the sun came up, Boomer drove the carriage to the edge of a river. He was thankful that it hadn't rained and driving across would be safer than before. Everyone in the carriage was sound asleep, but when the carriage stopped moving, Luther sat straight up and glanced around.

"Why have you stopped?"

"I thought we would cross the river and then make camp over in those trees. The animals need rest, and I could use a few hours of shut eye."

"Sounds good. Well, let's get going and be careful. I don't feel like traveling in wet clothes like we had to do before." Luther removed the blanket off his legs and tossed it over Sonny.

Slowly, Boomer drove the carriage across the river. After he got them on the other side of the bank, he helped the ladies out of the carriage. "Ya'll can have some privacy in those trees. When you've finished your business, would you please pick up some wood for a fire?"

Suddenly Jocelyn pulled on Boomer sleeve. When he looked at her, she was a white as a sheet. "Look," she said, "there's a bear."

Boomer hurried over to Luther. "Man, give me your gun. There's a bear coming this way."

"I ain't stupid. You aren't getting your hands on my gun."

"Well, you'd better start running or get ready to shoot that huge creature. He's coming faster now that he's seen us." Boomer grabbed Jocelyn hand and gave Mabel a shove. Hurry, go behind the carriage," he said, while pushing Sonny under it.

Luther surprised Boomer. He stood still, took aim, and pulled the trigger. He actually hit the big bear in the chest. The animal roared, bent down on all fours, and suddenly fell forward. Dead.

Boomer raced over to the bear and smiled at Luther. "I'm proud of you, boss."

Luther was shaking all over. He had never killed anything. He smiled at Boomer and said, "I did, didn't I?"

"Yep, you sure did. I'll hitch the horses to his legs and pull him out into the river. He can float away from our campsite. If we were home, I would have skinned him and have a beautiful bear rug or coat, but its best we just get him away from us."

The girls pulled themselves together and cooked breakfast over the campfire. Boomer watered the horses and hobbled them out in the open field to eat. Afterward, he told the girls to stay near him while he lay down for a few hours' sleep.

****

Matt awakened early. As soon as he saw light coming through the windows, he rolled to his side and sat up on the edge of the bed. He didn't know how long he had sat there praying, but he knew the posse would be arriving soon.

Cassie met him in the kitchen with a large cup of coffee. She had made him several sandwiches to pack in his saddlebags.

He noticed how nervous Cassie was acting. She was out of sorts, for sure. "Please try not to worry so much. You're going to make yourself sick. I'll bring Josh home, I promise you."

"Mr. Matt, I have something I need to tell you. I promised I wouldn't, but I know you're as upset as I am." Matt stood still and waited for Cassie to continue with whatever she had promised not to confess.

"Yesterday, Mabel, the wash lady, whispered to me that Jocelyn was safe. She wouldn't said anything else."

"Do you know where she lives?" Matt needed to speak with her.

"No, I don't. It can't be too far because she walks back and forth here, from her house."

"Thanks Cassie for telling me. I know how hard it was for you break a promise, but, I needed to know. I feel a little better." Matt walked out of the house and met the fresh posse at his corral. "Have you received any news as to their whereabouts?" Matt had prayed the sheriff might have good news.

"Sorry, we haven't discovered anything."

Matt was trying to keep his temper under control. He told himself that today they would find Luther and Jocelyn. He was determined to find them if he had to turn Amarillo upside down. His jaw clenched as he climbed on his horse.

"I'm going to take a few men and travel outside of town. There are lot of farmers who live on the outskirts, and maybe Luther is holding a family captive while hiding out."

"Good idea, "the sheriff said. "The rest of the men and I'll question all the store owners and people on the boardwalk. Somebody has had to see them. We'll find them today." The sheriff and his men rode toward town while Matt and his men rode in the opposite direction.

After traveling several miles, Matt asked one of the men, "Do you know a wash woman by the name of Mabel? You may have seen here come and go on my ranch."

"I believe she and her little boy live this way in a shack. I've seen her walking on this road, one of the men who sat tall in the saddle commented, as he pointed down the narrow trail. "She's a real nice lady and she take in people who are down on their luck. Let's ride down to her place and question her." The man led the way into Mabel's yard.

The men rode to the front porch, but there was no sign of anyone. Matt knocked on the front door, calling Mabel's name, with no response. He tried the lock and the door opened. Matt looked around the small room and noticed the covers on the beds had been removed. The cabinet door on the wall stood wide open. It was empty. He looked at the fireplace and noticed that there was no coffee pot sitting on the hearth, but the coals were still warm. He looked closely and determined that Mabel had moved out of the shack.

"I believe she's moved away from here. The blankets, foods and even the coffee pot and cups are missing." Matt didn't remember Mabel telling anyone that she wouldn't be doing his ranch's wash.

"Hey, Matt, come out here," a young man called.

"Look at these marbles on the ground. They must belong to the little boy that lives here. But, its funny how they're in a row on the ground as if he was leaving a trail."

"You know, I find it strange that this woman left and took things she might use for camping out. Let's see if there's more marbles on the trail.

A few minutes later, the young man found two more shiny marbles spaced yards apart. "I'm sure this trail was left for some reason. Something's wrong and they were smart enough to leave a sign." The young man said as he picked up the marbles.

"Let's go and keep looking for more marbles. I have a gut feeling that if this crazy Luther is involved, they are traveling to Midland by carriage. It will take them two or three days of traveling time. I may have to go to Midland by train and be there before they arrive."

After riding most of the day, the marbles had led the men to the river. After crossing the water, they discovered a campsite. Matt was sure they were on the right trail when a man found the word 'help' spelled out with marbles. Let's return to my ranch so I can pack a bag and catch the late train to Midland."

Chapter 26

Once Luther and his hostages arrived in Midland, he decided to go straight to the stagecoach platform and purchase tickets for all of them. He wouldn't be noticed if he had a family with him. There was chaos near the ticket window. A couple men stood directly in front of the ticket window in deep discussion with the stationmaster. Luther wanted them to move, but he didn't want to draw attention to himself by being rude to the older gentlemen. "I beg your pardon, gentlemen, but I need to purchase tickets for my little family. Do you mind stepping aside?"

"So sorry, mister. We haven't seen each other in a while, and we just forgot where we were standing. Please step ahead of us." The men moved to one side and allowed Luther to pull Jocelyn beside him as he asked for five tickets. I have my son, do I have to pay full price for him?"

"Oh, no sir, small children can ride free. So, you need only four tickets to where?"

Luther said softly, "Perryville."

"Perryville it is! Here you go and I hope you have a nice trip."

Luther tucked the tickets in his wallet and led the group onto the boardwalk. "The stagecoach doesn't leave for another hour."

"Boomer, I'm taking Jocelyn, the woman and kid into a back alley. Take this money and go purchase some sandwiches and a container of water. Make it fast and if you get any idea about seeking out the law, I'll kill the boy as soon as I sense danger."

****

Boomer hurried to the nearest deli and purchased sandwiches, a small bottle of cold milk, and a couple of apples. He wasn't able to get any water but there was a well in the back of the alley. Once he returned with the food, Luther grabbed the bottle of milk, turned it up and drank his fill.

"I got the milk for the boy, Boss," Boomer said as he handed the ladies a sandwich.

"Tough, he can have what's left if I don't drink it all."

Sonny pulled on Boomer's arm and whispered, "I don't have to have milk every day. I'm not a baby anymore."

"All right, let's walk toward the train station," Luther demanded. "Don't do anything to draw attention to yourself. Remember, I have a gun pointed at the kid's head."

****

The stagecoach ride to Perryville from Midland was a four-hour trip. Once they arrived, Jocelyn glanced up and down, one she knew well because she was born and raised there. While they waited at the livery for Boomer to procure them a carriage, the owner was over-joyed to see Jocelyn.

"My goodness girl," Mr. Hank Henderson said, "where did you run away to? We were at your wedding but, oh well, I see you're back with Luther. I'm so pleased that you two worked things out. Well, listen to me run off at the mouth when I should be helping your man with the horse and carriage."

Jocelyn moved close to Mabel and smiled at her. "I forgot that people might recognize me."

"It seems he remembered that you was going to marry . . . him," she nodded her head toward Luther.

Boomer appeared in the carriage in front of the livery. He jumped down and helped the ladies and Sonny into it. He tapped the horse's rump, and he moved toward Main Street. "Keep your face lowered so these nosy people won't try to talk to you," Luther said, as he looked all around. "Boomer, take us to the Norwood estate. We can stay there until you can deliver a note to my lawyer's office. We can freshen up while we wait to hear from him. I know he'll see us today."

****

As Boomer drove the small carriage around the circular drive of the Norwood estate, Sonny and Mabel's eyes were as big as saucers. "Miss Jocelyn, did you grow up here?"

"Yes, I did. I have a tree house in the back near the large hedges. I'll show it to you."

"Don't fill that kid with promises you can't deliver. Everyone will stay inside the house while Boomer's goes to town." Luther grabbed her wrist and squeezed it hard.

Boomer stopped the carriage at the front door. Luther jumped down and told Boomer to help remove the boards that were blocking the entrance to the front door. In a few minutes, they all entered the foyer. White cloths covered all the furniture, and the drapes were pulled closed. Jocelyn's eyes filled with tears as she stood in the center of her living room again. She was home, but unfortunately, this lovely place wasn't hers any longer.

"You, woman," Luther pushed Mabel, "go into the kitchen and see if there's any food in the pantry."

"Which way do I go to the kitchen? I've never been here before."

"It's to the right, down the hall under the staircase. Now, get going and hurry back and tell me," Luther said as he grabbed Sonny by his collar and made him stand next to him.

Jocelyn walked over to the large French doors and

found the drapery cord. She pulled the drapes open, and the sunshine flowed inside. Dust clouds floated all around but the place was still livable.

An older man appeared in the double doors and glared at the group. "What are you people doing in this house? You're trespassing," he demanded as his eyes were adjusting to the darkness in the room.

"Jackson, it's me, Jocelyn. I came home for a few hours." Jocelyn ran over to the older man and took his outreached hands.

"My word, miss. I'm pleased to see you safe and sound. We all have been praying for you."

"That is so kind of you and the others. You remember Luther Sullivan?"

"Don't tell me that you and he are together? Maria said that you had run away so you didn't have to get hitched to that bad boy." He removed his gardener's gloves.

"Listen old man. I'm standing right here and I'm not deaf. If you want to live another day, you'd better find a seat and keep your mouth shut. We'll be staying here for a few hours, and you'll be our guest whether you want to or not." Jocelyn whispered to Jackson to sit down and be real quiet. "I won't allow him to harm you."

Mabel came back into the living room and waited to be noticed by Luther. "Well, woman, is there any food out there?"

"I believe Jocelyn and I can cook something to eat. There's plenty of canned jars of food on the pantry wall," Mabel said.

"Good. Boomer, bring in buckets of water for a nice hot bath for me. These women can heat the water. While you're all busy, I'll write a note to my lawyer. You'll drive into town and deliver it to him." Later, Luther gave Boomer the note and told him not to be gone very long if he wanted to keep the little boy alive. "You'd better not get to feeling brave and tell the sheriff that we're here."

****

Boomer left the house and drove straight into town. He remembered the location of Mr. Taylor's office because he had driven Luther's father there many times. When he entered the impressive office, he told the secretary that he needed to see the lawyer. He had an important message to give to him.

"Give me the message and I'll give it to him. He's a busy man."

"He will see me. I will give him the note myself. Tell him that Luther Sullivan sent me." The secretary frowned but Boomer didn't bulge.

"Wait here," the stuffy woman said, as she walked into Mr. Taylor's office.

In a second, Mr. Taylor came out of his office ahead of the secretary. "Boomer, please come into my office. It's all right, Henrietta. I know Boomer." Mr. Taylor closed the door and turned to Boomer. "Where is Luther now? I know he made you leave town with him."

"Yes sir, he did. He ordered me here with this note." Boomer handed the note to Mr. Taylor and waited for him to read it.

"I'm too busy to see him today," he practically whispered to himself.

"You have to see him because lives depend on your meeting today," Boomer said, walking closer to the big oak desk.

"So, Luther is desperate. Does he have Miss Norwood with him?"

"Yes, and two more people. Please, it has to be today." Mr. Taylor recognized the urgently in Boomer voice and the sad expression on his face.

Mr. Taylor walked to the door and called to his partner. "Mac, come in here now. All right Boomer. Tell Luther to come and we'll see him."

"Thank you, sir." Boomer smiled, but pleaded. "Please

don't contact the law. Luther can be dangerous."

"I understand. We won't tell anyone he's in town."

Boomer drove back to the Norwood's estate and told Luther Mr. Taylor would meet with him as soon as he could get there.

"Good. Jocelyn, go freshen up a bit. I want you to look decent in front of Mr. Taylor."

****

Jocelyn walked into the water closet and washed her face and hands and combed her long hair. She twisted it into a neat rope and hung it down her back. She gave herself a lasting glance in the full-length mirror and sighed. With no bath or clean clothes, this was the best she was going to be.

****

"What do you think Mac?" Mr. Taylor asked his partner as he watched the big Black man climb into a carriage. "Do you think Luther has convinced Miss Norwood to marry him?"

"I'm not sure how he did it, but he wouldn't be bringing her with him if he hadn't. Shall I send for my preacher just in case the young fool has persuaded her to change her mind and ride off into the sunset with him?"

"Boomer said it had to be today and something about other people being involved. He's probably holding something over her head, or he's threatening someone she cares for deeply. I guess we will know which it is when he arrives."

"If they agree to marry, are we going to give him his inheritance?" Mac asked.

"We won't have any other choice, since that was the condition of his father's will. But, if he is attempting to force her into matrimony, that will be a different horse of another color." Mr. Taylor shuffled some papers on his desk.

"Should I have the sheriff present, just in case he's

trying something unlawful?"

"Best not. Boomer did ask me not to contact the law. Let's just wait and see what the pretty boy is going to say and do. This should be interesting."

Chapter 27

Jocelyn was so nervous she could hardly stand still as she prepared to marry Luther. He stood by her side, holding a tight grip on her arm that didn't allow any freedom. She would have run out of the office if given a chance. Luther was smiling enough to make her think he had lost his mind. She was sure that frightened state was the only reason for his happiness.

His smile faded when she refused to repeat the wedding vows. The old, preacher wouldn't continue with the ceremony until she did. Luther started squeezing her hand, then lifted it up pretended to kiss her palm. "Remember Boomer."

"I won't lie to the preacher man," she whispered loud enough for Luther to hear He didn't appear to be bothered by her words but gave her a wink and said sweetly, "Come now, my love, repeat your vows so we can allow these men to take care of my business."

Jocelyn lifted her face and looked straight into the eyes of the two lawyers who witnessed this farce of a wedding. They both appeared as if they'd been whipped.

The preacher coughed and asked the couple to take hands and stand closer together. As he cleared his throat, a rumbling sound of loud voices and stomping of feet preceded the door bursting open. The lawyers, Luther, Jocelyn, and the preacher stood gasping at the people who charged into the room.

****

"What's the meaning of this intrusion, Sheriff? Luther demanded.

"You know why I'm here, you lying weasel!" Cassie screamed and rushed to stand right in front of Luther.

Luther stumbled backward and spun around to the tall woman who loomed in front of him.

She posted her hands on her ample hips. "I traveled day and night to get here to stop you from marrying someone else. You broke my heart. You can't marry someone else until we've settled our arrangement. You promised to marry me and you will keep that promise or answer to the sheriff here."

"Who are you? I've never laid eyes on you, much less promised to wed a woman as large as my horse."

"Now, you look here, you scum of the earth," Jim pulled his pants higher, pushed the long sleeves of his shirt up, and shook his fist in Luther's face. "You'd better watch the words coming out of your stupid mouth. I brought this woman here from Midland, where you met and romanced her into a promise of matrimony. She told me all about you and I will put your butt in jail for breaking this lovely woman's heart." He stepped back away from Luther as he began to pace. Jim looked over Luther's back and winked at Jocelyn. Surprised, she realized that Cassie and Jim had planned this intervention.

"You all have lost your minds." Luther looked over at Boomer. "Tell these people that we weren't in Midland long enough for me to find a woman and romance her into marriage."

Everyone in the room turned to face Boomer who stood quietly in the corner of the room, next to Mabel and Sonny.

"I can't tell a lie, Boss. You left me at the livery to care for the animals and sleep there while you stayed in the fancy hotel. I didn't see you until you were ready to leave."

You fool. You're lying. I got robbed and beaten up. I didn't have money for days until you, Mr. Taylor, sent me money. I couldn't seek out a woman."

"That's right, you weasel. You came over to me while I was shopping in the dry goods store and asked for some help. You looked so pitiful, and my heart was nearly broken when I saw the sight of you. I took you to my room and nursed you back to health. Then I let you bathe while I bought you new clothes and fed you. And this is how you pay me back, by running off and leaving me? You said when you got money from your lawyer you and I would wed. My friends started planning our wedding. If I hadn't overheard someone talking about you kidnapping a woman and traveling back here to marry her, I would still be waiting at the altar." Cassie lowered her face in her hands and sobbed. Suddenly, she strode toward Luther, so close their noses almost touched. "You made a laughingstock out of me, and now I'm going to wring your neck." Cassie reached for his throat but he ducked and jumped behind the lawyer.

Jocelyn pulled herself together. Cassie spouted venom at Luther. How did they find her? Many thoughts flashed through her mind. "Oh, my goodness," Jocelyn said as she hurried over to Cassie and threw her arms around her shoulders. "Please, Miss, don't cry. He's not worth your tears."

Cassie laid her face against Jocelyn's shoulder and whispered, "Thank goodness you're safe." Cassie lifted her face and said loud enough for all to hear, "Oh Miss you are so sweet."

"Jocelyn, get away from that creature before I slap you."

The preacher's voice finally spoke. "Now, you look here, Mr. Sullivan. You won't be hitting anyone in my presence. This wedding ceremony is over until we can get to the bottom of your promise to this nice lady." He closed his Bible and took a chair.

"There is no promise, and Jocelyn and I are going to marry – now."

Cassie and Jocelyn both screamed "No" at the same time. Jocelyn nearly burst out laughing but managed to control herself. Her friend's body quivered next to her, so she was laughing as well.

"Luther, before we settle this problem about which woman you'll marry, I have some business to take care of with Miss Norwood. We can go into my office and discuss this business in private. It won't take us long, so you just take a chair and wait with the sheriff, if you don't mind."

Jocelyn strode into the lovely office of Mr. Taylor.

"Miss Norwood, this will only take a minute. I need your signature on some of your father's papers. You know about his gambling habit and the IOU he gave Mr. Johnson. Then, Mr. Johnson, in turn, sold to it to Luther's father?"

"Yes, she knows all about the IOU." A loud rough voice came from the lawyer's office doorway. Matt stood in the threshold.

"Oh, Matt," Jocelyn couldn't stop herself from smiling. Matt had found her. He stood straight and tall, looking just like a warrior. She couldn't tell what he was thinking, but she knew he was planning a battle.

"Miss Norwood, who is this man?" Mr. Taylor asked.

"This giant of a man is Matt Colburn, my boss, my protector and the man who has my heart."

Matt smiled. He walked over and took her hands in his. "Are you all right, sweetheart?"

"Yes, I am now. I prayed you would find me. And God answered my prayer". She grinned and fell into his open arms.

"All right, now that we know who you are, I need to return to the business I have with Miss Norwood. She needs to sign over the title of her former home and the property surrounding it. Her father lost a bet at the gambling table and wrote an IOU for this property to Mr. Johnson, but he didn't sign it. Later, Luther's father bought the IOU from Mr. Johnson."

"So, no one took the time to read this so call IOU?" Matt quizzed the lawyer.

"Well, I'm sure they did, but his signature was an oversight. We only need Miss Norwood's signature to make a wrong a right."

"You mean her signature will make this IOU legal, right?"

"Well, it is legal, but a signature will confirm it for the bank's legal department so the property can be sold."

"Hold on for a minute, Mr. Taylor. Miss Norwood will not sign anything until I discuss this with her. I do have a question, but if you feel it's not my business, you may so say."

"What is your question? But be quick, we must complete this business."

"There's a question about Luther's inheritance. I understand that he only had ninety days to marry to inherit from his father. Am I correct?"

"Yes, his father did put that in his will. He has never liked Luther's lifestyle and wanted him to settle down and marry." Mr. Taylor sat down behind his desk.

"Is there any way this 'death wish' of Luther's father can be removed?"

Matt knew that this man could do whatever he wanted, but he had to act dumb.

"Are you offering something in exchange for the removal of this demand in Mr. Sullivan's will?" Mr. Taylor seemed to perceive Matt wasn't just a plain old cowboy.

"Please give me a minute to discuss something with Miss Norwood." Matt took Jocelyn over to the corner of the office and spoke softly with her. He was sure she would readily agree to get rid of Luther in her life.

"I can't sign that IOU without Luther being punished

in some way for what he did to me. The man has hurt others, too. He kidnapped all of us and threatened to kill us all. Often Luther threatened to sell poor Boomer. To a mean slave owner. He mistreated my maid and has been so ugly to Mabel and her little boy. No, he must pay for his crimes and sheer meanness, not just walk off with thousands of dollars."

"Do you want him arrested for what he did to you? If you do this, you'll have to testify in court. It will be your word against his."

"No, he should have to give up some of his inheritance. Maybe half of it to me."

"But, Jocelyn, look at me." With his finger, Matt lifted her chin to look into his eyes. "When you become my wife, you will never need or want for anything. You don't need anything from that scum."

"I don't want the money for myself. Boomer needs money to help him start a livery business. My maid, Maria, lost her home and has to live with poor relatives. And Mabel, well, she and Sonny were terrorized by Luther. They live in a shack, and she works so hard. I want the money to help them. He doesn't deserve all that money." Jocelyn's face became redder with every sentence.

"All right. Let me explain your condition before you sign away your property. If you don't sign the IOU, they don't have any grounds to make you sign it. Your father's property will remain yours."

"I already figured that out for myself, but my father did lose everything in a card game. He knew the chance he was taking, so I really must honor the contract.

"Well, let's see what we can do." Matt took her hand, and both stood in front of Mr. Taylor's desk.

After Matt explained Jocelyn's demand for half of the inheritance, Luther slapped the desk and shrieked. "No deal. That's my money, and I will not split it with her."

"Well, Luther, do you have any other ideas on how

you can take hold of your money?" Mr. Taylor leaned back in his big chair and glared at his client.

"Yes, I'll marry that creature out there." He rushed to the office door and said for Cassie to come in. "All right woman, if you want to marry me, I'll call the preacher and we can say our vows right here and now. What if I confess my love to you now?"

Cassie stared at him like he had grown two heads.

"And you will be a very wealthy woman once we marry."

Smiling, Cassie rose on her tiptoes, reached for the front of Luther's shirt. She gave him a good shake. "So now you want to confess that you love me? Well, you little weasel, there's not enough love or money to make me marry a liar and kidnapper." Cassie lifted him off his feet and shook him.

"You don't have to, either." Jim Watson stood straight and tall and glanced at Cassie. Everyone in the room froze at the tone of Jim's voice. "Please let me finish before you react." Jim turned to Mr. Taylor and Luther. "This lovely creature, as you call her, is going to marry me. That is, if she will do me the honor of becoming my wife." Jim pulled Cassie next to him and smiled into her eyes.

Jim smiled at Matt's confused expression. "Cassie and I have traveled miles together, alone, and we've gotten very close. I love her and have from almost the first day she came to the ranch. I hope you'll be happy for us."

Matt looked at Jocelyn, and both of them laughed. Jocelyn glanced over her shoulder and said softly, "I couldn't be happier for you Jim, but I haven't heard Cassie give you an answer."

"Well, I can tell all of you now, I ain't taking *no* for an answer." He pulled Cassie into his arms, and she blushed a bright red.

"The word 'no' never crossed my mind. I would be proud to be your wife, Jim Watson."

Luther couldn't believe what he was witnessing. He seemed to have lost any chance of getting married today. He was going to have to give up some of his money or take a chance of leaving here penniless. Luther interrupted. "If I agree to share my money with Jocelyn, how long will it take to get me *my* money? I want to move away from this place and these people as soon as I can."

Mr. Taylor stood. "If everyone will go back into the lobby, you and I will discuss some private business that concerns your father's will."

Jocelyn rushed into Cassie's arms and gave her and Jim her congratulations. She pulled Mabel into her arms, too." Then she ambled over to Boomer who was holding Mabel's son in his arms while he slept. "Boomer, this is Matt Colburn." Boomer smiled and said he was sorry for all the trouble his boss caused. "I had to help him, but sir, I would have never let him hurt anybody, even though he threatened to kill us all."

"Boomer, I'm glad that you were on this adventure with her. She felt safer with you along."

"Can I ask how you were able to find us so fast?"

"“Well, our first clue was a trail of marbles that were dropped by someone. After we found your first campsite, we discovered the word 'Help' written out in marbles near the fire pit. From there, we figured Luther was taking Jocelyn to Midland and then to Perryville. Somehow, you all made it here several hours before my train arrived."

"Those were my marbles, Mister. I sure hated to have to give them up, but I didn't have anything else to use," Sonny said, his eyes lighting up. Boomer lowered Sonny to the floor but kept his hands on the boys' shoulders.

"Well, you're in luck. One of my men picked up all the marbles and put them in a bag. He'll be happy to return them to their rightful owner." Matt rubbed the young boy's hair. "You are very bright for your age." turned to Jocelyn as Mr. Taylor invited all of them back in his office. "Josh, are you sure this is what you want to do?"

When Jocelyn nodded, Matt grinned. "All right, I'll present your request."

"Mr. Taylor? If you can remove that one wish from Luther's father's will, Miss Norwood will sign over her father's house and property. She would like to be able to go into her home and collect a few pieces of her parent's furniture and paintings. She was forced to leave her home before getting some of her personal things. Also, Luther must promise never to come near her again."

"Please give me a minute to discuss this offer with my partner, Mac. I'll be right back." Mr. Taylor strode out of the office.

****

Jocelyn linked arms with her man. "Oh Matt, how did you find me? I have been so afraid." She wanted to snuggle with Matt, but she hadn't bathed or washed her long hair in a while. Even she could tell she smelled like a horse.

"I must admit that once I reached Perryville, I had a time locating where Luther had taken you. I went to your home, and it was boarded up, but an old man who was working in the rose garden told me that you left to go to the Mr. Taylor's law office. Thank goodness I arrived in time."

"I'm thankful, too," Jocelyn said. "I can't wait to get to a hotel so I can have a bath. Luther kept us hidden out in the woods or in alleyways."

****

Matt led the group back to the boardwalk, where he asked Boomer to drive them back to the Norwood estate so Jocelyn could choose some items to have shipped back to Amarillo. "I need to speak to Mr. Taylor one more time. I'll be right back.

As Matt prepared to knock on the lawyer's door, he heard Luther's voice.

"I tell you now, this isn't fair that I have to give that trash part of my money. She is Perryville's harlot and everyone who knows her will tell you the same thing. You even said that you knew her well."

"If you knew all this about her, why did your father want you to marry her?"

"He wanted me to marry, and he knew she was young and beautiful. With her reputation, she would be happy to marry a young, rich man. However, my father disliked my friends, and he wanted me to change my lifestyle. He figured she would jump at the chance to marry me, but she had already met a wealthy ranch owner."

Matt felt his blood drain to his toes. He didn't want to believe what he had just heard about the love of his life. But anger took over as he stormed to the waiting carriage.

Chapter 28

Jocelyn stood at the stove, humming a hymn. She was lost in thoughts as she pulled an apple pie from the oven and placed it on the counter.

Cassie was completing the lunch dishes. "Lordy child, I sure enjoy listening to your singing. You sound just like a bird."

"Thank you, sweet friend. I haven't had a lot to sing about in months. Have you and Jim decided when you want to get married? Matt and I want to plan a big party to help celebrate."

Behind them, the door opened and Jocelyn's spun round. She knew it was Matt before she turned to look his way. A whisper of fresh air came through the door with him. Yearning to see him up close to know that his eyes were upon her, she gazed at her handsome man. His hair was wet, as if his fingers had smoothed it into place. But below his hairline, his face was hard, with a deep frown. Something was wrong.

Cassie placed the last dish in the cabinet and said she needed to check on Mabel, who was washing clothes on the back porch. Jocelyn turned back to the stove, unwilling to look at Matt's expression any longer.

Matt came up behind her and touched her shoulder. "Are you all right?"

She glanced back at him. "Yes, why shouldn't I be?"

"We had a fast, tiring trip home, and you were up early

cooking. I had hoped you would have slept in and gotten some much-needed rest."

"I wasn't hired to sleep late when there are men to be fed." Mat frowned deeper.

"I overheard you speaking to Cassie about the wedding. Jim is ready to have the wedding today, but I asked him to give us a few days to prepare a nice celebration and invite guests. He said all he wanted was the men on the ranch and Cassie has no friends in Amarillo. What do you think about this Saturday evening? We can have a couple of men smoke and barbeque a big pig, and I can purchase food from the café in town. It wouldn't be right for Cassie to have to prepare her own wedding feast."

"I believe this Saturday will be fine. Regarding the food, Mabel and I can cook enough food to go with the smoked pig. I can bake a wedding cake, too."

She avoided looking at him. "If you're sure about the food, then plan to do that. I'd like for you to take Cassie into town and have her choose a new wardrobe. You know, girlie things, and whatever she'll need for a honeymoon. Buy her a new dress to be married in, for sure." Matt's face reddened. "I'll go tell Jim so he can invite the men." He hurried out the door, leaving Jocelyn frozen still. He didn't say one word about their up-and-coming marriage.

****

Cassie rushed in the backdoor with Sonny on her heels. "This young man is already hungry. I told him he could have two cookies."

"Good morning, Sonny. Have you had a chance to see most of the animals on the ranch?"

"Yes, ma'am. Mr. Jim took me all around and he said that he would get me a pony to ride. Boy, I can't wait to learn how to ride. Do you know how, Miss Josh?"

"I do ride but, Sonny, why did you call me Josh? My name is Jocelyn."

"I know, but I heard Mr. Matt calling you that. I'm

sorry." He hung his head down to his chest.

"That's all right. You may call me Miss Josh, if you like. I was just surprised."

"After I learn to ride, maybe we can ride together. Mama says she don't like to ride."

"Yes, that would be fun. I need to talk to your mama. Is she still here?"

"Yep, she's hanging up some clothes to dry." Sonny swallowed a large mouth full of milk.

"Young man," Cassie poked Sonny on the shoulder, "You don't say *yep* to a grown up, understand?"

****

"Good morning, Mabel," Jocelyn walked over to the basket of wet things and began hanging up the clothes. "I wanted to ask if you want to continue to live at your house, or would you like for Matt to sell it for you?"

"Gracious, where would I live if I sold my place?" Mabel sighed. "My husband and I had wonderful plans for our little homestead before he died." She held a wet shirt to her chest and smiled. "Lord knows, I miss that man."

"Well, if that's what you want, I can hire some men to make repairs to your house. They can replace the roof, and inside walls, and put in a dry sink and stove. There's plenty of space to add two more rooms to the back of the house and put in a water closet. How does all that sound to you?"

"Sure, sounds like a pipedream. I'd be crazy to turn something like that down, but I don't have any money for the stove, much less for a new roof."

"Mabel, I'll receive a lot of money from that crazy Luther who kidnapped us. I told Matt that I wanted the money to help you and Boomer, and maybe a few others. Let me do this for you and Sonny. And one more thing. I want you to have a horse and wagon so you can travel back and forth. Maybe, you should think about hiring another woman to help you with your cleaning business."

Tears streamed down Mabel's lovely face. "Oh, Miss

Jocelyn, I can't believe you would do this for me. I'll never ever be able to pay you back or thank you enough."

"You have paid me already. Sonny and you are like family to me. I want to do this. Jim will come over to your home and draw up plans. You can tell him how you want your house to look. He'll hire the men and oversee the project while they're building. Meanwhile, you can continue to stay here. I know Matt won't mind. As Jocelyn turned to go back inside, she turned back to Mabel. "Oh, I volunteered you to help me cook a wedding feast for Jim and Cassie this Saturday. You don't mind, I hope?"

"I'll do anything for you and my new friend Cassie. I'm so happy for her."

"Great, I knew you'd be willing to help. I'll make a list of foods that we'll need and go into town in the morning to purchase them. Matt wants Cassie to have a new wardrobe before the wedding so she'll go with us. We have a lot to do before Saturday, but it will be a wonderful day."

"Miss Jocelyn, what are your plans, you and Matt? When will you get hitched?" Jocelyn looked toward the moving white clouds but didn't reply.

"I mean, I kinda thought it might be a double wedding."

"I'm not sure. Matt has yet to speak to me about marriage since we left the lawyer's office. Of course, he's happy for Jim, who has been like a big brother to him for years. He doesn't want to take the attention away from his special day."

"Yes, that's probably true. Your time will come soon, and it will be grand."

****

Jocelyn and Mabel stayed busy cooking for the men while making preparations for the wedding party feast. The men stood around the fire pit where the pig was being roasted. They laughed and drank, while teasing Jim about his first wedding night.

Mabel was cooking and baking pies and large pails of potatoes while Jocelyn put the final touches on the wedding cake. It was a three-layer white vanilla with tiny fresh rose buds surrounding the bottom layer. One of the men made a light double heart out of iron and painted it red to stand on the top. It was a lovely cake like many had never seen before.

On the wedding day, Jocelyn had prepared a bubble bath for Cassie and filed her fingernails. She coated Cassie's body with a special cream that Gloria Crocker donated from her store. Gloria said it came from Paris. It smelled wonderful.

Mabel came into the bedroom and helped Cassie with her long, white gauze dress. Jocelyn had sat up the night before and made a soft white veil. She trimmed it with fresh small wildflowers. Mabel had Cassie sit while she slipped on a pair of white silk slippers that had been Matt's grandmother. Cassie was a lovely bride.

All three stood in a circle fighting back the tears when a knock came on the door. Jocelyn kissed her friend on the cheek while Mabel rushed to tell the wedding party that the bride was ready.

****

As fast as lightning, Jim took his place beside his bride. Her heart raced like it did every time he was near. Her eyes met his and she quickly glanced at the floor. One glimpse was enough because she felt like she might burst out in tears.

Jim lifted her chin and gave her a soft peck. "I have been waiting for this moment all my life. Let's do this."

Cassie gazed at the minister and then over to Matt. She smiled at both of them. Matt stood as Jim's best man while Jocelyn stood up for her.

Jim and Cassie stood side by side and waited. Jocelyn stepped forward and without music sang, *Nearer, My God, To Thee.*

Everyone smiled as the minister stepped forward. “Who gives this woman to be married to this man?” The minister asked.

Matt cleared his throat and said, “I do.” He bent over Cassie, slowly lifted her lovely veil and touched her cheek. “May you always be as happy as you are now,” he whispered.

The words that the bride and groom spoke were like a play, both new and unfamiliar to them. Jim slid a ring on Cassie’s finger. She was surprised to receive a ring. Probably Matt’s idea. When he turned the ring, she saw it had a dedicate carving but her tears blurred it so she couldn’t read it.

“I now pronounce you man and wife.” The minister voice made a chill run down her spine.

“You may kiss your bride.”

Jim lifted her face, and his kiss was brief but sweet. She leaned into him to receive his soft caress. Then Cassie took his arm and turned to everyone, and they were soon surrounded with an outpouring of affection.

Cassie glanced around, trying to commit this moment to memory. She was finally married, something she had only dreamed about. Never did she think she would find such a wonderful man. Then her thoughts turned to her new friend, and her heart was filled with love for Jocelyn. Soon, she would be standing in her place as Matt’s new bride.

Mabel set all the food on a table where everyone could serve themselves. After everyone was seated, different men made a toast with the champagne Matt had provided. Many of the toasts were beautiful and quite a few were funny. Jim and Cassie laughed along with all the guests.

Soon it was time to cut the delicious-looking wedding cake. Jocelyn gave Cassie the knife, and she had Jim help her cut the first piece. Cassie prepared to feed Jim a piece, but just as he opened his mouth, she speared the icing on his nose.

The men yelled, "Get her back Jim. Don't let her get away with that!"

Jim took a piece of the cake and acted like he would get revenge, but he only placed it in her open mouth. The men groaned but Jim grabbed Cassie, bent her over, and laid a big kiss on her mouth. When they stood back up, he had cake all over his mouth. That satisfied the men and they all laughed.

Three of the men soon broke out their instruments and played several lively tunes. Mabel danced with a few of the men while Jim didn't share Cassie with his friends. The men played a lovely slow song, so Matt took Jocelyn's hand and led her into the dance floor. Mr. and Mrs. Crocker joined them along with Jim and Cassie.

****

Jocelyn could feel Matt's strong muscles as she leaned into him. He was stiff and pushed her back from him. Certainly, he didn't hold her close like two people in love. She smiled and said, "It was a lovely wedding, wasn't it?"

"Yes, it was nice. Jim's a good man and he deserves a fine woman like Cassie. I'm happy they will continue to work here. For a wedding gift, I'm going to give Jim a piece of my land and build him a house."

"That's wonderful. Jim is like family to you. I feel like Cassie is a big sister to me." Jocelyn continued to sway with Matt until the song ended. He led her back over to the kitchen and walked outside for a breath of fresh air.

After a couple of hours, Jocelyn's lips curved into a smile as she watched the men begin to wander out as they congratulated the wedding couple.

Jim eased over to Jocelyn and expressed his thanks for all the work she and Mabel did to make them a grand wedding party. "I'm gonna take Cassie upstairs now."

"I've never seen you look so happy before," Jocelyn said.

"Now that I have Cassie, this is where we belong. This is home now." Jim grinned.

"Of course, it is. I think the rest of the guests will understand. She has already carried her personal things upstairs." Jocelyn smiled and gave him a tight hug.

Jim and Cassie stopped at the bottom of the stairs and waved at everyone. Jim stood behind Cassie and gave her a shove to start moving upward. Everyone laughed and some of the men gave a hoot or two.

Jocelyn, along with Mabel, cleaned the tables and stacked the dishes on the kitchen counter. Sonny had fallen asleep in one of the comfortable chairs. "Mabel, go and take care of your baby boy. He's had a big day."

"Yes, he has. I'll be back in a few minutes."

As Jocelyn was washing the dishes, Matt eased up behind her. "I should have hired some women from town to help you with this wedding party." His back was straight, and his shoulders wide as he placed his hands on her shoulders.

Jocelyn leaned her head sideways to touch his strong hands, yearning for his touch. She hoped he would say something about their future wedding. The warmth of his hands were gone in just a second. "Is there any coffee left? I feel I need some after drinking so much of that Champagne."

After serving Matt a hot cup of coffee, he said, "I didn't know you could sing. You have a lovely voice. Maybe you will sing just for me."

"Any time. You have to know that I'll do anything *for you."*

Chapter 29

Late into the night, Matt flipped from one side of his bed to the other. He couldn't sleep. All he could hear was Luther's voice screaming those foul words about Josh. He didn't want to believe his accusations. Josh had told him how he had mistreated her and caused her to be with child. She had good reason to hate the man. But, what was she like with other men? This is the part of Luther's words that had him so upset. He had to find out the truth. Maybe he would telegram the sheriff in Perryville and ask about her reputation. Surely, he would have no reason to lie to him. Yes, that's what he would do first thing in the morning.

****

Across the hall, Jocelyn couldn't sleep either. She should have fallen into bed and gone fast asleep. After all, she had to be exhausted from working from sunup to past midnight. Her heart was broken, and she didn't know the reason Matt had practically turned his back on her. Ever since they had arrived home, he treated her like a stranger working in his household. Before they left Perryville, he had said they would marry. He'd even wanted to marry her before reaching home. But, after meeting with the lawyer, his attitude had changed toward her. What could have happened to change his feelings? She couldn't continue to live like this.

****

Early the following morning, after the wedding, Jim

bounced down the stairs like a young man. He rushed outside, and in a few minutes, he was back with a sheepish grin, "Good morning, ladies," he said to Jocelyn and Mabel. "Cassie is still asleep. I hope you don't mind that she is sleeping in today."

"Jim, for goodness' sakes, you were on your honeymoon night. Of course, we weren't expecting Cassie to come down here and help us cook. Both of you relax and enjoy each other. Take a few days off, take a long walk, or go into town for lunch. We can manage without both of you for a while," Jocelyn said.

"Thanks. Oh, by the way, I saw Matt leaving for town while I was outside. Where was he going so early this morning?" Jim asked.

"I have no idea. He didn't come in for a cup of coffee." Jocelyn wandered over to the front door and glanced toward the barn.

"I guess he had some important business," Jim said. "He's getting ready to ship over two hundred head of cattle on the train to Midland. That probably the reason—he's making arrangements to reserve the boxcars. Oh, well, he'll be back soon. Cassie and I'll be down shortly and most likely have breakfast with the men."

Jocelyn pulled a pan of hot biscuits from the oven and drizzled hot butter over the tops of them. She knew Matt must have something on his mind, but she had no idea what he was thinking these days.

****

Early the next morning, Matt entered the dining room and sat down at the big table with the men. "I wanted to tell you that we'll be driving about two hundred cattle to the stockyard and getting them ready to board the boxcars on the train. Stan, you and two of the men go to the far pasture and cut out at least a hundred head and corral them in the west field. Jack, you take several men and cut out another hundred and bring them to the east field. We'll drive them to town and put them in the stockyard until the train arrives. I've reserved the train's boxcars for hauling them to Midland. We shall leave Amarillo the day after tomorrow. I already have a buyer for the herd. We'll stay the night so you can have some fun and celebrate. We'll travel back here on the next train at noon."

All the men stood, chatting among themselves, and left the house. Matt remained at the table to finish his coffee. Jocelyn walked into the dining room to remove the dishes. "Did you overhear my plans for the next few days? I have a buyer in Midland for two hundred cattle and mine are prime beef, ready to sell." Jocelyn nodded and continued to clear the table.

"I must go into town this morning to make the final arrangements. Do you need any supplies for the kitchen?"

"I'll ask Mabel to help me make a list." She picked up a tray of dishes and walked from the dining room. Matt followed her to the kitchen staring at her as she picked up a pencil and paper. She never looked at him. Finally, he whirled around and left the house.

****

After arriving in town, Matt headed to the telegraph office and sent a short questionnaire to the sheriff in Perryville. "Bill, you are not to discuss this with anyone, do you understand?

"Who do you think I am, Mr. Colburn? All telegrams are private." Bill rubbed the back of his neck as he faced Matt.

"Just make sure this one is. I'd better not hear my business discussed all over town. If I do, you'll regret it." Matt used his finger and pushed his hat back from his forehead.

"I understand, I sure do." Bill quickly sat down at his keyboard and began hitting the transmission key on the machine. "What do you want me to do with the answer?"

"If I am not in town, send a boy out to my ranch as

soon as possible." Matt left the office and healed over to the dry goods store.

"Good morning, Matt," Gladys Crocker greeted him. "Come on in and tell us when we can expect to be invited to your wedding?"

Matt felt embarrassed for a moment. "I'm not sure. I'll be taking a couple hundred cattle to Midland on the train in two days. I will be there for a day or so. Maybe after I complete this business and return home."

"So, we could be looking at a big celebration at the end of the week?"

"Now, I didn't say that." Matt pulled out a list of supplies that Jocelyn needed for the ranch. "Can you fill this list while I'm in the leather shop?" Matt hurried out of the store, leaving Gloria's mouth wide open.

****

"Well, I never," grunted Gloria to her husband. "If I didn't know better, I'd swear something happened between him and Jocelyn. What do you make of his answers about the wedding, Ben?"

"I think you need to mind your own business. Let that nice couple decide what's best for them." He took Matt's list out of her hand and began to fill the order.

****

The morning that Matt and the men were to leave on the cattle drive to town, Woody came riding hard up to the corral. "Mr. Colburn, Mr. Bill from the telegraph office sent me out with this here message for you. He said it was very important and I couldn't give this to nobody but you."

"Thanks, Woody. Here's a little something for your trouble." Matt flipped the young man a silver dollar.

"Wow, I've never had one of these. Gee, thanks."

"Woody, get down and go into the house and tell the ladies to give you a hot biscuit with some jam."

"Thanks sir, but I had breakfast already."

"Fine, but cool your horse down and give him some

water. You ride that animal of yours a little slower back to town." Matt placed the telegram into his back pocket and headed into the house. He didn't stop until he got to the privacy of his bedroom.

He reached for the message in his back pocket, then he sat down on his bed and read the answer from the sheriff in Perryville. The message read:

Matt Colburn . . . stop . . . Miss Jocelyn Norwood . . . stop . . . is one of the most . . . stop . . . prominent ladies in Perryville. She is a . . . stop . . . proper young lady . . . stop . . . honorable and worthy . . . stop . . . an outstanding lady . . . stop . . . She obeyed . . . and . . . served her father . . . stop . . . faithfully . . . stop. . . I hope this . . . stop . . . answers your questions. . . Marry the girl . . . stop. . . Sheriff J.P. Godwin.

As Matt read the telegram, his smile grew wider and wider. He knew all along that Luther was a liar. How could he had ever doubted her reputation? He felt ashamed of himself, but he could never tell Josh what he had done. She wouldn't understate that he had checked her background. He folded the telegram, sat it down on his nightstand and left his room.

As he went into the kitchen, he discovered Josh, Mabel and Cassie standing on the front porch speaking with Mr. Crocker at the front gate. He had delivered the supplies that he forgot to pick up yesterday. Matt needed to go, but he needed to speak with Josh and give her a reassuringly kiss. They would plan their wedding when he returned from this important trip.

Coming out of the corral, all the men were ready to go as were the cattle who took up the whole road.

Matt hoped to catch a glimpse of Josh and give her a big smile, but she never looked his way. He sure had some making up to do when he returned.

Chapter 30

Jocelyn nearly cried as Matt disappeared down the road with his men and cattle. She had prayed that he would seek her out and say something about their future, but he didn't. She tried to stay busy as he prepared to leave so she wouldn't cry in front of him.

After the kitchen was clean, Jocelyn went into her bedroom and dusted. She went across the hall and thought this would be an excellent time to give Matt's room a spring cleaning. At least, being in his room, she could feel near him. Jocelyn opened the two windows and pulled back the curtains so fresh air could flow. Walking over to the bed, she picked up his pillow and placed her face on it. She could smell his hair oil and the minty scent of his breath. After fluffing the pillow, she placed it back on the bed.

As she straightened the sheet and began to pull the quilt up to the pillows, a piece of paper floated off the nightstand. She reached down, and her eyes immediately caught sight of her name. It was a telegram. Jocelyn placed it down by her side. *Should she read his* private mail? But, it had her name in it. Why would this piece of paper have her name on it?

Jocelyn held the telegram and sat down on his bed. She slowly unfolded the paper and read the telegram. What's this about? It was from J.P., the sheriff and a friend of hers, in Perryville. It read, 'I hope this answers your question. So, Matt had written to J.P. and asked something about her. But why? She re-read the message, but it only had nice things to say about her and her reputation.

What reason did Matt have for writing to J. P. and asking about her? Was this the reason Matt had been acting so distant to her? Was he wanting answers about something? Did he not trust her? Of course, he didn't trust her. She jumped off his bed as if she'd been shot. That must be it. He didn't believe anything she had told him about her past. The paper floated out of her hand to the floor, but she didn't bother to pick it up.

Jocelyn trudged out of his bedroom. Cassie and Mabel stood in the kitchen but she couldn't bring herself to talk to them.

"What's wrong, Jocelyn? You're as white as a sheet." Cassie's lips turned down.

"Miss Jocelyn, would you like a cup of coffee or hot tea? You kinda look sick," Mabel said.

"I am sick. I'm heartsick. I need to go pack. Cassie, will you go and ask Jim to drive me into town, and if he can't, maybe Boomer will. I have to leave." Jocelyn turned away from the ladies and went back into her bedroom.

"Jocelyn," Cassie called to her. "Please tell me what's happened. Where are you going? You can't leave. You and Matt will be married in a few days."

"No, Matt will never marry me. I have to leave. Please tell him when my money is in the bank, I'll repay him for my passage here." Jocelyn closed her door and left Cassie standing on the other side.

Cassie rushed outside and called Jim who was working in the barn. He saw his new bride standing out in the bright sunlight. She was as beautiful as she was last night.

"What's can I do for you, Mrs. Watson?" he said grinning.

"Oh, Jim, listen to me. Jocelyn is leaving the ranch. She's leaving, do you understand?" She covered her face and cried.

"What are you saying, woman? She can't leave here. Where is she planning on going, anyway?"

"I have no idea. She wants you to take her into town. If you can't, she said for me to ask Boomer."

"Of course, I will drive her, but Matt ain't going like this. He might wring her neck when he gets back."

The front door of the house slammed and both of them turned to see Jocelyn standing on the front porch. Mabel was standing behind her, pleading with her not to leave. Jocelyn ignored everyone's pleas and placed her carpetbag in the carriage which was sitting in front of the house. "I love all of you, but I have to go. I 'll let you know where I am staying once I find a room somewhere or I may go back to Perryville."

****

Jim ran from the barn and jumped in the carriage, waving at the girls as he drove toward town.

As they traveled about a mile from the ranch, Jim stopped the horses. "Now, Miss Jocelyn, tell me what's this is all about. You have been my friend ever since the day you arrived on the ranch. Now, I ain't your pa or big brother, but I'm your friend. I can keep a secret."

"I don't understand myself, Jim. Ever since we arrived home from Perryville, Matt has been distanced to me. He's treated me like he did when I first came here. Something happened, and he's not shared it with me. Before we left Perryville, I thought we would be married before you and Cassie, but he hasn't even spoken about marriage to me. I discovered something today that convinced me he doesn't trust me. We can't be together without trust, so it's best I leave."

"What did you find out?" Jim almost demanded.

"It's only important to me. Since he doesn't trust me, he can't possibly love me, so it's best I go. Please just take me to town."

Jim grunted and turned to face the horses. He realized

he wouldn't get any more information from his dear friend. "Let's go boys," he snapped the reins.

After arriving in town, Jim stopped at the Miss Lilly's Ladies' Boarding House. "This is the nicest place for young ladies in town. Miss Lilly will take good care of you until Matt gets home. You must know that he ain't going to let you stay in town."

"I may work for Matt, but he doesn't own me. I can take care of myself. Thank you and know that I love you and Cassie. We will see each other, I promise." Jocelyn touched his arm and said she didn't need help getting down. She reached into the back and grabbed her carpetbag. "Bye, my friend. See you soon."

"You can bet on that."

****

Jocelyn picked up her carpetbag and knocked on the door at the ladies' boarding house. She waited and finally a short round little woman answered. "Hello," Jocelyn said, "My name is Jocelyn Norwood. I was told that this is the nicest place in town for a single woman to reside. Do you have a room that I can let?"

"Oh, my child, I'm so sorry, but I don't have a spare room. All my tenants will be with me for a couple of weeks."

"Please don't apologize. I appreciate you speaking with me. Thank you, I'm sure I will find something." Jocelyn stepped back off the porch and closed the front gate. She stood on the boardwalk, wondering which direction she should talk. Perhaps she should go to the dry goods store and visit with Gloria Crocker. Just maybe she would know where she could find a room. She crossed the street.

"Child, what are you doing in town, looking for a room? Does Matt know that you left the ranch? Ben? Come out here and talk with Jocelyn."

"What are you yelling about, woman. I was unloading

corn from Mr. Sellers. Well, Jocelyn, it is good to see you."

"Ben, she's in town looking for a room to let. Can you believe it? Something has happened between her and Matt, and she won't tell me." Gloria folded her arms across her chest, chatting a mile a minute.

"Dear, be quite and let Jocelyn speak." Ben joined his wife behind the counter, staring at her.

"Now, would you like to talk with us about your problem, or is there anything we can do for you?" Ben asked sweetly.

"I came in to ask if you know where I can find a room to stay. The ladies boarding house is filled so I don't know where else to look."

"You don't want to wait until Matt returns from his cattle drive?" Gloria asked.

"I only want to know if you can help me find a room. If you can't, I need to go and try to find something. Also, I need a job too." Jocelyn turned to walk away from the sweet couple.

"There aren't many places for a young woman to live in town. We don't even have a spare room to let you stay with us." Ben rounded the counter and walked with her to the door. "There is another rooming house about two street over, try that place," he said.

"Thanks, I'll see you both soon." Jocelyn gave them both a smile and left.

"Mercy, when Matt gets home and discovers she has left, there's going to be trouble. I sure hate to be that little gal when he returns." Gloria said, shaking her head.

Jocelyn found the rooming house that Ben told her about, but there wasn't a spare room available. The landlord didn't offer her any other place to look. He just slammed the door in her face. Dejected, she plodded down the street. As she headed down the boardwalk, she heard piano music and a lady singing, if one could call that singing. The person couldn't carry a tune. Jocelyn stood on her tiptoes and looked over the batwing's door into the dark, smoky room and saw a drunken older woman sitting on top of a piano. If she wasn't careful, she would fall off. Jocelyn wondered how the woman got up there to start with.

Without warning, Jocelyn felt her feet removed from the ground. Two burly men picked her up by her arms and carried her inside the saloon. "Look. . .ee who we found peeking in the door. I believe she wanted to come in and have a drink with us." The men stood her on her feet with triumphant grins.

"Sorry fellows, I wasn't coming inside. I was just listening to that lady sing."

"First, that ain't no lady, and second, she can't sing. Now, I bet my hat that you can sing."

"Why do you think I can sing? I was just standing there by the door." Jocelyn laughed at the two men, who would have scared a younger person to death, but for some reason they didn't frighten her.

"Would you like a drink?" before she could answer, one of the men called to the bartender. "Bring our pretty new friend a drink."

"Just a glass of water, please." Jocelyn said quickly. The bartender smiled and set a fresh glass of cool water in front of her.

****

Jay Butler, the owner of the saloon came out of his office and starred at the two men with the pretty young woman. He couldn't imagine who she was or what she was doing in his place of business.

"Bert and Willy, who is your new friend and what is she doing in here?" he asked.

The two men looked down at Jocelyn and both removed their hats. Bert said, very nicely, "Miss, please tell Jay your name. I'd tell him, but we haven't been introduced." He gave her a proper bow.

Jocelyn turned to the owner of the saloon. "My name is Jocelyn Norwood. I was peeking in your door when these gentlemen invited me to come in. I was listening to your lady sing." Everyone turned to look at the old woman leaning up against the wall on top of the piano, dead to the world, asleep.

"Joey, help her down from there and see that she packs her bag and gets out of here. She doesn't work here anymore." The bartender shook his head, went over to the piano, and reached for the older lady who batted her arms at him.

Jay turned to the pretty lady. "Now, Miss, my name is Jay Butler, and I am the owner of this place."

"It is very nice meeting you, sir. I'm sorry, but I must go. I'm in need of a room and I'm looking for a rooming house."

"Where have you looked?"

"I have been to two different places but they're full and I need to find some place to live before dark. Sorry to have bother you."

"Maybe your luck has changed. Can you sing?" The owner asked.

"Well, many people say I have a nice voice, why?" Jocelyn said, her face warming,

"As you can see, I need a singer and I have a few rooms upstairs. One of them can be yours if you'll sing every night for my customers."

"Oh, I could never work in a place like this. My reputation would be destroyed for sure."

Well, if you sleep on the street, more than your reputation will be destroyed," Jay said with a grin.

"Well, you do have a point." Jocelyn placed her carpet bag on the floor. Where is my room?"

"I want to hear you sing first. Billy, come and play this pretty gal a tune of her choice."

"All I know are songs that I learned in church. I can sing *Amazing Grace*."

"Shoot, I know that by heart. You start, and I will play." Billy waited until Jocelyn sang the first line and then he joined in with soft piano music. Jocelyn smiled at him, and they sounded beautiful together. Everyone in the saloon chapped and hooted their approval.

"That was wonderful," Jay said. "Tomorrow you and Billy can work on a couple songs that the men will enjoy and attract more customers from outside." Jay motioned for one of the other girls, named Lulu, to come and escort Jocelyn up to her room.

Chapter 31

Jim was worried about Jocelyn. He had stayed in town for several hours after dropping her off at the rooming house just to make sure she got a room. Speaking with the Crocker's at the dry goods store, they told him that she didn't find one. He wanted to find out for himself, so he headed to the other rooming house and was told they were filled and not rented to a Miss Norwood. After looking around for a while, he was walking back to the livery when he heard a sweet voice coming from the Lady Luck Saloon. He couldn't believe his eyes. There was Jocelyn standing next to the piano.

He pushed the door open and stepped inside. Many people surrounded her, so he left before she saw him. On the way back to the ranch, all he could think about what Matt was going to do when he discovered her new residence.

****

Early the next morning, Jocelyn woke up from a restless night of sleep. She washed, fixed her hair, and dressed in an old day dress. She didn't bring anything that she had received from Matt. Easing down the stairs to the back of the saloon where there was a small kitchen, she found coffee and a coffee pot so she made a big pot. In the icebox, she discovered milk, eggs and a slab of dried bacon. Under the cabinet was a bag of flour that had never been opened. She made a pan of hot biscuits and a pan of white gravy.

Jay dressed and opened his bedroom door. He immediately smelled coffee and hurried down to the kitchen. "Well, what a lovely surprise," he said, as he poured himself a cup. "I always enjoy starting the day with a lovely creature."

"Thank you for the comment, sir. It's nice hearing sweet words."

"What are you doing up so early? The other ladies sleep until noon every day." Jay watched Jocelyn spoon eggs, biscuits and gravy on a plate and set it down in front of him. "What are your plans today?" Jay asked.

"Sometime today, Billy and I are going to practice a few songs. Other than that, I don't have any. I haven't had this much free time in months."

"Really? Where did you come from?"

"I have been working on the Colburn Ranch a few miles out of town."

"Working on a ranch? What kind of work?"

"Oh, I was the cook and housekeeper. I came from Perryville, Texas on the bridal wagon train months ago. Surely, you heard about all the brides-to-be arriving here. It caused a really big stir for a time."

"Actually, I've only been in Amarillo a few months. I haven't heard about that wagon train. So, you came here as a man's bride-to-be?"

"No, I arrived on the train, but not as a future bride. I was to be a cook for a rancher and his men. That's how I came to work on the ranch."

So, now you aren't a cook on the ranch any longer. Why did you leave?"

"Let's just say, I had my reasons. I don't belong to anyone so I can do whatever I please. So, for now, I'm going to stay here and be your singer."

"Well, Josh, how would you like to take a ride with me? I'm looking at purchasing a small farm a few miles from town and I could use a woman's opinion."

"All right, I'd enjoy some fresh air and would be happy to go with you," she replied. "I have one request. Please don't call me Josh. I don't like it."

"Whatever you say." He smiled and kissed her hand. "I'll be waiting for you in about two hours."

Jocelyn smiled down at her hand and thought, *what a gentleman.*

After cleaning the kitchen, Jocelyn straightened her room and looked at the clock. It was a little after nine. She grabbed her bag and headed for the bank. She was hoping her money had arrived from Perryville. Mr. Taylor had said the money should arrive in a couple of days.

Luck was on her side this beautiful sunny morning. The money from Luther's inheritance had arrived and was in her account. It was much more money than she ever dreamed it would be. Now she could make plans to leave Perryville once Mabel's house was repaired and Boomer was set up in business.

Later that afternoon, she'd send word to Jim and hire him to start work on Mabel's house. Boomer was already working at Matt's ranch, so she was going to send him a note to come into town and see her too. She was thrilled to be able to help them.

At ten a.m., Jay stood at the bottom of the stairs dressed in a black leather jacket, a colorful silk vest with a pocket watch dangling, and black boots a girl could see her face in. His head of cold black curly hair was covered with a handsome Stenson hat. He certainly was a handsome man, Jocelyn thought.

"Come my lady, take my arm and allow me to escort you to my carriage." Jay gave her a bow and reached to give her a kiss on the cheek. Jocelyn leaned back and said, "Now kind sir, aren't you attempting to take advantage of a young lady?"

Jay laughed, "I knew you were a lady. Come, let's go.

As Jocelyn got in the carriage, she noticed a large basket covered with a checked cloth, a blanket, and two fishing poles.

"Are we going to fish?" Jocelyn laughed.

"If we run out of other things to do." He gave her a wink.

After traveling several miles out of town, they came upon a pretty stream and parked the carriage under several shade trees. Jay hands lingered on Jocelyn's waist as he helped her down from the carriage and purposely had her slide down the front of his body to the ground.

She frowned at his actions then hurried over to the water's edge to watch ducks floating down the stream. Out of the corner of her eye, Jocelyn watched Jay untie the two horses from the carriage and hobble them. They could eat the green grass and roam the area but wouldn't stray too far.

Just then she felt his lips on her neck. "Now, Jay, I asked you not to get too personal with my person. We have just meet and I'm not a loose woman."

"I know, sweetheart. That's what I like about you." He circled to face her and pulled her tight to his chest.

Jocelyn smiled at him and pushed him away. He lost his footing and tumbled backwards into the cold stream of water. A large splash and scream came at once.

Jocelyn stood at the bank and placed her hand over her mouth to keep her from laughing. She pretended to be surprised as she offered to help him out of the water.

He refused her hand and shouted, "You did that on purpose, and I won't forget it." Jay whirled around, took off his soggy jacket, and headed to free the horses. "Get in! This day is ruined." He didn't offer her a hand to get aboard. Once they arrived back in town, he stopped in front of the saloon and didn't even look her way as she climbed down.

Jocelyn hurried inside and rushed up the stairs. Lulu

was lying on a bed with a small brown cigar in her mouth. A cup of coffee sat on the nightstand.

"Hey, gal, how come you're back so soon? I figured you would be gone with the boss until dark."

"Well, the funniest thing happened. Funny to me, but not to Jay," she said, trying to be serious. "He tried to get a little fresh with me, and when I pushed him away, he fell in the stream. I wish you could have seen him splashing and slapping the water while trying to climb up on the bank. His pretty clothes were a mess. I backed a good distance away from him because I wasn't sure if he was going to hit me." Jocelyn bent over laughing. "He was so mad." Her laughing made Lulu laugh, too.

"You know he isn't going to forget it. If I were you, I'd stay away from him for a while," Lulu warned her.

"I know. He said he wouldn't forget that I pushed him in the water. However, he was only mad because I rejected his advances." Jocelyn pulled out a black ruffled dress with sequins trimmed down the front. "Whose dress is this? It's so lovely."

"Jay bought it for you to wear tonight. I wouldn't disappoint him by not wearing it. He's been bragging to others how you will fill the house with your lovely voice and new clothes."

"But, look at it. It doesn't have a top. Mercy, my shoulders will be bare . . . for all the men to see and maybe more." Jocelyn held it up to her and whirled around the room as she judged how it would look on her.

"That's the point, honey. The more they can see of you, the more they will drink and spend their hard-earned money. You're gonna be their main attraction, with your songs or whatever. Of course, the more you move around the room, the safer you'll be. The men will enjoy your singing and the wiggling of your backside, but they won't touch you as long as Jay is present."

"I can't wear something like this and he can't make

me. It's not decent."

"He can toss you out in the street, where you came from, if I remember." Lulu sprang off the bed and took the dress from her. "Go on and wear it tonight. Jay is a pretty nice fellow. If you draw a big crowd, he'll forgive you for pushing him in the water today. He likes money and that's all he'll be thinking about."

"I guess I can try it on and maybe, just maybe, you can help me make a few adjustments. I don't have the nerve to go out there the way this dress is now."

"Yes, I bet you do have a case of nerves." Lulu poured Jocelyn a small glass of amber liquid. "Here, drink this. Down it in one swallow and it will give you courage."

Jocelyn shook her head after downing it. "That's awful and my throat is on fire. What is it?"

"Um, nerve medicine. Here, drink another one. Swallow it quick and the burning will stop."

"Oh my, that wasn't as bad as the first. She handed the glass back to Lulu, but instead of taking the glass she refilled it again. "Once more and you should be ready to tackle the world that awaits you downstairs."

Jocelyn took the glass and downed it, just like Lulu instructed. She coughed twice and took a deep breath. "My throat feels numb now." Lulu laughed and tossed Jocelyn a hand full of underclothes.

"These things go under the dress." She tossed her a black corset, and a pair of long black silk stocking with a black garter belt. "Let me know if you need any help." Lulu grinned to herself and lit another cigar. Two things I like are a cold beer and a fresh cigar.

Chapter 32

After finalizing the cattle deal, Matt got on his horse and rode back to Midland, instead of waiting to catch the train the next day with his men. He had to get home and straighten things out with Jocelyn. Matt knew he'd been acting like a stubborn jackass for a week or more, and he was ashamed of himself. His gut told him that Jocelyn wasn't the type of woman that Luther described to Mr. Taylor, his lawyer. But once burned by a woman, a man doesn't forget it. Matt had been fooled by a gal when he was young, and the ordeal left a bad taste in his mouth. He had a hard time trusting, but he'd fallen hard for his new cook and bride-to be and he never doubted one thing she told him. Still, Luther's words still haunted him. All the old memories of how he felt betrayed came rushing back and he couldn't allow that to happen to him again. So Matt did what he had to do-- checked out her reputation. He wouldn't tell her what he had done, only that he had a lot on his mind, and he was ready for them to marry.

Matt rode into the ranch yard where Jim met up with him. "You're home earlier than we thought. Cassie was going to have a big supper for you and the men tonight."

"I decided to ride the fifty miles on horseback instead of waiting around to catch the train. The men celebrated last night, but I needed to get home to Josh. Please take care of my horse, while I go in to see her. I could use a good cup of coffee." Matt tossed his horse's rein to Jim and headed for the house.

"Matt, wait. Jocelyn isn't here."

"Where is she? I'll go into town and meet up with her." He reached for his horse's reins.

"Jocelyn left soon after you and the men left. She was cleaning the house then all of sudden she started packing. I had to drive her to town."

"You mean to say that I have a run a way bride, again?"

'I don't know if I would put it that way, but she told Cassie that you didn't love her enough to trust her or something like that. You know women, how they repeat things." Jim didn't dare tell Matt that he had seen Jocelyn is the Lady Luck Saloon. He would have to find that out for himself, if she was still there.

"I'm going in the house, eat and take a bath. I will be going into town and bringing my bride home, on her own two feet or over my shoulder. This is one time I am not putting up with her tears or temper tantrums."

Matt stormed through the front door and yelled at Cassie who was at the stove. "Please have hot water brought to my room so I can take a bath. I'm going to town, and I am sure you know what I'm going after."

Matt entered his bedroom and found the room all tidy. He found his telegram lying folded on the bed. A thought flashed through his mind. Had Jocelyn cleaned his room and discovered the telegram and read it? If so, she would know that he had questioned her hometown sheriff. He hurried to the kitchen and questioned Cassie. "Did Jocelyn clean my room after I left?"

"No sir, I did, why?" she asked, worried that she did something wrong.

"Oh, no reason, except I found this note on my bed."

"Oh that. I found it lying on the floor beside your small table and just placed it back on the bed. I didn't know if it was trash or something important because I can't read.

Now, it won't be but a second and Mabel and I will bring in buckets of hot water." In less than an hour, Cassie stood next to Jim and Mable on the front porch and watched as Matt and Boomer drove the small black carriage toward town. "I should hate to be in her shoes when he discovers she's working in a saloon." Jim spit a stream of tobacco juice in the grass.

"I was so surprised when you told us she was singing there. Oh, Jim, he won't hurt her, will he?" Cassie asked very concerned for her friend. "I have heard that he has a fierce temper, and he looks really mad."

"I don't believe mad is the right word. I wouldn't be surprised if he didn't paddle her behind once he gets a hold of her. He's tired of her running away."

The ladies stood watching Jim as he stormed to the barn, muttering to himself.

"My wash isn't going to get clean by its self, so I better get busy," Mabel said.

"I've a lot of baking to do myself, but however Jocelyn comes home, I'll be happy to have her back. I sure have missed her," Cassie murmured.

****

Matt rode into Amarillo and decided to check Miss Merriweather's ladies rooming house. Surely, if she was still here in town, she would be staying there. Once the landlady greeted him, she told him that Jocelyn had come by, but she didn't have room for her. "Sure is good seeing you, young man. Did you get one of those brides off the bridal wagon train?" Before he could answer, she went on to say that his mama would want him to get married."

"Thank you, Mrs. Merriweather. I'll think about marriage very soon. Good day to you." Matt had forgotten that his parent's old friends owned that rooming house.

After standing on the boardwalk for a few minutes, watching people stroll up and down both sides of the street, he decided to go see Ben and Gloria Crocker at the dry goods store. It was getting dark but it wasn't six o'clock yet and he was sure they were still open.

"Matt, it's so good to see you. Did everything go well with your cattle drive in Midland?" Mr. Crocker glanced at his wife giving her a warning to keep her mouth shut or else.

"Yep, everything went just fine. My buyer was there waiting for me so I was able to come home sooner. There's just one problem." Matt noticed that Gloria wouldn't look at him. She busied herself with arranging some material on a table.

"All right, Gloria, out with it. Where is my runaway bride? I know you know, so please tell me before I tear this town apart searching for her." Gloria glanced at her husband and bit her bottom lip. "I can't tell you, but Ben can."

Matt looked from Gloria to Ben. "One of you tell me, please. I need to find her and make amends. I want to marry her as soon as possible."

Ben looked like he wanted to strangle his wife. "Matt, that's wonderful news. We've wanted you two to get together for some time." Ben walked over to stand beside Gloria. He wanted to pinch her so bad.

"Look Matt, Jocelyn needed a place to stay, but as they said in the Bible, there was no room at the Inn so she found the one and only place she could."

Matt frowned and said, "Where would that place be?"

"The Lady Luck Saloon. She's working and singing there for Jay Butler." Ben looked down at his shoes. "We didn't have room for her to stay with us, but we never dreamed she would wind up there. If I'd known, we'd put her on the floor in the back room, but she never came back. We're very sorry."

"Did you say that she's singing?"

"Yes, I haven't been there, but I have heard others talking about her. I heard her sing at Jim and Cassie's wedding, but I didn't know she could sing the kind of rowdy songs cowboys like to hear." Ben walked to the front door and could see men going into the saloon. There wasn't any sound coming from the piano or any woman singing.

"Matt, you know that Jocelyn is a good woman. I'd bet my last dollar the only reason she's working there is to have a roof over her head. Amarillo is busting at the seams with people, and the man who could afford to build a hotel would be a rich man in a year. There isn't a bed in town that isn't already taken by someone. Give Jocelyn the benefit of doubt."

"I'm going to give her something once I find her. Josh won't be staying another night in that saloon. She'll be going home with me, and you'll be invited to a wedding soon." Matt stormed out of the store.

****

Ben turned to his wife and saw the biggest smile on her face. "I really didn't want to be the one to tell him that Jocelyn was working in that place, but I hope he'll be gentle with her once he confronts her."

"But, Ben, what about him having to confront that Jay fellow who owes the place? I heard that he has feelings for Jocelyn, and he may not allow her to leave." Gloria said as she moved close to her husband.

"Matt won't care about that man's feelings. He loves our little friend and he'll be taking her out of that place, just like he said. Come, let's close up and get upstairs. There may be fireworks coming from the saloon and we can watch from our big window."

"Ben, I'm surprised at you. I can't believe you're as nosy as I am." Both of them laughed as Ben locked the front door.

****

The bat-winged doors banged against the wall as Matt stormed in the Lucky Lady saloon. Jocelyn froze in her tracks. Matt was home. Her Matt was here. He looked fiercely angry. He had come to take her home, she was certain of that.

She noticed Jay leaning up against the bar waiting for Billy to start playing for Jocelyn. When he saw Matt, he straightened. She had to do something, so she hurried to the bar and threw herself into Jay's arms. If Matt was coming to get her, she'd give him a show.

"What the devil? Now this is what I have been waiting on, sweetheart."

Billy started playing *Camp town Races* and Jay took her arms from his neck and said, "Sing for my men, Sweetheart."

Jocelyn stood close to the piano, using it like a body shield. Her stomach felt uneasy, but she swallowed and began singing with gusto. She put everything she had into the loud, fast song that the men enjoyed. All the drinking customers started clapping as she moved around the room being careful not to get close to Matt.

****

Matt started walking toward her but she side stepped him twice before he was able to get a grip on her upper arm. He couldn't believe the garment she was wearing. All of her chest and upper arms were bare. He'd give her a good shake. She tried to make him turn her loose. A man jumped out of his chair and swung at Matt. "Turn my woman loose before I shoot you."

Matt's fist flew up and hit the man so hard he did a back flip over a table. All the other men backed away from the angry man. Not one attempted to help Jocelyn. She ran across the room to where Jay and Billy were standing.

Matt turned as he rubbed his fist and bellowed, "Woman, get over here, now!"

"You talking to me, cowboy?" Trying to impersonate Lulu, she hiccupped, and felt like she might through up.

"Don't play games with me, Josh. We're leaving this

place."

"Never," The dandy, owner of the saloon, yelled loud enough for the whole town to hear. "You have no right busting in here and demanding to take my woman." Jay stood beside Jocelyn and gripped her upper arm.

"Josh, if you want to see this man unharmed, you'd better tell him who you belong to. Tell him you're going home and, in a few days, you will be Mrs. Matt Colburn."

"Matt Colburn." His name spread across the room to the other men. "I haven't ever known him to come into a place like this," one man said to some of the others.

"He's a rich rancher and a mean son of gun, I'm told." Another man said. "If I was Butler, I wouldn't tangle with him."

Matt pulled Josh to look directly at him. "Get upstairs and put on some clothes or I'll put you over my shoulder just like you are. Now!"

Jocelyn shook herself loose from Jay and hurried up the stairs. She stopped halfway up and looked down at the two men. Matt noticed that she had stopped climbing the stairs. "Do I need to dress you?" Matt said.

Without answering, she continued until she practically fell into Lulu's arms.

"Help me out of this dress." Lulu unhooked the back and let it fall to the floor when she froze, then scooted out of the room.

"Where are you going?" Jocelyn said, then saw Matt standing in the doorway. Jocelyn grabbed for a wrap to cover herself. Had Matt seen her stepping out of the black dress? She stood dressed only in the black corset and silk stockings.

Instead of wrapping the silk robe around her, she faced Matt in the black underclothes. "Well, is this what you wanted to find out? Did you want to know if I fit the role of a harlot?" Jocelyn was so angry that she dropped the colorful silk wrap. "Do I meet your approval of what a saloon gal looks like?" She placed one leg up on a chair and slowly slid one of the black stockings down her long slim leg.

Matt watched her remove the stocking, and she saw his eyes linger on her leg, "Put this on. We're leaving now."

"Please Matt, let me put some decent clothes on. I 'm coming with you, but don't embarrass me anymore than I already am."

"You have five minutes, and if longer, I am coming back in and you'll go dressed or not. I don't have any patience left my dear runaway bride." He said every word through gritted teeth.

In less than five minutes, Jocelyn opened the dressing room door and saw Matt standing straight as an arrow. He came in the room, reached the bed, and grabbed her carpetbag. Taking her hand, he practically raced down the stairs. At the bottom of the stairs, Jay Butler stood waiting. Matt stopped when they stood nose to chin, since Jay was much shorter. "What do you want now?" Matt spit out. He took Jocelyn's carpetbag and using it as a ramming rod pushed Jay against the wall.

Jay stood on his tiptoes and glanced around Matt's large frame to see Jocelyn. "I want to know if Jocelyn is going because she wants to or is she leaving because you're forcing her?"

"Answer the man, Josh. Be quick about it." Matt said, softly.

"Jay, Mr. Butler, I want to thank you for everything you did for me while I was working for you. Everyone has been very kind." She paused for a minute. "I am going home with Matt because I want to go. I'm his *cook and housekeeper*."

Jay shrugged. "If you ever need anything, Josh, please come to me. I will always be here for you."

"Don't hold your breath waiting for her to need you. I'm all she will ever need. So, step aside, little man," he said, using the carpetbag to give him a shove, "before I have to remove you."

Jocelyn quickly looked toward the piano and bar. She smiled at Billy and the bartender. Both men had been good to her.

As she went out the door, Lulu said to Billy, "Why couldn't I be so lucky."

"Lucky? What do you mean, lucky, Lulu?" Billy watched as his songbird went out onto the boardwalk.

"A gracious hunk of a man just came storming in here to take her away. A rich cowboy to boot. Yes, lucky.

Chapter 33

A hush came over the big room as Matt pushed Jocelyn ahead of him toward the batwing doors. The men removed their hats and stood as they passed by. Embarrassed beyond words, Jocelyn lowered her eyes. Once they made it out the door, Jocelyn saw Boomer patting their horse's head at the front of the small black carriage.

"Boomer, it's so good to see you," Jocelyn said as Matt lifted her into the carriage. Boomer returned a reassuring smile.

"Let go home, Boomer," Matt said. Boomer leaped into the driver's seat and chucked at the horse. Matt took Josh's hand and held it between his two palms.

There was only silence between the three of them for a long while. Suddenly, Jocelyn said, "Stop." Boomer pulled the horses to a stop and turned to look down at the couple. She leaned over the side of the carriage door and emptied her stomach. Matt leaped down and rushed around to her side, sidestepping another bout of vomit. "I'm sorry, I'm sorry," Jocelyn cried and laid her head against the rim of the carriage door.

Matt gave her his handkerchief, and she wiped her mouth. "I feel sick all over," were the last words she spoke."

****

"Matt jumped back in the carriage and moved Josh

onto his lap. “Turn around and head to the doctor’s office off Main Street. Something’s terribly wrong with her.”

Thankful the doctor was still working in his office when Boomer drove up. He jumped down and pounded on the door. “What in the world? Couldn’t you have just knocked?”

The door flew open, revealing a stooped man with a brush mustache.

“Sorry sir, but Miss Jocelyn is very sick. Mr. Matt is bringing her inside now.”

Matt carried Josh to the back examination room as instructed by the doctor. “What is her problem, Matt? He lifted Jocelyn’s right, then left eye lid. She was unconscious and smelled like a brewery.

“What was she doing when she fainted?” the doctor asked as he listened to her heart.

“After I brought her out of the saloon where she was singing and started home, she started throwing up when we were a few miles out of town. After she wiped her face, she said she felt sick all over. Then she passed out. I couldn’t wake her.”

“Her heart is beating rapidly. How much has she had to drink?”

“Drink? I never knew her to drink anything.” Matt said, confused.

“Man, her breathe smells like whiskey. She drank liquor and my guess she drank a lot. She could have alcohol poison.” The doctor turned her over on her side and listened to her back. She was totally out.

“When she recovers and wakes up, will she be all right?”

“I’m not sure. Sometimes, the alcohol can affect her brain or memory. She could be sick from this for weeks.”

“What can you do for her, now, I mean?’

“Sleep is what she needs now.”

“Can I take her home? Cassie can take care of her

personal needs, and I can sit with her while she sleeps, but when she awakes, what should I look for?"

"Look for loss of memory, no appetite, and listen to her speech. I will come out late tomorrow afternoon."

"May I borrow a blanket to wrap Josh in while we travel home? It is a little cooler now and I don't want her to catch a chill."

"Of course, Matt. I feel that she'll be just fine when she wakes up. She's in good hands now," Doctor Adams smiled and patted Matt on the back as he carried Josh to the carriage.

Boomer drove the carriage slowly, careful not to hit any deep ruffs. Matt held Josh as tight as he could without causing her any harm. A couple of hours ago he was ready to tan her backside for running off and getting tangled up with that Butler fellow. He still wasn't sure why she ran away from his ranch, this time. If she hadn't read the telegram, then she wouldn't know that he had her investigated. Something had caused her to leave him again, and he would get to the bottom of it as soon as she recovered. It was very hard to believe that this sweet girl would drink enough whiskey to make herself so sick.

Matt surmised that the person that gave Josh the liquor encouraged her to drink it for some reason. Did that Butler fellow plan on seducing Josh while she was unconscious? That wouldn't surprise him at all.

****

Jim and Cassie were sitting in front of the fireplace enjoying a cup of hot chocolate when they heard the carriage stop in front of the house. Jim jumped up and hurried to see who were arriving this late at night. Boomer was holding the front gate while Matt carried Jocelyn in his strong arms. Jim rushed up to join him. "What's wrong with her? Is she--?" He couldn't say the word.

"No, she just sick. Passed out."

He blew out a sigh of relief, then turned to his wife

who stood on the porch. “Cassie turn down Jocelyn’s bedcovers. She’s sound asleep in Matt’s arms.” Jim held the door and offered to take Jocelyn from Matt, but Matt nodded toward her bedroom. “Let me get her in bed, and then I’ll tell you both what’s happened.

****

Matt lingered a little longer after placing her in her bed. He rubbed her forehead and squeezed her hand. She didn’t stir. He placed a kiss on her forehead and left the room, leaving the door partly open.

“Where did you find her, Mr. Matt?” Cassie asked.

“She was working in the Lucky Lady saloon, serving drinks, and singing. The reason she seems to be asleep is because she’s unconscious. She got sick to her stomach on the trip home and then she fainted. I had Boomer turn around and take us back to the doctor’s office. After a thorough examination, he said she had alcohol poisoning. She had drunk a lot of whiskey.”

“Will she be better in the morning?” Cassie asked.

“The doctor said she could be sick for a while. Sometimes people lose their memory, don’t want to eat and maybe their words might be slurred. Let’s just hope she awakes and be back to her old self.” Matt poured himself a cup of the hot chocolate and sat down in a rocker.

“Cassie, did you know how well Jocelyn can sing?” Matt asked while studying her reaction.

“I knew she could sing, yes, but only sweet Christian hymns. Two of the other girls on the wagon train would come to our camp at night and she’d sing along with them. I never dreamed she could or would sing in a saloon,” Cassie just shook her head back and forth.

“I have to admit I was impressed with her singing, but her attire left a whole lot to be desired, but those rowdy men loved her and that skimpy dress. I wanted to grab her and take her out of that place. I guess that’s what I did in the end.”

Cassie yawned. It's been a long day. They were all exhausted from worrying about Jocelyn's whereabouts and it was getting late for ranch hands to be up on a weeknight. "Matt, you go on to bed. I'll make a pallet and sleep next to my dear friend. Mabel and I'll take good care of her."

Her yawn was contagious, and he stifled his own. "I am worn out, but if she awakes, please knock on my door. I want to be with her."

"I'll be sure to wake you," she said, reassuring him. "Jim, you go up to bed. I'll see you first thing in the morning."

"I don't know if I'll be able to sleep. I've gotten use to you snuggling against my back," he whispered and patted her on the backside.

"Oh, go on with your old self. I love you," Cassie said, patting his face.

Chapter 34

Very early the next morning, Jocelyn opened her eyes. Where was she? She needed to get out of bed and relief herself.

Cassie sat up when she heard Jocelyn moving around. "Oh, it's wonderful to see you awake."

Jocelyn pulled the bedcovers up to her chin. "Who are you and where am I?" She glanced around the room. "I need to go outside."

"Here, let me help you get up. My name is Cassie and you're at Matt Colburn's ranch. You've been sick but you're going to be just fine." Cassie offered her a hand and steadied her on her feet. "The water closet is right here in this room. No need to go outside. Do you need help with your nightdress or anything?"

"No, I can manage on my own."

****

A knock sounded on the door waking Matt up. He raced to the door. "She's awake?"

"Yes. She's using the water closet, but Mr. Matt, she didn't know me."

"Thanks for telling me. I'll be more prepared to help her. You go on upstairs to your room, and I'll take over."

In a few minutes, Jocelyn shuffled back into the bedroom. She almost screamed with fright when she saw a strange man standing beside her bed. She saw a tall powerful, masculine man she wasn't sure she could cope with him. His size was enough to put any woman at a disadvantage.

"He lifted his hands. No need to be afraid of me." He walked closer to her and pulled back her covers on the bed. My name is Matt. You know me well, Josh, but right now you're having a problem remembering. The doctor said this is normal. You have alcohol poisoning."

"I'm sorry I don't know you. It's like I am in a bad dream." Her voice was shaky, and her lips trembled.

Matt listened but made no reaction. He could hear the despair in her tone as she struggled to remember. "Don't push yourself to remember anything. It will come naturally back to you. For now, just know that you're safe and loved here."

"You said I have alcohol poisoning. How could I get that?"

Matt didn't know how to answer that question, but before he could try to respond she asked. "Loved by whom?"

"Me, of course. And Cassie and Jim."

"Who is Jim?" Jocelyn asked. Puzzled by these strangers but not real *strangers?* She had a flash of memory but she was trying to put it together.

"Jim is Cassie's new husband. They've only been married two weeks." Matt watched for any reaction of memory on her part, but none came. He yearned to console her in his arms, give comfort and tenderness, but he didn't dare reach for her. She didn't appear to be afraid of him, but to her he was a stranger. He wanted her to warm up to him on her own, so he kept his distance.

"Are you hungry? I can make coffee and toast. We have a lot of different jams." His cooking skills were limited but he could prepare something light.

"No, thank you, but I'm still very tired. I'd like to go back to bed, if you don't mind."

"No, sleep will be good for you. Here, let me help you

back in the bed." After she was nested back under the covers, Matt told her he was going to build up the fire in her fireplace so the room would be cozy later.

As he placed logs on the fire, he peered back over his shoulder and watched as she snuggled with the covers. It appeared she was already asleep. She closed her eyes and remained that way until he left her room.

He walked back into the kitchen and found Cassie mixing up a big batch of cinnamon rolls, one of the men's favorite. "Couldn't sleep either?" he commented softly.

"You know Matt, one minute I was sure Jocelyn knew me, and then I wasn't too sure. I hate to say this, but I'm going to anyway. Could she be pretending to have lost her memory? She knows how angry you have been since finding her in that saloon."

"Surely, she wouldn't be playing a silly game like that. She wouldn't dare have us worrying over her health, would she? If I thought she was pretending, she'll be sorry. I don't know what I might do to her, because we are getting married."

"Oh, Matt, I believe she will come around soon as she is sure you'll forgive her for taking a job with that Butler fellow."

"Maybe, that is what I need to do. Have a long discussion with her and see how long it takes for her memory to return. Cassie you are one smart woman.

"Lordy, Mr. Matt, don't let her know any of this was my thinking."

"Oh, I won't do that? I know how to charm a lady."

****

Early the next morning, after Cassie motioned to Matt that Jocelyn was awake and moving around in her bedroom, he tapped on her door and pushed it open all the same time. He was carrying a large breakfast tray with a small vase of flowers on the corner.

"Good morning sunshine," Matt said, as he watched

her quickly grab her house robe and tie it at the waist.

"I never expected to have such special treatment. And I can walk to the table."

"Of course, you can, but I wanted to share a quiet, intimate breakfast with you—just the two of us. Come and join me in front of the fire." Matt pulled up both rockers and placed the tray on the small table between them. "Now isn't this nice. Here let me pour you some coffee or would you prefer tea? I can have Cassie brew you a cup."

****

"Coffee is fine, I believe" A flash of Matt sitting in the big dining room with a large mug of steaming hot coffee after all the men had gone outside, whisked past her thoughts.

She had a strange expression on her face so Matt asked, "Is something wrong?"

"No," she responded quickly. "I was thinking how if I knew I liked my coffee."

"Well, why don't you taste it black, then if not to your liking we can add milk and more sugar."

"Good idea," she responded and made a frown at the black stuff. He added cream and then she spooned several teaspoons of sugar. "This is very good, now."

Matt placed some scrambled eggs and a slice of ham on her plate. She chose a slice of buttered toast while he emptied the remainder of the food onto his plate. They ate in silence for a few minutes. Finally, Matt ask if she had a dream or a memory of anything she wanted to share or ask him about.

"No, but I was wondering how I got alcohol poisoning. I can't believe I'm a person who likes to drink. Most of the stuff smells awful."

"I'm thinking that since you don't normally sing in a saloon, you may have drunk some to give you courage to perform. A lot of performers will do just that before they stand in front of a large audience. Maybe that's what happened to you?"

"That's possible. I have no idea why I would be in a place like that."

"Well, that's over with now. You are home where you belong. After you're back on your feet, we'll plan our wedding, if you're still in agreement to marry me? I want you to be happy."

"So, I am here on this ranch to be your bride?" She knew better. Suddenly, she remembered every little detail before last night, but she wanted to hear what he was going to tell her.

Matt could tell in an instance that something changed in her eyes. "Yes, I paid for your passage from your hometown to come here on a bridal wagon train and you were chosen to be my bride. So, that's the whole story."

"That had to be an adventure for sure." She sat quite as a mouse and watched the big grin spread across his face. He knew that she knew he was telling a big fat lie, but he was enjoying it. She couldn't call him a liar without giving herself away.

"What, after I get on my feet, I am not ready to marry you or anyone, what will you do with me."

"Do with you or to you?" He laughed. "Well, Sunshine, I will send you packing and wish you well. "Eat up so I can get to work."

Matt kissed her on the forehead and started whistling as he left the room.

After Matt left the room and Cassie had removed the tray with the dirty dishes, Jocelyn was fuming. Matt could have come in the room this morning proclaiming how happy to have her home and how much her loved her, but no. He acted like she hadn't been there very long and she'd better marry him or she would be right back in the street again."

She knew he loved her but she couldn't believe that he'd investigated and now he was lying to her. "Oh, but what a messy web we weave," she thought to herself.

Once she dressed, she went into the kitchen to see if Cassie would allow her to help with the cooking. "Good morning, Cassie, is it? I am terrible with names."

"Yes, it is Cassie, and your little game is up with me, Missy. I have been with you for months now and I can read you like a book. Why are you pretending to be sick? Lost your memory or whatever?"

"Oh, Lord, thank you dear friend for being honest with me. I'm so tired and afraid."

"Well, all I gotta say is, you'd better be afraid of Matt. That man is worried sick over you. He nearly torn this country up searching for you and to discovery you in a saloon, of all places."

"Cassie, there was nowhere else to go. That was my last resort or come back here. I was sick when Matt came in the saloon. I had drank too much nerve medicine, that's what Lulu called it. My corset was so tight I couldn't breathe. The wild ride home made me lose my stomach." She rubbed her middle.

"When Matt came in the saloon looking for me, he was furious. I was really afraid of him for the first time. He was ready to shoot Jay Butler, the handsome saloon owner. Once, I awoke and heard the doctor tell Matt that I might have memory lost, well, I thought if I was sick for a day or two, he would calm down and listen to reason. You know, why I left this time. Cassie, he had me investigated like a common criminal." She busted into tears.

"When did he do that? He never asked me anything about you." Cassie replied.

"When we left Perryville. He said as soon as we arrived home, we would plan our wedding. We have been home for weeks now and he hasn't even tried to kiss me or even mentioned our wedding. He spent hours with me planning your wedding to Jim."

"When he left for the cattle drive, he said we would

talk when he got home. Nothing else." She wiped her eyes. "I went into his bedroom to give it a thorough cleaning when I discovered a telegram on his nightstand. I would have never read it, but my name jumped out at me. He had written to the sheriff in Perryville questioning him about my reputation and character. He didn't trust me or anything I had told him." She saw the surprised expression on Cassie face.

"I was shocked to my toes. I hurt all over. I couldn't believe that the man I had given my heart and soul didn't trust me. A man and woman cannot love without trust. So I left."

"Now, dear friend, you and I both know that man loves you very much."

"Oh, Cassie, you should have heard him telling me lies about how I came to be at the ranch. He thinks he can fool me into marrying him. I will never marry a man that doesn't trust me."

"Well, you go ahead with your memory loss plan and see how far it gets you with him. I won't say anything to him. If you feel like it, I would appreciate some help in preparing pies for lunch. I have spoiled this bunch of men with sweets, and they have sorely missed your cooking."

She offered a weak smile at her friend. "Let me grab my apron. Is Mabel still working on her wash here? I want to get Jim working on her house. Guess I have to get well before we can do that."

"Actually, Matt had Jim order a great deal of building supplies to make repairs already. Some of it was delivered yesterday. She is so excited." Cassie's grin spread across her face.

"Great, I am not supposed to remember any of that yet." She glanced at Cassie, and both smiled broadly. "I've to be careful until I'm ready to forgive him for not trusting me."

Chapter 35

Matt came in with the other men for a nice big dinner. They had worked on new fencing and several of them had broken ground to allow the river to spill over to the new pastureland that Matt had secured months ago. He went straight to his bedroom, washed, and changed into a clean shirt. His mother never allowed her men to come to the dining table dirty and with unkempt hair. As he entered the kitchen, he noticed Josh's bedroom door open. He tapped on the door but received no answer. He entered the room but she wasn't inside. Wondering where she could possibly be?

Once in the kitchen area, he saw her coming from the dining room with an empty tray. "My goodness, Josh. I'm glad to see that you're feeling better tonight. Have you been helping Cassie with dinner?" He also noticed that she didn't correct him from calling her Josh.

"Yes, Mr. Colburn, I'm so much better, thank you." she smiled sweetly at him.

"My name is Matt. You don't need to call me Mr. Colburn. We settled that when you first arrived."

"Come on Matt. The men are going to start eating without you," Jim said.

"I'm sorry fellows. My future bride distracted me." When Jocelyn whirled around at his comment, he gave her a wink, daring her to make a rebuttal.

****

Once the men had seconds, Cassie cut the strawberry and apple pies. She placed them on the tray and Jocelyn carried them into the dining room. She was greeted with big smiles and a hallelujah was voiced by one. "It great to have our pie maker home/"

"Well, I didn't see any of my pies left on the plates, boys. Just see if I cook any more for you." Cassie acted like her feelings were hurt, but the men knew she was only teasing them.

"Oh, Miss Cassie, you're the best biscuit maker in Texas. That Jim snatched you away before I could lay claim on you." One of the men teased until she blushed.

She waved a dismissive hand. "Oh, go on with your old self and leave me to clear this table." The men pushed their chairs under the table and filed out the front door, thanking the ladies for a fine supper.

"Josh, after you've have finished helping Cassie in the kitchen, I want you to come out to the yard swing where we can visit privately. I'll be waiting for you." Matt didn't wait for a response. He walked outside toward the corral.

****

Jocelyn was looking forward to going out the swing. Early in the evening after supper, some of the men would gather in the bunkhouse and play cards. Several would pull out their instruments and play western tunes on their guitars and fiddles. It was a very peaceful, restful evening before bedtime.

"Go on outside and meet Matt, Jocelyn. Mabel is here now, and she and Johnny will help me clean the kitchen. Don't keep him waiting." Cassie said.

Jocelyn went into her bedroom and ran a brush through her long blonde curls and added a touch of rosewater on her wrists. She took a deep breath and went out the side door to the swing beside the house.

Matt stood when he saw her coming. "That was quick." He said as he waited for her to take a seat.

"Mabel and Johnny are eating now, and they said they would assist Cassie in cleaning the kitchen."

"So, you met them?"

"Yes, I had seen Mabel washing clothes today and her son is a nice young man."

"Yes, they are good people. The ranch is lucky to have a woman who works hard. She keeps my things in order and most of the other men's too. She is going to have to hire another lady to help her with her laundry business."

"So, Matt, what do you want to talk about?"

Oh, this and that. Nothing special. Mostly I wanted to know how you're feeling and if any of your memory has returned?"

"My stomach is so much better. I believe that alcohol poison is out of my system. My memory comes and goes. Sometimes, I'm sure I am about to remember something, but it goes away."

"Don't rush or try to force it to come back. It will come when your mind is ready. That's what the doctor said, anyway." He leaned toward her. "I was wondering if you remember anything of your past life in Perryville, Texas, before you got on the bridal wagon train."

"No, I can't seem to remember anything about myself, or my family? Why do you asked?"

"Just thought something might have come to you, that's all. Well," Matt took his boot and stopped the swing from moving. I guess we'd better go in before the bugs start having us for their supper. Sleep well."

Matt took Josh's elbow and led her into the house. "I'll say good night here." With a slight bow, he went down the hall to his bedroom.

****

"Get over here Boomer," Luther said pointing a gun at his stomach. "I didn't think that bunch of folks would ever turn in for the night."

"Now you look here Luther. I ain't going to help you

kidnap Miss Jocelyn again. I would rather let you shoot me. I mean it, now. I 'm not going to do any harm to her or Mr. Matt. Those people are good to me."

"I only need you to help me get in the house and keep the horse quiet while I go into her room and have a discussion with her. When I come out, you can help me get back on my horse and then I'll be gone. No one is going to be kidnapped or killed."

"Now, let's just sit here and wait until we're sure everyone in the house is asleep." Luther said, pointing for Boomer to sit on the damp ground.

****

A light tap disturbed Matt as he lay thinking. He stood, walked over to his bedroom door and inched it open praying it was Josh, but it wasn't. "What's wrong, Jim?"

"Be very quiet and stay away from the bedroom windows. Come over here and peek in the edge of the woods. I believe it is Boomer, two horses, and that vile Luther. He's up to no good. I think he's come for Jocelyn again for some reason."

"Yep, I can see him now. The moon is very bright. The fool hasn't realized that the whole world can see him even if it is late. Let's wait until he makes a move to get inside Josh's room."

"He might hurt her," Jim said, shifting from foot to foot.

"No, he won't have time." Matt said, as he put on his clothes. "I can't believe he had the nerve to come here again. He must be desperate."

After thirty minutes, Matt and Jim watched as Luther scrambled across the yard to stop under Jocelyn's bedroom window. They watched him raise the window and crawled inside. He stood to get his eyes adjusted to the shadows in the room.

Jocelyn watched as the man entered her room. She flipped the covers back and slipped out of the bed. She eased quietly over to the table and lit the lamp. Luther appeared to be shocked as he slammed his gun into the lantern and it shattered when it hit the table and floor. The bedroom door burst open with a spear of light coming in behind the two men.

Jocelyn screamed. “Matt, its Luther!”

“Don’t move Luther or I’ll shoot you down like the sneaky dog you are,” Jim shouted.

“Don’t shoot, please. I wasn’t going to hurt the b. . . her.”

“Jim go into my room and bring a new lantern. Let’s get some light in this room.”

Matt eased over to the window and bent down. “Boomer, you out there?”

“Yes sir, I ‘m here.”

“Get in here and be quick about it,” Matt yelled.

“Josh, are you all right? Did that lantern glass cut you?”

“No, I’m not hurt. I’m so glad I wasn’t asleep when I saw him climb in my window. Did you know he was out there?”

“Will talk about it later.” Matt watched Jim lit the fresh lantern and sit it on the table. The room soon flooded with light. “Jim, we’ll have to lock this fool up in the storage room for the night. I’ll take him into town tomorrow.”

He motioned with his head toward the chair in the corner. “Sit down here, Luther. Come inside the bedroom, Boomer. I’ll have to question you after I listen to this fool’s story.”

“First of all Luther, you were told never to come near Josh again, so why are you climbing in her bedroom window?”

“I came after the money you, and Mr. Taylor stole from me. You took part of my inheritance since Jocelyn wouldn’t marry me. I never wanted to give her any of my money but you forced me to agree." He shrugged. "I've changed my mine. I want my money back."

Jocelyn frowned and posted her hands on her hips. "I can't give you any money because I told you I didn't want your money for myself. I only wanted it for Maria and Boomer. I gave Maria money and I have purchased land and building materials to build a business for Boomer. We had money left so Matt is repairing Mabel's house. You see, all your money went to a good cause."

"I got my money back from Maria. She didn't want to give it to me but with a little force, she gladly gave it to back. Now, I want your money, too. Your rich husband can afford to give it back to me."

"How could you hurt my dear maid? I will claw your eyes out." Jocelyn raced around the table and reached for Luther's face with her long fingernails. Boomer grabbed her around the waist and pulled her away from him.

"Settle down Josh. I'll take care of this fool. "Now, look Luther. You signed papers and agreed to the settlement where you wouldn't have to go to jail for the harm you had inflicted on a young lady months before her father died. You can still go to jail for doing harm to Maria. And added to that breaking and entering a young lady's bedroom window to do her harm."

"I never intended to hurt her. Tell them Boomer. I only wanted my money, and I promised Boomer I wouldn't do her any harm."

"Yes sir, he promised he wouldn't hurt Miss Jocelyn. I couldn't trust him to come out here alone. I was afraid for her so I tagged along with him. Plus, he had a gun in my side the whole time."

"I understand and I appreciate what you did to help protect Josh. You aren't in any trouble." Matt patted the big guy's shoulders.

"Luther, Jim is going to lock you in our storage room. I will take you to the sheriff's office in the morning. Now, go along peacefully, and you won't be hurt."

"Mr. Matt, I have got two horses I need to put in the corral. May I spent the night in the bunkhouse and ride into town with you tomorrow?" Boomer asked.

"That will be fine." Matt watched as Jim left with Luther, Cassie went back upstairs, and Boomer went to retrieve the two horses. Everyone was gone their separate ways except Jocelyn, the new recovered love of his life.

Jocelyn rushed into Matt's arms. "Oh, Matt, darling, what are you going to do to Luther?"

"Matt pushed Josh from his arms and looked down at her teary face. "If I was you, I would be thinking *what is Matt going to do to me*?"

He gave her a big grin and walked over to a rocking chair still holding her hand loosely. "But Matt, aren't you glad Luther helped make my memory return?"

"Oh yes, darling, I am. I am so pleased that you remembered all that took place with Luther. What I want to know is why you ran away from me this last time and took a job, dressed like a harlot, singing and drinking in a saloon. Also, I'd like an explanation why you was romancing that dressed-up dude when none of that was necessary. You waited until I was on a cattle drive and gone for a few days."

"I had my reasons," she said, as she tried to shake her hand lose from his. "I happened to know that you have never trusted me. You had me investigated like a common criminal and it won't be easy forgiving you for that. A man who loves his woman would've trusted me and you didn't. You had to drag the sheriff in my hometown into our private business and asked him personal questions about me. I felt I had reasons to *'punish*" you a little," she said pouting a little. "After we got home from Perryville, you'd turned your back on me and treated me like a stranger."

"Just listen to yourself," Matt said, staring at her with his hands on his wide hips. "You thought to punish me by pretending to have lost your memory and being very sick. Well, you're going to regret making all of us worry about you. You've giving me many reasons for not trusting you and this is one time you are going to regret your actions by running away from me for a petty reason. You aren't going to be able to sit down for a week. He grabbed her, but she dodged him and raced across the bedroom. She picked up the lantern and drew it back as to throw it at him.

"Matt took three giant steps and gripped her arm. "Put that lantern down, now." She lowered it on the table. "Matt, I'm sorry," she lowered her face and tried to shed some tears.

"I know you are and you're going to be really sorry after I blister your spoiled, sassy backside." He dragged her over to the rocking chair. He flopped down in it and flipped her over his lap, smoothing her night gown down on her back side.

She screamed, twisted and turned. "Turn me lose you big Ape!"

He slapped her hard, and suddenly his hand paused. He wanted to continue but he just couldn't. He flipped her back over onto his lap and hugged her like a small child. "I wish I could punish you like you deserve, but I can't hurt you." He held her tighter. "We've both been wrong in our treatment toward each other. I've misjudged you because I was hurt by another woman years ago and you were hurt by someone you knew. Now it's time for both of us to forget and forgive. We love each other and its time we start behaving and acting like grown people. I love you and you love me."

Jocelyn sat up in his lap and faced him. "But Matt, why did you change toward me after we came home from Perryville?"

Matt sighed and took Jocelyn's face in his hands. "I had to have you investigated. I was wrong and I pray you'll forgive me. When we were in Perryville, I went to ask the lawyer one more question. I heard Luther discussing your reputation and character. I didn't believe those things Luther was saying, but I had been burned badly a long time ago by a young woman and I couldn't allow that to happen to me again. I always believed in you, but I had to know for sure. I guess you read the telegram in my room?"

"Yes, I did, but I wasn't snooping. I picked it off the floor and I saw my name. I couldn't help but read it. You didn't trust me, even though I always told you the truth about my past. It hurt to know that the man I had given my heart didn't trust me. That is the only reason I left. I tried to find a place to stay in town, but it was getting dark, and the saloon was the only place that had a room. The owner never asked anything of me. Oh, once he got fresh, but I shoved him in the stream." Smiling she said, "He treated me like a lady afterwards."

"I'm sorry my temper got the best of me, but you'd pushed me to my limit." He kissed her and she responded over and over. "I love you . . . love you . . . love you. He saw tears well and slip from the corner of her eyes as her lips formed the words he desired to hear.

Matt removed her arms and held them close to his body. "We'll be getting married in a couple of days and I don't want any sass about it. I love you with all my heart and I promise you I'll never harm a hair on your head again."

"Oh, Matt, I've wanted to be your wife for a long time. But I wasn't sure if you felt the same way about me." She leaned up to kiss him again but he held her tighter.

"We've better take things slow and easy or will be having the honeymoon before the wedding."

Once more, slowly, deliberately, his mouth covered hers, pressing gentle at first. Caught up in desire, he held her tighter against his chest, her arms winding around his neck with surprising strength.

"Oh, Matt, I'm so happy." Leaning back, she giggled.

"I'll need a few days to prepare my dress and a few personal items."

"I hope you brought that black corset you wore in the saloon. I like to see you in that again," he said grinning.

"Oh, you, I did pack it, but not on purpose. Just maybe I will wear it for you." Jocelyn smiled as he stood her on her feet.

****

Matt stood in front of the window. "I'll contact the minister while I'm in town. I really don't want Luther to spend the rest of his life in jail. Those terrible men in jail would kill him in a couple of months. They love men who are different. What do you think I should do with him?"

Jocelyn thought for a moment. "We aren't that far from the border. Maybe you could have a couple of men escort him into Mexico and let him live there. He should have enough money to live there comfortably. Make him promise never to come back to Amarillo, Texas.

"Yes, I will think about that. Good suggestion." Matt said.

"Matt took Jocelyn's hand and led her over to the bed. He pulled back the covers and motioned for her to get in. "This is the last time I'm tucking you in bed. In a few nights, we'll be together in my big bed." He leaned down and gave her a deep kiss, but quickly pulled himself back. "I better behave myself or my poor mother will be turning over in her grave for not treating my bride properly."

Jocelyn smiled and whispered again "I love you, Matt Colburn."

"I love you, too. Good night, Sweetheart. See you at breakfast." As Matt strode to the door, he said, "Oh, by the way, Jim is standing outside your bedroom door waiting for me to come out." He threw her a kiss from the doorway with a shy grin.

Chapter 36

Jim and Matt stood at the storage room door. "Are you sure you don't want to just turn the fool loose and be rid of the whole problem?" Jim asked.

"No, I'm afraid he might show up again, and I don't believe I'd be able to control myself around him. "Let's ask for a couple of volunteers to escort him to Del Rio, and they can take him across into Mexico. I'll offer them a bonus for taking him."

"I know just the two who will want to make the trip. They can stay a day or two and sow some wild oats while gone," Jim laughed. He unlocked the door and handcuffed Luther. "Come with me to the outhouse and then you can have breakfast in the bunkhouse. Afterward, we're taking you to the train station."

"Why would I want to go to the train station?"

"You're taking a trip to your new home, old Mexico."

"I don't care to live in Mexico."

"Listen, you little fool, you'll go peacefully to Mexico and live like a king with the money you have, or you'll go to the state prison and live among the meanest men in the West. Take your choice."

"All right, but I need more money. I had debts to pay after I received my pittance of an inheritance after my lawyer gave Jocelyn half of my money. Her new rich husband could give me some of my money back."

Matt had been standing outside of the storage room

when he heard Luther speaking about needing money. He turned and went into his office where he sat. Matt sat at his desk for a few minutes and finally turned around and bent down to open his safe. He fumbled through some papers and pulled out a stack of green- backs. He counted out two thousand dollars and put them in a brown envelope. Scribbling Luther's name on it, Matt placed it in his vest pocket.

After the two volunteers arrived who would accompany Luther on the afternoon train to Mexico, Matt faced the man. "Luther, I never want to see you again. Here's two thousand dollars. If handled correctly, you can live on it for a long time in Mexico. You can have your own house and land, cattle, or whatever else you want. But you'll be one sorry man if you ever come back here and bother Josh. Do I make myself clear?"

"Thanks for the money. I really wasn't expecting you to give me any. You'll never see me again."

Jim and Matt watched as the two young men drove Luther away from the ranch. "Now, I have a wedding to help plan. I'll need your help with reaching out to the community and inviting most of them. Josh said she wanted a small wedding, but I want the whole world to know that I've found the most wonderful, and beautiful woman in the territory. So, let's celebrate."

"Cassie and I'll be thrilled to help. Everyone who knows you will be at your wedding."

****

Matt sat at the breakfast table and informed the ladies that Luther was out of their lives forever. They would never have to fear him again. "He will be on the afternoon train to Mexico. Now, we have a wedding to plan. Saturday is the day after tomorrow. I thought we could be married this Saturday at 5:00 p.m. What do you think about that?"

"Cassie, do you think we can plan enough food, and have my dress ready for this Saturday?" Jocelyn looked to her friend, her eyebrows furrowed.

"We'll hire Gertie from town to come out and work on your dress. The men can smoke a slab of beef and a pig for the meat and most of the ladies from town will bring a covered dish to help with the food. "

"I can purchase kegs of beer from the saloon, and cases of Champagne can come from Midland on the stage tomorrow after I send a telegram to the winery there today."

"I believe the wedding is on." Cassie said, laughing along with Mabel.

****

The room was crowded with guests that Jocelyn scarcely recognized but she didn't care. Matt and Jocelyn stared at each other with their pulses racing and their stomachs tied in knots. They both stood toe-to-toe in the hallway of the living room. Their wedding would be talked about for years. The love that shined from their eyes told the whole world that these two beautiful people shared great love for each other.

Reverend Watson was waiting in the living room with a question, "Who gives this woman? He waited as Jim stepped between Matt and Jocelyn and smiled broadly, "I do."

Jim took the bride's hand and tucked it into the crook of Matt's elbow. He took the basket of fragrant yellow daylilies and English ivy from Jocelyn and passed it to Cassie.

"Dearly beloved . . . "Reverend Watson offered a meaningful message of what it took to make a successful marriage; the importance of giving of oneself and the willingness to forgive. He spoke of the rewards of the love that they would receive from one another. The pastor mentioned the children with which this marriage might be blessed.

Jocelyn cut a sideways glance to find Matt's gaze

fixed on her face when the pastor mentioned children. After the short sermon the two ladies that had traveled with Jocelyn on the bridal wagon train stepped forward and sang, "*Wondrous Love*" in their faultless, crystal-clear voices.

Facing each other, the bride and groom held onto each other as if one of them might take flight. Jocelyn's hand trembled, but she wasn't the only one shaking.

"I, Matthew Wayne Colburn, take thee Jocelyn Marie Norwood . . ."

His voice was deeper than usual and carried a light tremor. His dark eyes, conveying a depth of emotion, never wavered from hers as he spoke his vows.

Her heart swelled with so much love that it created a sweet hurt in her breast. She only heard a few of his words until he said . . . 'till death do us part."

Then it was her turn. "I, Jocelyn Marie Norwood, take thee, Matthew Wayne Colburn . . .

****

"As Matt held Josh's hands and listened to her soft voice, he saw a glimmer of tears on her eyelids and was touched at her sincerity. He squeezed her fingertips to let her know he understood how she felt.

"The ring . . . requested the minister.

Matt removed a small diamond from his little finger and slipped it over her knuckle. This small piece of jewelry bound them together forever. Their gazes united over their joined hands as their vows were sealed with the pastor's words. "I now pronounce you man and wife."

Matt's leaned toward Josh's blushed red cheeks and their lips touched lightly. The kiss ended, and he turned his beautiful bride to face the crowd of well-wishers. Many of the ladies were wiping their eyes while the men pounded each other on their backs.

Matt walked Josh over to a beautifully polished table in the dining room where the family Bible lay open. There on the page already bearing many entries, Matt wrote;

October 6, 1876
Matthew Wayne Colburn
Married to
Jocelyn Marie Norwood.

Then he kissed her again, this time exuberant. Then he whispered, "I love you so much."

The crowd separated them, and strangely enough they saw each only for a few minutes during the remainder of the evening. There were so many guests for Jocelyn to meet and many old acquaintances for Matt to renew.

Cassie and Mabel served the guests buffet-style with the help of many of the neighbors. The men had set up a bar in the front yard. Many of the guests scattered onto the lawn, wandered around the small garden or visited inside the house. The musicians set up in front of the barn door where the ground had been swept clean. They'd played slow songs at first, but as the party got into the spirit of things, they played louder and faster tunes which all the dancers enjoyed. The children chased the peacocks that Jim had purchased for Cassie to have as pets. Many fed apples and pieces of cake to the corralled horses. Everyone was enjoying themselves except the bride and groom. Every time they were caught together, someone would interrupt and carry one of them away.

****

As the evening moved on, Jocelyn noticed Cassie's face had lost its color and she touched her stomach as if she were sick. When she rushed out of the room, Jocelyn excused herself from chatting with one of the guests and followed Cassie.

Cassie was wiping her face, when Jocelyn opened the water-closet door. "Are you sick?" Jocelyn asked. In the many months she'd known Cassie, she'd never once been ill.

"Well, I didn't want to say anything until I was sure, but for several nights I have been sick to my stomach." She waited for Jocelyn to guess, but when she shrugged, she said, "I'm with child."

"Oh, my goodness, this is wonderful news. Have you told Jim, yet?"

"No," she laughed. "I'm sure now, but I've been waiting to tell him. I didn't want our news to spoil your wedding."

"Something like this is great news. It could never spoil our day. It makes me so happy for you and Jim."

Matt and Jim came rushing into the bedroom. Jim quickly closed the door. "Now, what's going on between you two? We both saw you rush in here like the house was on fire," Jim said to Cassie.

Jocelyn eased into Matt's arms and pulled him in front of the fireplace. She brought her fingers on her lips and motioned to him to listen to Cassie.

"Jim, you know how you said you always wanted to be a father?"

"Yep, but I'm too old for that now . . . Wait, are you telling me that I am going to be a papa?"

"Yes, in about seven months. We're going to have a baby. Are your happy?" Cassie winked at Matt and Jocelyn over Jim's shoulder.

He reached for Cassie and spun her around. I'm beyond happy, woman. I feel like a bridegroom myself right now." The four of them joined arms and rejoiced together.

A pounding came on the door, and it opened before Matt could reach it.

"Is everything all right in here," Mabel asked while holding Sonny asleep on her shoulder. "I need to leave the guests while I put this big boy to bed."

"We've coming Mabel. Do what you have to do and

come back to the party."

As the clock approached midnight, Matt and Jocelyn stood on the front porch, thanking their guests for coming and wishing them a safe journey home.

****

Once Matt and Jocelyn were alone in his bedroom, he locked the door. Jocelyn's heart fluttered as Matt took one step toward her and then another. He reached her and pulled her into his arms. His absolute love reflected in his eyes as he covered her face with kisses.

Both began to undress each other when a knock sounded at the door. "Ignore it," Matt whispered. Filled with frustration, the knock came again so Matt went to the door. He opened it to find the pastor standing on the other side.

"I'm sorry to trouble you, Mr. Colburn. But one of the young men said you wanted to see me before I went home?"

"Oh yes, I did, I do." Matt rushed over to his suit coat and pulled out a white envelope with the minister's name on it. "Yes, I wanted to give you a donation to you and your church, of course, for performing the wedding. You did a great job and I thank you."

The minister took the gift and said," It isn't often I get to perform a beautiful wedding like this one with so many people." He turned to leave and stopped to say, "I wish you a lifetime of happiness. Looks to me like you're well on your way to that already."

Matt held the door wide open for the minister and watched him continue down the hall to the kitchen. Matt again locked the door and then leaned up against it. Grinning, he walked toward his bride who was still dressed in her wedding dress.

"He wished us a lifetime of happiness. Hopefully, tonight will be filled with privacy and many surprises," he said, as he nibbled on his bride's neck and shoulder.

Epilogue

"Josh!' Cassie screamed. Over their months together, she had begun calling her best friend by her husband's pet name.

"Josh. help me, please. Get this baby out of me. I'm dying for sure." Cassie was in the worse pain of her life. She never dreamed having a child could be this bad. There were too many children in the world, and many women had multiple births. How could they? No woman in her right mind would ever go through this more than once.

"Doctor Murclock, can't you do more for her? I've never known Cassie to carry on so. She's a strong woman," Jocelyn said.

"Let's see, Mrs. Colburn. You have about five more months to experience what Cassie is going through. Every woman's childbirth experience is different. I don't want you to be afraid when your time comes."

"How will my time be different from hers?"

"Now, I don't have time to talk about it now. We need to make Cassie comfortable. Go and get more ice and dry cloths."

Jocelyn hurried out of the room, happy to have something to do besides standing beside her suffering friend.

Jim met her at the door and asked if he could do anything.

"If I were you, Jim, I wouldn't go in there. She might

decide to get out of bed and strangle you for putting her in this condition."

"I never dreamt I would get her with child, but I'm thrilled."

"Don't tell her that until she's calm and happy with the baby in her arms." Jocelyn was trembling from fright. Her forehead was damp, curls were plastered to her neck, and her skin felt clammy.

****

Matt had come from town where he had finalized turning the ownership of the brand-new livery stable over to Boomer Moore. The big barn sat at the end of town and would board up to a dozen horses at one time. Boomer had hired a young schoolboy to help him every afternoon. He had plans to hire a blacksmith to help build and repair wagon wheels and carriages. Matt rode away smiling as he remembered the big smile on Boomer's face.

He stopped by Mabel's house to check on all the repairs to the small structure. It had doubled in size with a large closed-in porch on the side for her laundry business. Mabel had lined up another woman to work with her. Matt was certain she would be hiring more than one woman because she had a lot of future business.

Matt strolled into the kitchen and saw how pale Josh was. "Are you all right? Is Cassie's baby doing fine?" He took her in his arms, and she bit her bottom lip, trying not to cry.

"Yes, Cassie is fine but the first baby is taking more time than normal to show itself, so the doctor says." Jocelyn placed the clean cloths over her arm and picked up the bowl of ice.

"Here, let me carry that for you," Matt said, but Josh wouldn't allow it.

"You must stay out of that room with Jim. Right now, Cassie hates all men." Jocelyn offered a weak smile, but Matt realized that childbirth has really scared his wife.

"Maybe, you should allow Mabel to help with the delivery. She's witnessed this sort of thing before."

"That's why I need to be with her so I'll know what to expect."

"Sometimes being ignorant is better than knowing too much." Matt's father had told him that many times.

"I need to be with her. She's my best friend. So, please let me get back to her." Matt stepped aside and watched his sweet wife go back into the torture chamber.

After a long day, just as Mabel was putting supper on the table, a baby's cry came from the upstairs bedroom. All the men that had come inside cheered and slapped Jim on the back.

"It a boy!" The doctor yelled down the stairs and said that mother and child were both fine.

Matt hugged Jim and then heard his name.

"Matt, come upstairs and bring Mabel. Your wife has fainted, so she isn't any help to me." Matt froze for a quick second and then made a mad dash up the stairs to the bedroom. Over on a side chair, his chubby wife was sprawled out in a dead faint. She looked so peaceful Matt hated to disturb her. He scooped her up in his arms and carried her down to their bedroom. On the way, he passed Bryan and two other men serving the food that Mabel had prepared. The men were a great group who would pitch in whenever needed.

"Mabel will be busy for a while and Josh is feeling poorly, so you guys just help yourselves. I'll be out as soon as I can."

****

Jocelyn came to as soon as Matt stretched her out on their bed. He was removing her shoes when she tried to sit up.

"Now, you just lay still, little momma."

"Oh, Matt, I wish I could say that childbirth is a beautiful thing, but I only saw a glimpse, which I guess was enough for me."

Matt sat on the side of the bed and took his sweet wife's hand. "You know, honey, the first time my pa asked me to help him deliver a calf, I lost my breakfast, lunch and dinner all at one time. I cried and cried."

"How old were you?"

"I guess I was about five. He only wanted me to hold the cow's head but I saw too much. It was a long time before he asked me to help him again."

"But Matt, I didn't see a cow." She grabbed at his shirtfront. "I'm the one who's going to have our baby in a few months. I hate to admit it, but I'm really afraid." She laid her face against his chest.

"I know honey, but I won't leave you for a minute. I'll be holding you the whole time, I promise. Childbirth is beautiful, and when you hold your baby in your arms, all the pain will be a thing of the past. You ask many mothers, and they'll tell you the same thing."

"Cassie will never have another child. She screamed her head off."

"I bet Cassie is holding her baby now and loving it and Jim for all the world," Matt said. "After you rest for a while, I'll carry you upstairs to see your friends' beautiful baby boy." He used a damp cloth and wiped his beautiful wife's face. "I promise you, when you see Cassie and Jim holding their baby, you'll be ready when your time comes."

Jocelyn tried to smile but her only thought was, *if I could only runaway.*

The End

Coming soon, fall of 2023

Untitled (as of now)
Introducing the story . . .

Chapter 1

It was a sunny, windy day as Lizzy Winters stood out in the backyard, hanging the Monday wash. She was singing *Oh, what a wonderful day* when she felt a tug on her skirt. “Lizzy,” Joshua, one of her seven-year-old twin brothers yelled, “you gotta come to the front of the house. A man is lying over his horse. I think he’s dead. Come on now.”

“Oh, Joshua, I don’t have time for any of your shenanigans. Can’t you see I’m busy?” she said, picking up another piece of wet laundry. She could hear Blue, the kid’s dog, barking.

Joshua wasn’t giving up. He jerked the shirt out of his big sister’s hands and began pulling her across the yard. “I ain’t playing. His big horse is drinking water from our trough. Come on, hurry!”

Giving up, she gave him her full attention and hurried to the front of the house. “Quiet Blue and get back under the house!” Lizzy waved her apron at the dog, who was growling and barking at a strange horse. “Oh, my goodness, Joshua. Go to the barn and round up Jake. Tell him to hurry and help us.” Lizzy was surprised to see a rider and horse in front of her house. He appeared to be severely hurt, maybe even dead.

Easing over to the stranger laying sideways on his large horse, Lizzy saw his tan chaps and hands were bloody. “Come on, boy,” she spoke softly to the horse, hoping he would allow her to lead him to the porch, which was three feet off the ground. Blue was steadily jumping close to the horse’s hoofs, growling.

After hearing a commotion outside, five-year-old Pearl, Lizzy baby sister, stood in the doorway. She placed her doll on her hip and pointed to the man. “Who’s that, mama Lizzy?”

“I don’t know, sugar, but collect a clean sheet out of the chest in our bedroom. I need to place it on the porch so we can drag this man into the house.”

“But, Lizzy, you said never let a stranger in. Are you sure you want to drag him come inside?”

“Please do as I asked and hurry with the sheet.” Lizzy smiled at her sweet little sister.

Jake came running from the barn. With cow manure between his toes and hay in his hair, he stopped with wide eyes and asked, “Who’s this man, Lizzy?”

“He’s a drifter, but he’d been hurt. Wash your feet so you can help me drag him off his horse and inside the house. First, make Blue behave and stop that barking. He’s upsetting the stranger’s horse.”

Jake yelled, “Quiet Blue. Under the porch, now.” Blue lowered his face, crawled on his belly to the porch’s edge to stand guard.

Jake hurried to the water trough, stepped in it, rubbed his toes clean, and hurried back to his sister. “How will we get this big boy down onto the porch?”

Lizzy studied the man and horse. “Joshua, you hold the horse’s head, and Jake and I’ll pull him off his saddle down to the floor onto the sheet. Then, after we straightened him out, we can drag him inside and help him on my bed.” She looked at her two brothers and asked,

"Are you ready?"

Jake was standing next to the horse, grabbed the man's long leg and tossed it over the saddle. The stranger moaned and cried out when his shoulder landed on the porch. Joshua walked the horse away from the porch and tied his reins to the hitching post. He quickly helped Lizzy and Jake straighten the man onto his back. "Lizzy, look at all that blood. He's sure gonna ruin your sheet."

"It'll be all right. I'll soak it in cold water, but let's pull the stranger inside." Lizzy and both boys had a corner of the sheet and dragged him into the living room. "Come on, let's move him in my room. He can't lie out in the front room while I care for him."

After a few more tugs, they had moved the stranger into Lizzy's and Pearl's room. "Now to lift him onto the bed."

Lizzy stood and looked at her three siblings. There wasn't any way they were going to be able to help her with this tall, lanky man onto the bed until Jake offered a suggestion.

"Try to wake him, Lizzy. Maybe, he can help us."

"Good idea. He did make some noise while on the porch." Lizzy knelt and took the man's face in her hands. She slapped his sweaty face softly to try to wake him. "Hey, fellow, can you hear me? I need your help." After a couple more tries, the man moaned and opened one eye. He saw a beautiful young girl with a scarf wrapped around her wild, blond hair. He was sure she was a windblown angel.

"Help me," he mumbled.

"We're trying to, but you have to try and stand. Can you try, please?"

This time the stranger opened both eyes and groaned. "Help me up," he said, offering his arms to Lizzy. He shuffled his boots under his lower body while Lizzy and the boys pulled his arms to a standing position. They immediately allowed him to sit back onto the bed. Sighing big, he fell unconscious again.

"Thank the good Lord," Lizzy said. "Jake, please bring me a pan of hot water and Joshua, retrieve my medicine box and bring it to me. Pearl, you can remove his boots and socks. Boys, please remove his chaps and jeans."

All the children fell into action while she went to find her scissors. Lizzy lay them on the table beside the bed and rushed outside to complete her laundry, before she had to redo it. After the wet clothes were hung to dry, she went back inside to find a sheet covering the stranger from his waist down.

Lizzy was thankful that the children had undressed the stranger and he still lay asleep. "Thank you all so much. I can take it from here, except boys, take the man's horse, unsaddle it, and place him in the barn. Give him some oats and rub him down good."

"If he dies, you think we can keep that fine horse?" Jake asked.

"Jake Winters, I won't have no such talk. We all need to pray for this poor soul." Lizzy didn't get her feathers ruffled often, but she was surprised to hear her brother coveting another man's possession.

Walking closer to the young man, she saw a sheen of sweat on his bare chest. As she pulled the sheet up on his body, she felt a radiating, unhealthy heat coming from his body.

Lizzy knew she had to take care of this stranger immediately. She hurried into the kitchen, got a bottle of vinegar and poured some in the hot water that Jake had fixed for her. She sponged his face, neck, arms and chest. After straightening the sheet, she left a cold compress on his brow to bring down his fever. Next, she needed to check his wound on his side.

Holding her breath, Lizzy slowly lifted the cover. Flames of embarrassment shot through her body at the sight of his nakedness. Thank goodness the wound was just below his waistline. She gasped as she looked at the hole in his side and knew she had her work cut out for her. The bullet had penetrated all the way from the front to his back. It was a raggedy wound that would need to be cleaned and later, sewn together.

Chapter 2

After Lizzy thoroughly inspected the bullet wound, she knew he'd been shot a few days ago. The wound had festered, and it would need to be cleaned. The man needed Doctor Hayes, but the last time he came by, he said he would be gone to St. Louis to learn more about surgeries. He would be out of town for several weeks, but would drop by as soon as he returned.

Doctor Hayes was a dear friend who had delivered the twins and little Pearl. Several weeks after Pearls' birth, Lizzy's pa had run off and left the family stranded. Her mama was in poor health and at the age of sixteen, Lizzy had to be the caretaker of all of the family. Doctor Hayes helped by giving advice and instructions on how to care for the little ones. He stopped by often while visiting others in the area.

As she looked at the stranger's busted side, all the years of caring for the little ones and her poor deceased mama, had not prepared her for this. As she leaned over his body, she heard his stomach grumbling. "Good gracious, if he got shot a few days ago, he is most likely starving," she said aloud.

Lizzy covered his body with the sheet, rushed into the kitchen and pulled down her string of ginger root that she kept close to the kitchen window. She pounded a piece and placed it in a small pan of water to make wild gingerroot tea. This would treat him from the inside, too.

He lay still as death when she carried the tea back to him. She blew on the tea and attempted to spoon-feed it to him. The liquid only dribbled from his lips. It rolled down the side of his face, which she quickly wiped away. She tried again to force another spoon full, but it only made him cough.

She pressed her hand to her mouth, almost in tears, as she tried to find a way to get nourishment in him. Suddenly, she thought of the tall cat tails at the river's edge. They would make great straws. Yes, she could have him sip the liquid into his mouth.

"Pearl, please sit in the padded chair at the foot of the bed and watch over our patient. You can be his little nurse. Do not touch him, understand. I'm going to the river and get something. I will tell the boys where you are, all right?"

"Yes, mama, I will be the *nightingale nurse* while you're away." Lizzy smiled at Pearl, remembering the children's story written by Hans Christian Anderson that she had read to her many times about the *Emperor and a Nightingale*.

Walking and running as fast as she could, Lizzy tiptoed into the water at the edge of the bank. She plunked a cat tail and then another. She raced back inside the house and found her little nurse and patient both sound asleep.

Taking a knitting needle, she reamed out the pith from its center. She poured water into a cup and tried using the straw to sip some. It worked. Being pleased with her new tool, she lifted her patient's face and pried open his mouth with her fingers. She placed the cat tail down his throat, gagging herself at what she was doing to him.

Lizzy was so close to the man, her pulse did strange, forbidden things. She had never felt this way about any man but she knew that she must continue to feed him.

She couldn't keep the liquid in the cat tail, so she filled her mouth and blew the ginger tea into the straw, down his throat. As she lifted the straw a little, he swallowed. Again and again she forced him to swallow the tea. Finally, he moaned and clapped his teeth closed, letting her know he had enough. She tried to open his teeth, but he only opened and closed his sharp teeth down on her two fingers. Immediately, she held in the scream but sucked the blood off her fingers.

The stranger seemed to be more relaxed. Lizzy decided she had to check his wound and see what she could do to remove the infection before more gangrene set in. She didn't have any medicine to apply to the injury. All she had in her cabinet were alcohol, vinegar, mineral oil, and turpentine. But she remembered reading about an old ancient treatment; maggots.

The thought made her skin crawl, but she had to do something. She knew that the insect was creepy and slimy. The slime is a great healing balm that will consume the infected tissue and leave the good tissue unscathed. Cold chills ran up and down Lizzy's spine just thinking about the treatment but what other choice did she have.

Walking to the front door, she called the boys to come inside. "Now listen to me, please," she said to Jake and Joshua.

"I need you to scout inside the old hog pen and search for some old rotten wet boards. I need a board that has some white maggots clinging to it. Don't touch the bugs, understand?

"What are you going to do with those awful things?" Jake asked. "You ain't planning on cooking them for us to eat, are you?

"Mercy, no. I need them to help make our patient better. Just scoot and bring me several boards. Leave them on the back porch. I will attend to the bugs."

Lizzy stood at the front door and watched her two brothers run around to the old hog pen. They were wonderful boys who never gave her trouble and would do anything she asked.

Realizing it was near noon, she washed her hands to prepare lunch. She walked to the side of the house and opened the cellar door. She removed eggs and potatoes from the straw. Reaching up on a hook, she took down a smoked ham.

While the boys were gone on their bug hunt, she fried ham, and scrambled eggs with small potatoes, which was one of the children's favorites. She sliced the freshly baked bread and covered it with yesterday's homemade butter.

Once the boys returned with a large plank that held the awful white maggots, she made them wash their hands until they shined. "But Lizzy, we didn't touch anything but the boards," Joshua said. "You would never catch me touching one of those nasty creatures."

Pearl had awakened from her long morning nap. "Something smells good and I'm hungry. I think that man is hungry too or he has a bear in his tummy. I heard it growling."

"Come here, sweetheart and let me wash your face and hands. I have cooked some lunch and I want you to eat real good for me. I may need you to help me again."

"Jake, would you please say the blessing so everyone can eat?" Lizzy asked.

"I guess, but why can't Joshua ask it sometimes."

"I did," he fussed. "I said it last night at supper."

"I wanna say it," begged Pearl.

"All right, Pearl, go ahead and pray so we can eat." Lizzy said, watching the boys bow their heads.

"Oh, Lord, come into our hearts and help us not to sin because we will go straight to hell. Amen. Pearl looked up, proud of herself.

"Pearl, what kind of blessing is that and where did you hear such awful talk?" Lizzy was shocked, almost speechless.

"At the meeting place last week. That old man

standing in front of the room was yelling at everybody said we better not sin because we will go to . . . you know where. Mama Lizzy, what is sin and where is that bad place?"

Lizzy stood her head in utter disgust. "Let's eat and later you and I will talk about prayers and blessings. I 'm sorry you misunderstood what Preacher Booker said."

****

After filling Pearls' plate, Lizzy entered her bedroom to check on the stranger.

Dear Lord! He'd turned over on his injured side. She pushed and grunted with his limp weight until she managed to flip him on his back. She knew before she looked what she going to find. His wound was bleeding again.

Linda Sealy Knowles is originally from north Mobile, Alabama. She presently resides in Niceville, Florida, near her two children and three beautiful granddaughters. Linda's writing is a God-gifted talent that brings joy to her heart. When she receives a compliment or review from one of her fans, it warms her soul, and she feels like a New York bestseller.

More books by Linda Sealy Knowles

The Maxwell Saga (six books series)
Journey to Heaven Knows Where
Hannah's Way
The Secret
Bud's Journey Home
Always Jess
Ollie's World
--
Kathleen of Sweetwater Texas
Abbey's New Life
Sunflower Brides
Trapped by Love
The Gamble
Joy's Cowboy
Anna, The Lawman's Problem
A Stranger's Love
Forever Mine

Made in the USA
Middletown, DE
08 June 2023

31717352R00156